Acut

Ruby Lang is the author of the acclaimed Practice Perfect series and the Uptown series. Her alter ego, Mindy Hung, wrote about romance novels (among other things) for *The Toast*. Her work has also appeared in *The New York Times*, *The Walrus*, *Bitch*, and other fine venues. She enjoys running (slowly), reading (quickly), and ice cream (at any speed). She lives in New York with a small child and a medium-sized husband.

Also by Ruby Lang

Practice Perfect

Acute Reactions
Hard Knocks
Clean Breaks

Acute Reactions

RUBY LANG

CANELO

First published in the USA in 2015 by Crimson Romance, an imprint of F+W Media, Inc.

This edition published in the United Kingdom in 2024 by

Canelo
Unit 9, 5th Floor
Cargo Works, 1–2 Hatfields
London SE1 9PG
United Kingdom

A CIP catalogue record for this book is available from the British Library.

Print ISBN 978 1 80436 771 1
Ebook ISBN 978 1 80032 414 5

This book is a work of fiction. Names, characters, businesses, organizations, places and events are either the product of the author's imagination or are used fictitiously. Any resemblance to actual persons, living or dead, events or locales is entirely coincidental.

Originally published in 2015 under the pseudonym of Mindy Hung.

Look for more great books at www.canelo.co

Printed and bound in Great Britain by Clays Ltd, Elcograf S.p.A.

1

Chapter One

The man with allergies never got the girl, at least in the movies Ian Zamora had seen, and Ian had watched enough of these films to last a lifetime. The man with the allergies couldn't enjoy life because he was busy sneezing in his soup or looking for tissues. He was fussy. He was hapless. He was the one who the girl always dumped after she met the hero. Well, Ian was going to be the hero this time. He certainly had the other credentials. When they weren't itchy and watering, his brown eyes glinted with steel. He could run a mile in seven and a half minutes (okay, eight) and use a belt sander. He looked good in jeans. Ian Zamora did not hunt for goddamn tissues – usually. Most of all, Ian was determined to get the girl, so the only solution was to get rid of his allergies.

If only his doctor would turn up.

The office of Dr. Petra Lale was completely empty that Tuesday afternoon. There was no receptionist in the waiting room and no one to greet Ian after he had climbed the stairs from the busy Portland street. The room was silent. At least it was clean, he thought, taking a step inside. Three magazines sat on a square coffee table, and the reception desk was clear of everything except a colorful paperback. In fact, except for a vague antiseptic tang in the air, there was no indication that any testing, checking, or healing was taking place at all in the white-walled office.

Ian glanced at the door again. Petra Lale, MD, Allergist, it said, in shiny new lettering. He nodded to himself, of course — who else was there to acknowledge him? —and sat gingerly in one of the shiny plastic chairs. It glistened like a gummy bear. At least it was comfortable.

Okay, so he didn't *really* want to be here.

He wasn't scared of doctors, or blood. He could bear needles with a minimum of flinching. Still, the idea of being tested for itches, then returning week after week for more jabs, just so that he could coexist with Danielle's cat — well, it wasn't his idea of the best time in the world. But he was determined to make a go of it with his new girlfriend and he was willing to think of the long game. That meant accommodating Snuffmaster Six — Snuffy for short. And because Ian preferred to live his life clear-eyed and clean-nosed — and his colleagues at the restaurant liked him that way, too — allergy shots were the order of business.

This relationship had better work out.

Just think of a cozy, domestic future, Ian told himself, squaring his shoulders. Danielle was smart and optimistic. She smelled like a cupcake. She was just the kind of woman he needed. For some sort of stable relationship, he was ready to endure a hundred thousand pricks of the needle.

At least.

Probably more.

The doctor had probably just stepped out for a moment. Or maybe she had been called away on an allergy emergency. Maybe some teenager had ingested too much pollen on a dare. Flowers: the natural high. All the kids were doing them. They'd have to license and regulate all the florists, hire extra security at the botanical gardens.

Where the fuck had that come from? Maybe he *was* scared of needles.

This was ridiculous. He had spent half his life in mining towns all around the world, crawling under fences, getting mud all over himself, learning how to use Swiss Army knives, and getting splinters while making lean-tos. He had a scar between his thumb and forefinger from the time he had accidentally grabbed some barbed wire while trying to help his friend retrieve a soccer ball. Hell, he was comfortable with drills and axes, and he worked around knives now. A couple of thin, stainless-steel needles administered by some chilly old woman in a lab coat would hardly hurt him.

He called out an irritated "hello," and stood up. In the restaurant business, you didn't keep people waiting. There was always something to offer: a glass of wine, a basket of bread, a refolded napkin, new silverware, a lighted candle. Professionals knew how to distract before they struck. He liked to train his wait staff as if they were assassins. Each little gift, each inquiry, each movement was part of a master plan.

Evidently, someone had heard him, though. After a thump and a muffled curse, the doctor finally swept open the door to the inner office. Ian pressed his lips together, ready to face a cranky old woman who didn't know or care about the state of her waiting room. He was going to march in, get poked, and march out. It would be easy.

A woman strode through and looked right at him.

Wow, he thought for a dazed minute. *Wow.*

She was definitely not old. In fact, she looked a lot younger than his thirty-two years, a fact emphasized by her elfin features, her pointy little nose, tawny skin, and short, dark hair. He shook his head to clear his addled

3

brain. This small, vivacious woman with the sharp gray eyes was the doctor, he reminded himself. Suddenly, the thought of receiving a thousand hurts from her hands was nothing compared to the way her eyes flashed when she caught sight of him.

Then he remembered. He was beginning something meaningful with a great, wonderful woman. He certainly wasn't attracted in any way to a disorganized, jumpy-looking *allergist* – his doctor, for heaven's sake. He was here for shots to smooth his way to move in with his girlfriend and her damned cat and live happily ever after. His time in this office was sure to be unpleasant, and full of stabbing and bleeding and itching. As she approached, he told himself that Dr. Lale smelled nothing like baked goods. She probably had chilly fingers and cleaned her skin with alcohol swabs. She probably wore latex gloves to bed.

Dammit, he was *not* picturing the allergist's lithe little body in bed, was he?

Eyes on the prize, he reminded himself. *Eyes on the prize.*

He thought of his plans for the future and gave the doctor a dark glower for making him forget.

–

Wow, Petra thought, taking in her new patient's dangerous glare, *this guy really doesn't like me.*

Granted, she was supposed to stick him with a bunch of tiny needles today, and some of those pricks were bound to itch. But he was one of the first patients in her new office, and she needed all the allergy-ridden bodies she could bring in to keep her fledgling practice afloat. She needed him to like her or, at least, return.

Petra led him into her office and stifled a sigh. She hadn't honestly thought that attracting people to her practice would be so difficult. She was already a worrier, and her puny patient base was making her desperate. She wasn't asking for much, just enough money to keep her in sensible shoes and make regular contributions to her retirement fund. She was fascinated by the immune system and all the little signals and subtleties that made it go haywire. But she admitted that she also thought allergy and immunology would afford her some measure of comfort and serenity. She would have regular hours. Patients would come by for shots, maybe a panel or a breathing test. Sometimes she would deal with a patient's asthma, but, for the most part, no shrieking at nurses in the ER, no crazy hours, no loonies, no nonsense.

No patients.

Well, no, there was one patient, right here, right now, with molten brown eyes framed by silver glasses. He glared at her as if she had already plunged a syringe into his arm. She wondered how long he had been sitting in her waiting room, and why she hadn't heard him come in. Somehow, somewhere, she needed to locate a scrap of professionalism.

She took a deep breath and reminded herself that she was the physician. She was in charge and she had some big needles. "You're here for an allergy screening, is that right, Mr. Zamora? I'm sorry there wasn't anyone to greet you today. My receptionist must have stepped out."

That wasn't exactly the truth. Business was so slow, Petra could only spring for a part-timer named Joanie who studied acting at the Willamette Academy of Drama. Joanie read from the complete works of J.R.R. Tolkien when the phone wasn't ringing – which was almost always. So, yes, the receptionist had stepped out.

For the rest of the week.

The Two Towers still lay on Joanie's desk.

Ian Zamora was making Petra so nervous that she was lying.

Petra put on a perky smile. She noticed that he waited until she sat down. Good manners, nice hair, *great deltoids*, she told herself, then tamped down the thought immediately.

"Maybe I should tell you a little bit about the test. It's called an allergen-specific IgE panel," she said, straightening her spine.

As she spoke, she cast her trained eye over the patient. Fit, she thought. Lean. Tall. Dangerous.

He's a patient, she reminded herself before her thoughts meandered in an unethical direction. Fibulae, tibulae, T cells, and lymph nodes, pecs, those deltoids again – well-developed deltoids outlined subtly under a tailored, blue button-down – beautiful, long quadriceps under his jeans. A runner maybe? He was certainly rangy but gifted with a graceful elasticity that was evident even in the way he walked and sat down. She shied hastily from that thought. An image of Hippocrates, the father of Western medicine, appeared in her head. He waggled his finger and tried to make himself heard over the shrill voice of Petra's hormones. *Do no harm*, he intoned, *and quit ogling your patient*. But really, did this Ian Zamora have to have such piercing brown eyes? Did he have to have knife-like cheekbones?

"Um, did you need me to fill out any paperwork?" he asked, shifting his athletic frame in the chair.

She gave a startled jump. Christ, she'd forgotten about the insurance forms. She straightened and tried to look like she'd been doing this forever and that he wasn't one of the first patients in her practice.

Maybe he hadn't noticed. "You can fill it out while we're waiting for the results of the test," she said. "It'll keep your mind off things."

"That's actually a good idea."

"Hum. Yes. Well, let me get a few more of your particulars, Mr. Zamora."

"Ian."

"Right," she snapped. "Ian."

She took out her smartphone and began asking him the standard questions about medications. The next moments flew by. She felt soothed by the familiar rhythm of the exam. She loved being a doctor. Even the routine things felt good: washing her hands, listening to heartbeats and checking blood pressure, pricking and marking the skin. It was the peripheral stuff – filling out insurance forms, figuring out the copays, even just talking to her receptionist (when she was there) – that threw her for a loop. She took out the panel and settled it into his skin, then withdrew it carefully. She gave him his paperwork, took his insurance card, and told him she'd be back in a few minutes. In front of the photocopier, she held her head between her hands.

Six years of med school, hundreds of thousands of dollars in debt. Now, Petra was standing in front of a combination fax/copier/printer that she barely understood. She stabbed at a button with her finger. It worked! *You are awesome!* she told herself.

It was the little things.

She looked around her. The honey-colored floors of the office were unscuffed by feet, and the coffee table shone glossily at her, polished to within an inch of its life. There was no dust lurking in the corners or curling under desks. She had beautiful equipment: an automatic blood pressure cuff, a customized records system, a USB spirometer that plugged into her laptop, a slim, European medical refrigerator with rows of tiny bottles filled with allergens. Her office was perfect. It was everything that she had ever dreamed of. Except...

Except, if she didn't start getting patients soon, she would tear through her savings and the money her father had left her. And if she lost all of her nest egg, she'd definitely have to close up the office. She rubbed her forehead. She would have to go work at Pronto!Docs, known among her classmates as The Factory, a multi-armed practice with offices in malls across the city. A couple of her medical school buddies worked there and they loathed it. Patients shuttled through the offices as if transported in and out on conveyor belts, and physicians acted like prescription-writing machines. But business poured in regularly and everyone got paid, which was far more than Petra could say for her own modest office.

She took a deep breath. She could stick out this early dry spell. She had a few patients. Ian Zamora could potentially be another. She just had to be friendly, helpful, and knowledgeable. *Professional*. She knocked on the office door and let herself in, then scrutinized his forearm. She touched his skin gently and for a moment, they were silent.

"Looks like you reacted to the dust," she said, blinking. "Cats, too. But that's all."

She took her hand away.

"I want the shots," Ian Zamora said, delivering the line with the coldness of an aristocrat. His eyes behind his glasses were inscrutable.

Was this guy for real?

"Uh, yes. Well, we can book them for your next visit, but first, I should probably discuss some of the options open to you," Petra said, pursing her lips to keep from an irrational urge to laugh. "Immunotherapy – the shots – will certainly lessen your reactions. But you'd have to come in once a week for the jabs and stay here for at least half an hour afterward so that we can monitor your reaction. It takes a long, long time – some people do this for years. And since you're only really allergic to dust and cats, you might be able to control the reaction with medication and avoidance of allergens."

Ian Zamora cleared his throat. "So if I understand you correctly, Doctor, you're actually trying to discourage me from coming here, week after week for a year or more, for your services?"

"I'm just trying to make sure you know all your options."

Ian Zamora shook his head and the beginnings of a smile finally began to play on his face. "That is what we call bungling the upsell."

"What does that mean?"

"It means that you should try to convince people to use the full extent of your services, no matter what."

His face changed suddenly and his voice dropped into the discreet tones of a waiter. "May I suggest a bottle of the 1927 Grapé de Welch's to go with your entrée, ma'am? Our sommelier can recommend a wine pairing for your salad. Dessert? Coffee? Tea? Dessert wine? Cookie plate? Surely a woman of your beauty hardly need watch her figure. An aperitif to go with your crème brûlée, perhaps?"

"I'll take it all," Petra said dryly. Then she flushed. She wasn't here to joke around. "But it's not really the same thing. I'm not out to make piles of cash off of people's ailments. Although I do need to start thinking of it more as a business. But my main duty is to make sure that patients stay well and, I don't know, live to come in another year. I don't believe in making people do something completely unnecessary and potentially harmful."

Ian looked wry, and a dimple appeared at the corner of his mouth. "So earnest. You're new at this, aren't you?"

"How can you tell?"

"The last doc told me I was allergic to ragweed, oaks, elms, dogs, and feathers and twenty different kinds of flowers. She recommended that I come in for a whole fusillade of needles, prickles, and ointments and pills. She wanted me to buy four different medications, and she told me we should do some food allergy testing. I balked, of course. Until now, I hadn't seen a reason to do anything about my allergies."

"Well, I'm not saying that she's wrong about your other sensitivities," Petra said carefully. "But some physicians find it, um, worth their while to err on the side of caution."

This time, Ian Zamora gave a real laugh. His eyes crinkled at the corners and his mouth opened wide to reveal slightly snaggled teeth. It was appallingly charming. Petra felt the full force of it in her solar plexus. "You're not saying she's wrong, but you *are* trying to find a nice way of telling me that she was full of shit," he said.

"If we must use layman's terms."

They exchanged a long look.

"Well, I want to receive the full, long treatment, Doc. I won't avoid cats because I have a special fondness for crazy cat ladies. My girlfriend is one." He smiled at Petra for some unspecified reason. "And nothing's going to persuade me to clean under my couch. I've got a little dust-bunny commune going there. They're like my room-mates." He paused, and glanced at Petra almost coyly. "I'll bet your place is immaculate."

Underneath the glasses, he had long lashes.

Petra grimaced. "Uh, no, my place is not immaculate. Why would you think that?"

"I guess I imagined it would be like this office."

They both glanced around at the shiny floors and Petra's bare desk. The glass and steel refrigerators hummed quietly in their corner. Petra laughed again even as she felt a little pang. "It's very spartan, isn't it? But it is supposed to be a place of business. It doesn't reflect who I am."

Not that she cared who he thought she was under the white coat, of course.

He quirked an eyebrow, which caused Petra to stop breathing.

"No, I suppose not," he said. "Besides, I hate to think what my office says about me."

Don't ask him any personal questions. He was clearly too dark and intense and masculine for the likes of her. It wouldn't inspire confidence if the allergist began hyper-ventilating in her own office. She turned away to hide her blush, and let out a small stream of air from her nose. "Okay, because you've decided you want to come in for the full course of shots, let me write out a couple of prescriptions and set up the first appointment for you for next week."

Rattling off instructions about nasal spray and pills helped restore her competence, in her own mind at least. She loaded his arms with leaflets about immunotherapy and a pile of samples, and practically pushed him out the door.

When he was safely gone, she sat down in one of the waiting room chairs. Her body tingled. She had never had this kind of reaction to a patient before. She hoped it would get better over time.

Chapter Two

Somewhere, in some handbook about single life, there was a chapter on what reasonably attractive, professional women should be doing at eight o'clock at night in the city. Staring at the ceiling while lying in bed, twitchy and alone, was probably not one of those things.

But it was hard to think about going out when she didn't have any money, or rather, when she was acutely aware of the trickle of pennies clinking from her purse. Ramen noodles had started to seem outrageously expensive.

It wasn't as bad as that, Petra chastised herself. She had an apartment and a fancy smartphone. She went out for brunch. But there was a gulf between the airy apartment that the world probably thought she could afford as a doctor and the dark, cramped space that she hid in tonight. She had grown up without luxuries, accustomed to waitressing, re-balancing her checkbook, forgoing backpacking abroad in favor of camping out at the financial aid office. Money, truth be told, was part of the reason that she became a physician. She liked the idea of financial security, and she thought it would put her mother at ease about Petra's future. Lisa Lale was a worrier, too. It was no wonder, having had to support first Petra, and then Petra's half-sister Ellie, after Lisa's husbands divorced her. But she hadn't been one of those strong, silent women. Lisa was a clucker, a hand-wringer, a sobbing, sighing second-guesser. She had a tendency to fret over every decision that she had to make, and now that Petra was on her own, Lisa agonized over her daughter's practice, too. Petra learned long ago not to tell her mother half the things that went wrong in her life. Her mother's quavering would probably kill her.

I should probably take off my shoes, Petra thought, staring at the ceiling. It seemed a gargantuan task.

The phone rang. Luckily, it was on her night table and she only had to move her arm to find it. "Tell me. Tell me why I'm already a failure at age thirty-one," Petra said, without bothering to see who it was. It could only be one of her best friends: Sarah or Helen.

"You need a good fuck is all," Sarah said.

"Why do gynecologists always think that everything begins and ends in the vagina?"

"Well, it does, in most manners of speaking."

"I can hear you smirking."

"You can't hear a smirk. It's a facial expression."

"I can hear yours. Your lips smack away from your gums like a rubber band."

"Gross."

"Yeah, I associate that twang with smug amusement now. You'd be funnier if you didn't laugh at all your own jokes, Sarah."

"Feisty. What's wrong with you, anyway? Tell the doctor your troubles."

Petra jumped from the bed and began to pace. She felt embarrassed. She and Sarah were friends, yes, but competition had also been inevitable. Medical school and residency fostered envy and tension, especially among people who were used to being smart and in control of

14

everything. But she didn't feel smart or in control now. Sarah and Helen were great. They didn't take bullshit and they didn't celebrate when others failed. But Petra didn't want to be the one they pitied. She didn't want to be Poor Petra.

"You don't need to hear me cry," she told Sarah.

"Sob on me, Petey. I'm like a washcloth. I can be wrung out. I love terrible dating stories. Besides, I need the distraction."

Petra could hear Sarah was moving around her apartment, folding clothing or straightening her papers. Sarah collected file cabinets the way other people collected Shaker furniture. Raven-haired Sarah was the most organized person that Petra knew. Sometimes, Petra could pretend to be like her. People even thought she was like that: Dr. Lale, organized and calm. But at most, she achieved a kind of superficial neatness. The bathtub sparkled and there were no weird smells from the refrigerator. But under the bed lay unmatched socks, playing cards, pennies. The closets were jammed with oversized, undersized, and just plain dirty clothing. Copies of her tax returns sat in piles on her desk. Pen caps and more nickels and dimes lurked in the drawer. Late at night, she thought of scraping together all the loose change in the apartment, rolling it up, and taking it to the bank. But usually, she abandoned the project halfway through and left little piles of money, like pots of gold, scattered throughout her apartment.

Sarah would never have made a mistake like opening her own practice right after residency. She had gone to work for The Factory and now she could afford premium-steel file cabinets in all colors of the rainbow. Petra, on the other hand, had spent all the money that her father had left her on renting the Pearl District office space, an examining table, a fancy spirometer, and countless little boxes of sterile pads, bandages, syringes, and creams. Oh sure, she had told herself at the time that it was a sensible decision grounded in theories about long-term versus short-term fulfillment and projections about customer base – no, *patients*, not customers – and so forth. But, really, her main impulse had been to build something, to own something, to say that it was hers and hers alone.

"The problem is that I'm a loser," Petra said, finally giving in. "I can't attract patien— I mean, people. I can't hang on to the ones that do get lured in. I don't know how to get myself out there. I don't know how to attract the right... er... men and others to come in for all the things I have to offer."

"We're not talking about boys, are we, Petey?"

Petra sighed. "No, we're not talking about boys."

"Why can't we ever talk about boys?"

"I promise, we'll talk about them later." Unaccountably, her thoughts flew to Ian Zamora. Now there was someone worth giggling about with one's girlfriend. With that crooked smile, the shiny glasses and shinier eyes, and very nice arms.

Except he's your patient, her inner Hippocrates yelled. *First do no fucking harm.*

Clearly, inner Hippocrates needed his own T-shirt line.

But it was true. Ian Zamora was a patient. She was going to have to be able to take care of him without drooling over him. Petra shook herself. "Right now, I have more pressing problems. Like, how am I going to drum up more business? What am I going to do if I have to shut down my practice? How am I going dispose of all those shiny, lacquered office chairs I picked out after

I'm destitute and unable to afford a cell phone to call the Salvation Army to pick them up? I love those chairs, Sarah."

She heard Sarah open a drawer. "It's hard striking out on your own," Sarah said. "That's why so few of us did it."

"I think I lost my head when my dad left me that money. It was so unexpected. I hadn't talked to the man for fifteen years. Figures he'd be the one to get me in over my head."

Petra tried to sound light, but Sarah understood. "Anything I can do?" she asked.

Sarah had snapped into advice-giving mode. Petra did this, too. She was, after all, a physician. Nevertheless, she braced for some of Sarah's straight talk.

Petra gathered a deep breath. "I know they frown on sending patients away from The Factory farm, but maybe you could nudge some my way. Those teenagers you treat must break out in hives sometimes."

"Not the ones I see. Most of them are too horny to care whether they're allergic to anything. Look, I know things are tough for you right now, but at The Factory, I'm a pill vending machine. Scratch that. I'm more of a handy birth control prescription printer. If I were a vending machine, I'd take in cash and that would be awesome. Stupid physician drug dispensary laws. And as for hospital work and research? Even Helen's not happy with that. What I'm saying is that you shouldn't beat yourself up. It's not like I'm ecstatic with my life. You didn't make such a bad choice."

"It'll be a bad choice if I go under."

"It's a brand-new practice. Give it a while. Besides, if there's anything I've learned from working at The Factory, it's that you have to advertise and network. Do you have a web strategy?"

"I have a website."

"That free website from Brazil?"

"St. Barts. St. Barts is classy."

"Petra, if you feel the need to qualify something as classy, it is usually the exact opposite of classy. Let's examine the facts. You've got a free website that proclaims its cheapness with its name: Freeeeebie with five Es, dot BL, slash server, dot number sign, exclamation point, DocPeetra. And what's with all the extra Es everywhere? Were vowels on sale? And how about the flashing banner ads on all sides? It's in Spanish."

"French."

Sarah snorted. "Right, because language choice is really going to help. Pete, darling, you know I love you. But… you're cheap when it comes to the things that make an impression."

"I'm frugal."

"No, you're cheap. Remember when we all decided to go on that health kick in third year, and you wore scrubs to the gym instead of exercise gear?"

"They were perfect workout clothes."

"And you used a rubber band to hold up your hair?"

"What's wrong with that?"

"I think it still had the words 'romaine lettuce' and the code stamped on it. Cheap, cheap, cheap, Petra, that's what you are. How is anyone ever going to find your site with that web address? And if they do, what does it say about you?"

"Websites aren't that important anyway."

"They're something. And you, my friend, have nothing. Zero, zippo, zilch, nothing, nada."

"Not helping, Mr. Roget."

"Okay, let's forget the website for now. What about those physician-ratings type sites? Are you on them? Have you Googled yourself to see how you're doing? You have to make sure all the doctor-review pages have your name and information down correctly – you know, credentials, office location, what insurance you take. You have to get some reviews up—"

"Reviews?"

"Yeah, patient ratings. Testimonials. Get someone to write something nice about your staff, your bedside manner, the damn magazine selection. Ask all your patients to do it at their appointments and have them give you a bunch of stars."

"Do people even read the magazines anymore? Don't they have smartphones to keep them entertained?"

"Please tell me you have magazines in your waiting room. Or a TV, or something."

"I have a copy of *Time* and *People*. Maybe a *Us Weekly*. I could put out my old *Scientific Americans*."

Sarah was very, very quiet.

"Oh hell," Sarah said, finally. "This is going to be more work than I thought."

-

Gerry, Ian's head chef, business partner, and buddy, noticed the bumps on Ian's arm right away. "You could kill the cat," Gerry said, spearing a meatball with his fork. He shrugged when Ian sent him a glare. "What? It's a lump. And mangy. I never knew what mangy meant until I saw a picture – or five million – of that cat. Who has the mange nowadays, anyway? It's like scurvy or leprosy. That cat was probably around when people still suffered from those diseases."

"You're suggesting I get rid of a woman's beloved pet because it's got an unfashionable ailment?"

"I'm not suggesting you throw it in front of a trolley or anything. I mean, put the darn thing out of its misery. It's, what, ninety in cat years? It would be a mercy killing. Better than what you're sentenced to. Shots once a week? Are allergies even real? Besides, it's not like Danielle and you are really, really serious yet. You're just gambling on the long-range possibility of a stable relationship. Just because you hate living alone in your glass tower—"

"I don't care where we live, Ger. She's perfect for me. Smart, pretty. But more importantly, I've finally met a woman who understands about my schedule—"

"Maybe if you eased up, you wouldn't need a woman who doesn't care that you're a workaholic."

"I'm okay with the shots. The shots are fine. And soon, cat dander won't bother me. With a little immunotherapy, I'll get over it."

Gerry drew a disgusted face and made a big show of pushing aside his plate. Most of the kitchen staff had already left the table to begin pounding, chopping, and cursing at high volumes. One of the bussers, Marco, started clearing the table from the staff meal. Gerry stood up and stretched. "All right, all right. You're trying with the cat lady. I shouldn't insult her. Plus," Gerry admitted grudgingly, "she's plugged in to the food scene here. And her voice is so honey-sweet that you can almost forget the fact that she's a lawyer and she's fleecing you left and right."

It was high praise from Gerry. Ian grabbed a pile of dirty plates and headed toward the sinks. He helped Marco load the huge industrial dishwasher. Idly, he thought about Petra Lale. "Plus, I like my allergist. If I'm going to get stuck with needles, then at least she'll be a good person to see week after week. She's… very nice."

And she has a beautiful laugh.

"Lady doctor," said Gerry, brightening.

"Yes, I'm told they're allowed to practice medicine now. They even vote and ride bicycles astride."

"I wouldn't mind having a female's healing hands on me, even if she is an allergist. If the woman's loaded, I could live with being man candy. I'd drown my shame in baubles and bonbons."

Remembering the talk he'd had with Dr. Lale, and the empty state of her waiting room, Ian shook his head. There was no way this doc was pulling in the big bucks, if that was the way her practice operated. He wondered if he should try to send people her way. He remembered what it was like to start a new business – *No*, he told himself. He could not afford to start seeing her as a woman in need. She was his physician. End of story.

"Trust me, she's not your type, Ger, fiscally or physically."

"Introduce me anyway," Gerry called as Ian walked away.

Ian was still shaking his head as he entered his basement office. Field, his restaurant, forced him to put in long hours at his computer, on the phone, at the front of the house, in the kitchen, in the alley, and even in the supply closets. He had only one day off a week, and even then, he often found himself coming in to make phone calls and interview staff. When he got really stir-crazy, he went for a run. If he couldn't leave, he did pushups in the corner of his office. He had a silly boxing ball hanging from the ceiling, and he stuck pictures of critics and bloggers on it. Sometimes, he felt like a troll under a bridge, hardly seeing sunlight. Back before Field had gotten popular, he played soccer on weekends, but now Saturdays and Sundays were his busiest days. Danielle was a saint to put up with the constant phone calls that had him dashing off to fix leaking roofs, remedy produce emergencies, and mediate wait staff wars. Yet, here he sat, devising ways to keep his allergist out of Gerry's clutches. Not that Gerry was a terrible person. But Petra Lale seemed so vulnerable in her empty office.

He pushed up his glasses and rubbed his face. He hadn't seen Danielle in a week. Maybe his mind kept dwelling on his allergist because he couldn't remember what his girlfriend looked like. It wasn't terrible to admit that he found other people pleasing to the eye, he reasoned. Petra Lale was an attractive woman. He was allowed a tiny, harmless crush.

By the afternoon of his next visit, he was feeling much more sanguine. He'd had an aberrant reaction to her last time. Luckily, Dr. Lale's professional manner had also improved. She flew out of her inner office and administered his shots efficiently. She ushered him to a seat to wait out his reactions. Another patient, a kid sporting angry red welts on his upper arms, soon joined him. Then, all was quiet again – except for the kid panting loudly through his mouth. Every thirty seconds, he seemed to make a snort deep in his throat. Ian wondered if he should summon Dr. Lale. But just as he was about to rise up, the kid looked up from his iPhone, right at Ian. He seemed to be breathing in regular intervals despite the fact that he sounded like a llama working up to spit.

The kid smirked, then seemed to choke on a cough. Served him right.

Ian settled back down. They were the only ones in the waiting room.

The doctor's office door was partly open and she was on the telephone. She seemed to be trying to soothe someone. She had a musical voice and when it pitched lower, it stirred the hairs on the back of Ian's neck.

He decided that now would be a good time to call his girlfriend.

"How's it going?" he asked Danielle.

The kid sitting across from him raised his eyebrows.

Ian turned a little in his seat. He lowered his voice. "I hope I'm not interrupting anything."

"Oh, everything's great," Danielle chirped. "We're fine-tuning the Hammerstein contract and eating some lunch. Chinese, from Golden Palace. We got the crystal dumplings and the chicken mixed vegetables and those funny little spicy noodles that you like. I told Mark and Janet to try them and they loved them."

Danielle always assumed that he wanted a full report on what she was eating, even if it was a cookie from the break room. It was cute, if a little annoying. "That's great," he said. "Listen, are you going to be working late tonight? I was thinking you could stop by the restaurant—"

"Sorry, baby, I have to stay a lot longer. Billable hours, you know. We've got widows to swindle. Could you do me a favor, though? Would you stop by this afternoon and fill Snuffy's water dish and give him some dry, grain-free kibble? No wet foodstuffs, not even if he begs for it. And if you'd entertain him for a little while with the feather toy? The vet says he's becoming overweight and we need to exercise him more, but I haven't had time to engage him in productive calorie-burning behaviors lately."

"I could feed the cat," he said, a little dubiously. "I can't stay with him long, though. Allergic, remember?"

"Key's under the flowerpot. Thank you. Love you."

"Right. Okay. See you."

Ian tucked away his phone.

"Was that your girlfriend?" the kid asked.

"Yes," Ian said.

"Is she a model?"

"Uh, no," said Ian.

"Then why were you sucking up to her?"

"I wasn't sucking up," Ian said. "I just happen to be around to feed her cat."

"You're allergic to cats. That's why you're here, isn't it?"

"Agreeing to feed her cat isn't buttering her up. She doesn't usually make demands on me, which is how we like it."

The kid shrugged, as if not quite believing him.

It might have been wise to retreat at this point, but Ian couldn't bring himself to give up to a preteen. "I actually like the cat, you know."

Mild disinterest.

"It isn't polite to eavesdrop."

"It's not like I can help it," the kid said. "You're right across from me, and I don't have anything better to do. I read all of these *Scientific Americans* already. I thought Tesla was a car, not some guy."

Ian was saved from replying by the doctor.

"Tesla was the man who invented the alternating current," Doc Lale said, sweeping in. "The AC in AC/DC," she said, cocking her head. "Kevin, are you going to be okay out here? I'm going to have Mr. Zamora come into my office for a few minutes. Cough really loudly if you think you're dying."

She grinned and ruffled his hair. The kid smiled smugly at Ian, as if Ian should be jealous. Ian resisted the urge to kick him and instead simply followed Petra Lale into her office. She told Ian to roll up his sleeves again. His cuffs felt too tight. The spots where she had injected the allergen were red and puffy. The doctor murmured something about putting cream on them, and turned away. In a moment, she began to smooth a white ointment on his itchy arms. He swallowed hard and suddenly felt very aware of her fingers on his skin.

Why had he never realized how small the room was? It was almost a closet, really. He turned and noticed how close her head was to his. He could study the sharp arch of her brows, her thin, dusky lips. If he moved just a little bit, he would be able to rub his cheek on her curls. Her breath fanned lightly over his neck.

He felt a hot slide of lust and immediately tried to dampen it. So much for thinking that he wouldn't react to her again.

His face was on fire, although whether it was because his lower body had tightened or because he was embarrassed, he wasn't sure. He thought of penguins in Antarctica and ice-cold waterfalls. He thought of glaciers and meat lockers. In fact, he became so busy ignoring her that he almost failed to register that she was asking him a question.

"I was wondering," she was saying, hesitantly. "If you have a chance, would you mind writing a review of the practice for one of those doctor rating sites? I can send you the links, if you'd like. DocStars.com is really popular, I've heard."

She was still swirling cream into his bicep as she spoke, concentrating hard on her task, as if she were deciphering Braille rather than just soothing him. Her cheeks were pink too, Ian noticed. He shifted uncomfortably in his chair.

She must have misinterpreted his silence because she added, "You know, be honest, of course. But I'm trying to raise the profile of the practice and every bit helps."

She returned his arm to him. They both stared at it, unable to look at each other. Ian tried to form a coherent thought.

"I'll try to think of things to write," he said.

She looked so sad and embarrassed that a stab of pity penetrated his confusion. She had been honest with him and had even tried to tell him that he might not need shots when others had clamored to give him more drugs and more tests. She seemed competent. Then again, he'd only had two appointments and her front office left a lot to be desired, especially with that kid around. Not that it was her fault.

"I understand what it's like," he said. "All reviews make a difference. I'll try to be fair."

He began to roll down his cuffs again, giving his unruly body more time to settle. He allowed himself to peer over at the doctor.

"I'd rather get a rave," she confessed.

Ian laughed. "Do you have any other patients?"

"Drowning in them," she said. She gave a crisp nod. "We probably shouldn't talk about this anymore. I'm stepping over the line."

"No, I don't mind," he said quickly. He forced his business mind to take over. "I noticed that you're running the show solo most of the time. It might be a good idea to have things more solid before you ask for people to assess you. Have your receptionist in place, maybe have more magazines, or books, or maybe get a water cooler for the waiting room. You wouldn't want superficial things to cloud customers' – I mean patients' – judgment. I speak from experience."

"Yes, I remember you told me that you were in the restaurant business. Is it someplace I know?"

"Have you heard of Field? It's a block or so from here on North West 11th Street."

She looked impressed. Ian tamped down the surge of warmth. "That place is supposed to be great," she said. "My friend went last month. She couldn't stop talking about the hush puppies. Oh, and I think she mentioned warm buttermilk biscuits. Helen likes her carbs."

"Sounds like a girl after my own heart. You'll have to come with her next time. Stop by after work sometime and mention my name," he said. "We'll feed you real well."

Despite his offhand manner, his legs shifted restlessly. He had managed to get his heart rate down again, but for some reason, he felt guilty inviting her. Hell, he suspected that he had broken at least seven commandments while she rubbed cream on his arm. Luckily, Dr. Lale didn't sense his discomfiture. She laughed. "Someday, when I strike it rich," she said lightly. "You're good to go. Same time next week?"

He nodded and stood up. Not a moment too soon. He needed some distance from Petra Lale. He needed to think long and hard before he did anything rash, even though in his mind, he'd already come to a decision. Plus, his arm itched like crazy.

Chapter Three

"Petra, Petra, Petra," her friend and former classmate Scott Santos said. "Tell me, why didn't we ever…?"

Santos never finished his thoughts. He didn't have to. Usually there was some love-struck girl hovering, ready to complete his sentences, and often that woman used that implied *sympatico* to convince herself that she and the Saint were soulmates. He was good, Petra admitted to herself, assessing his strong wrists and solid forearms as he swirled a glass of something golden and expensive-looking. His flexors flexed, as they should. Scott Santos was a beautiful man. Idly, she compared him to her patient, Ian Zamora. They were both dark-haired and about the same height. They were also both healthy, athletic specimens. But where Scott was big and bluntly handsome with strong arms and pretty lips, Ian Zamora was craggy, lean, and raffish. He looked like he could do real mischief, despite the preppy tailoring of his button-down shirts.

And then he smiles, and the world tilts on its axis.

She wondered where he was right now. Probably not drinking down soda and sucking up to former classmates. His business kept him occupied at night, and he had a girlfriend who was probably gorgeous and charming and polished – nothing like Petra. This was a dangerous line of thought, and it was one that she shouldn't sustain. She'd had several appointments with him now and at the end of each one, when she took his arm to check his reactions, she felt her own skin grow hot. She was responding to him, yes, but she was also flushing because of the guilt she felt. She hardly knew what she was doing tonight; she certainly couldn't afford to dream of someone else's evening.

Santos raised the bourbon to his perfect mouth and smiled at her before swallowing. "So why didn't we—"

"As a matter of fact, we did," Petra said tightly. "For a week, in the middle of our psych clerkship."

Actually, it had been more like five sloppy encounters. But clarifying that their hasty hook-ups took place over the length of a business week made it sound so pathetic. Then again, so was remembering the whole affair when Santos had clearly forgotten.

"Of course," Santos said smoothly. "What I meant was, why didn't we ever try it again?"

He edged away as he said it, though, and began scanning the crowd. A few eyes blinked dewily at him. It was obscene. Even though most here at the alumni happy hour knew his reputation, he still attracted lovely, otherwise-intelligent women. She wondered if Ian Zamora had women sighing for him over their hush puppies. Hell, the man had his restaurant where he could line the ladies up and charge them for viewing. No wonder he had a girlfriend.

Petra gulped down her club soda and wished she were somewhere else instead of trying to drum up referrals. Helen, a neurologist, had come with her, but she was arguing with her ex-boyfriend in the corner. *No help there*. Petra would rather be home drinking boxed wine and reading *The Lancet* on the Internet than barging in on conversations and generally making an ass of herself.

Buttonholing people was so out of character for her. Her embarrassment made her punchy and time was wasting.

"Santos," she snapped, as Scott started to creep away. "Attention back here for five more minutes, please. I was going to ask you a favor. I just started my own allergy practice over in the Pearl District and I was looking for referrals."

"I was wondering why you showed up at this thing. You never usually do."

"It's not really my scene. I'm not good at flattery and batting my eyelashes, or even pretending that you interest me anymore. Will you help me or not?"

She was not being smooth at all. She was going to hate herself in the morning. Maybe she should start drinking. But slurry Petra wouldn't be able to convince any one of her peers to send her patients. She sighed and began to turn away. Santos took her arm.

"Petra, I'm sorry," he said, looking slightly shamefaced. "I'm at that huge group practice, Westside Associates, and we're really working to compete. Plus, Ray Khatri – he was a couple of years ahead of you, I think – his office is right next to mine, so I usually try to send people his way. He's a good guy." He attempted a smile and shrugged.

"Asshole," Petra muttered into her club soda. Louder, she said, "Just throw me a bone, Santos. One out of every five patients, or something. Ray won't notice if it's infrequent. Please," she added.

Santos sighed and rubbed through his hair. "I forgot what an intense little person you are, Petra. Guess Ray can't complain if I keep it on the down low. I'll see what I can do." He relaxed a little more and pursed his lips. "Good for you for striking out on your own. If I didn't have all this debt from med school, I'd love to start a solo practice instead of dealing with the bullshit. I don't know how realistic it is for me, though. I guess we all think we can make our own hours, not have to see eighty coughs and colds a day."

He looked at her with lazy jealousy, or at least as much envy as a hot, single, male physician could muster up for a desperate woman. He slid nearer to her once again. "So, Petra, maybe sometime we can get together and reminisce about the time we spent in the…"

His smile gleamed in the night.

"The utility closet?" Petra finished for him. "And the seventeen minutes door-to-door that we took off to screw in the apartment I shared with Helen? That sounds unbearably romantic, but I think I prefer to leave those memories pure and sacred. You know, something to keep me warm in the cold nights."

Santos laughed again, pecked her on the cheek, and started to stroll toward a knot of fresh-faced dermatology residents. "Actually, Petey, I think we went to my place," he called softly. "And we took at least twenty-two minutes, if not twenty-three."

Petra watched him disappear and swore softly. The bastard was right on the location, at least. She turned and went to rescue Helen from her ex. This was definitely shaping up as one of the most humiliating nights in recent history.

–

Ian raced to get the check to table sixteen. It was going to go down as a bad night. Two of his servers had called in sick, Gerry was having some sort of meltdown over pork bellies, and Danielle had popped in while he was in the middle of plunging a toilet in the men's bathroom. She only had two minutes, she said. She was meeting sorority sisters for drinks, so he had settled for kissing her on the cheek instead of the long talk he'd wanted to have with her.

It wasn't working out between them and she didn't seem to know it.

Then again, he hadn't much noticed it either, until he realized in his allergist's office that he would rather make time for a series of painful shots than actually spend time with his girlfriend.

Ian sighed. He and Danielle had managed to miss each other for nearly a week now. She had recently made partner, and she had hundreds of very close friends whom she did not want to disappoint. And he was busy cajoling suppliers, fixing plumbing, and dealing with health inspections by day, while by night he was defusing tensions between Gerry and hostess Lilah, and Gerry and the pastry chef, and all of the front of the house staff. He was greeting guests, hiding mops, finding mops, and doing the floors, and everything in between.

He could have pushed it. He could have set aside some time to take her to a movie, or drink a cup of coffee, or even just drive her to work. Not once had he even tried. He couldn't muster the interest.

He looked down at his stained shirt and sighed. He was no prize, either. No wonder she hadn't wanted to stick around tonight. He smelled like steak and sewage. He mentioned that they needed to chat, and she had agreed before breezing out the door. Maybe she was feeling the same way.

He checked his phone and grimaced. It was already eleven. The guests wouldn't see him, but the staff would.

It was times like these that he hated being the person in charge. He tramped down to his office and stripped off his offensive clothing.

A knock sounded at the door. "Everything okay?" Gerry asked, sauntering in.

"Aren't you supposed to be upstairs being a chef?"

"Isla's working it," Gerry grunted. "Although she under-salts everything. You'd think she'd have learned that from the fancy institute of culinary ass-lick she attended."

Gerry had a grudge against culinary school. He was largely self-taught.

"I'd hit that, though," he added.

"Harassment," Ian said ominously.

"Oh, please, you've been hanging out too much with lawyers. Us restaurant people are constantly horny. Comes from not enough sunlight and lack of exercise. And don't you try to pretend that you're above it all, Lord Military Pushup of the Washboard Abs. You may look like a goddamn footballer, but underneath it all, you're a troll like the rest of us."

"I am," Ian said gloomily.

He paused, gauging what he should say. If he told Gerry how distracted he'd been and that his doctor was the one doing it to him, he'd never hear the end of it. Still, he had to give Gerry a warning shot.

"I'm breaking up with Danielle."

"Wow." Gerry shook his head. "Really. Wow. I was resigned to a lifetime of that woman. And yeah, she's all wrong for you, but wow, Ian Zamora is backtracking on the master life plan."

"Thanks, Ger. Way to rub it in."

"Sorry, sorry. I can't − this is really unlike you. I've never seen you deviate from long-term goals before. I mean, raising the capital, finding this space, building the place, the business – I've seen you over the years. This has never happened before."

"Okay, Gerry, I get it."

But Gerry wasn't done. He dropped into a chair then sat up abruptly. "It's the shots, isn't it? It's all fun and games until someone sticks you with a needle."

Ian grimaced and debated what to tell his friend. "I'll still be going in for them for a while."

"What? Why?"

"It's good to… not be allergic to dust. And cats," he said.

"O-kay," Gerry said. "You're not planning on opening an antiques store soon, are you?"

Luckily, a knock sounded on the door and a fresh crisis blew in. As he and Gerry raced up the stairs, Ian berated himself for not admitting to his friend that he had enough of a crush on Petra Lale to keep going back for more of her medicine. Then again, the less Gerry knew about some things, the better.

At the end of the night, Ian stuffed his soiled shirt in his backpack and checked his pockets for his iPhone. After a terse farewell to his staff, he set out into the humid air.

His apartment was only a few blocks from the restaurant. When he had first started Field, he lived by the airport with four roommates and three messy dogs. On nights when he couldn't be bothered to drive home, he would spend the night on the cramped floor of his office. Now he lived alone in a nice enough apartment. He should have loved the high ceilings and the big windows that faced the sun. But he was never there during the day, and at night, when he returned, he found the dark and silence depressing.

He had no family left. His mother passed when he was a teenager and his father died on a night very much like this one, when Ian was in his twenties.

Gerry was right. Ian wasn't one to abandon the plan. But he'd started this relationship – all of his relationships – hoping it would be serious. Yet he still felt alone. Part of it was that he worked a lot. But then, he worked because he had no one else. He assumed that when he met the right person that he'd be able to relax – that he'd want to enjoy that feeling of togetherness that he'd never had.

Ian sniffed the air. He was in the mood to make reckless decisions. He could avoid his apartment if he walked toward the water to Chinatown. He could go to a bar and drink. He could get into a fight, steal a motorcycle, TP someone's lawn so that he wouldn't have to be lonely and vulnerable for another goddamn night. He could abandon the weeks he'd spent cultivating one girlfriend so that he could pursue this indefinable and possibly imaginary thing with a gray-eyed woman who stabbed him with two needles every time they met.

He paused as a taxicab discharged a passenger in front of him and with a start, he realized that it was Petra Lale. It was as if his loneliness had conjured her.

"I am never, ever wearing shoes again," Dr. Lale was muttering as she bent to adjust the strap of her shoe.

The jolt of seeing her under streetlamps, instead of the harsh fluorescent glare of her office lights, made his heart race. Deference for her healing skills was not at the top of his mind right now. She was wearing a short trench coat and high, very wobbly heels. She had nice, if unsteady, legs. He wanted to close his fingers around her ankle and slide his thumb up. He tried to cover his lechery with fake heartiness. "Petra Lale, MD," Ian said, as she turned slowly. "Are you *drunk*?"

Her head whipped up. "Ian." A pause. "No, I'm not. I swear, it's just that I'm not used to these stilettos. I can't move more than six steps without feeling like the Little Mermaid after she grows feet."

She seemed even more twitchy than usual. She smoothed down her coat and shifted to one foot. "Hans Christian Andersen wrote a very tragic story," she said. "Not as pathetic as the evening I just endured at the hands of my esteemed colleagues, but sad nonetheless. In summary: not drunk, just hobbled and defeated."

She gave him a collapsed smile. Ian was concerned. "What was so terrible?"

She squeezed her eyes shut and whispered, "I just spent the night *networking*."

He laughed. It was the first time that had happened this evening, he realized, and it felt very good. "Oh come on, it couldn't have been that bad."

She peered at him, her face still scrunched up. "It was exactly as horrible as that. I know I shouldn't say this, but I kind of hate doctors, even the ones I'm friends with. A whole roomful of them, drinking dirty martinis, talking about emergency sedation, and trying to one-up one another is some kind of hell. I'm just not built for that kind of jousting, especially when they're all trying to act nonchalant while bopping their heads to Coldplay. You've heard me talk. I get nervous and spout obscure facts about T cells and Serbian inventors. It's not like I dazzle anyone with my jokes and good looks. Not like you," she added quietly.

He gave her a quick look. Her volubility was quickly chasing away his dark mood. "You have your own charm."

37

Another half smile. "If I were charming, I'd be telling you that you were charming, thus charming you. But I'm not and you are, and that's why."

"Are you sure you're not drunk, Doc?"

"My point is that this sort of thing is probably effortless for you. You go out onto the floor with all that going on" – she waved her hand up and down at him – "and people just swoon at your feet."

"Are you trying to tell me that you find me irresistible?"

"No. I mean – no."

She looked at her feet. It was too dark to tell if she was blushing, but he was pretty sure that she was. Without the dignity of her white coat, she seemed vulnerable and human. Well, she had always been human to him, but now, even more so. It appeared that the good doctor was not immune to his attractions either.

"It's not all about looks and glibness," Ian said. "And you can't actually be telling me that you think you're utterly without wits."

She brushed her hair aside and looked wry. "I know that I look acceptable and that I can engineer a proper turn of phrase," she said. "I didn't mean to imply that you had nothing going on besides the lean and dangerously handsome thing. Obviously, you're confident and successful. And you have a natural ability to make people laugh and set them at ease. It's no wonder your restaurant does so well. I just don't have that, especially lately. Maybe because I'm just starting out and the waiting room is empty. I guess when I begin to see failure on the horizon, I start to think that maybe there's something fundamentally wrong with me."

"This isn't about you. This isn't something you necessarily have control over."

He took off his glasses and rubbed them. They were gazing at each other, and speaking more and more quietly. Cars drove by, streaking their headlights across her face. She looked unhappy and tired, and Ian felt the irrational urge to kiss the sadness away. More than a kiss. He wanted to take her into his apartment and strip the trench coat and dress off of her. He wanted to put her in his shower and wash her small body and lay her on his bed so that she could relax and sleep. In the back of his mind, Ian realized that his thoughts had gone entirely too far. This conversation had become personal and he had no wish to stop it.

"When I first started out in the restaurant business," he said, "I wasn't this way at all. It's a notoriously difficult field to survive in. A lot of people go into it thinking it's going to be glamorous. They think it's tablecloths and chocolate cake appearing from nowhere. I was twenty-seven and was still getting my MBA when I met Gerry, my chef and business partner. My father had died the year before of a melanoma. He was a geologist. He was really smart and interested in how everything worked and in learning about the world."

Petra touched him on the arm. He wanted to slide her palm up, across his shoulder to his chest. Her face was turned away slightly, as if she were trying to hear him better.

"Anyway," Ian continued, blinking, "his death spurred me to make my MBA project into a reality. It's a terrible business to go into if you want a life of your own, but at the time, I just wanted to bury myself. Everyone thought I was a naïve, dumb kid, and they were probably right. I might as well have been chewing on a piece of hay while a banjo played in the background."

"And now you're thirty-two and everyone thinks you're the shit," she said softly.

"Oh, I wouldn't say that. If you'd seen me on plunger duty tonight, you'd change your mind. My point is that nothing comes effortlessly. No one is without doubt." He rubbed his forehead. "Anyway, how did you know how old I was?"

"I have your medical records."

They looked at each other for a long moment. The air was stirring with something warm and humid. Rain was probably approaching, but Ian felt no urge to hurry home. "How old are you?" Ian asked, unable to contain his curiosity.

"I'm thirty-one," she said, almost shyly.

"Have you always wanted to be a doctor?"

"Almost always," she said. "But I guess I didn't understand then how much of it would be paperwork and just calming people down."

She made a vague gesture toward the sky and Ian looked that way, as if he could actually see what plagued her, written in the dark clouds. One question and one answer wasn't enough. He wanted to know things about her: where she had grown up, if she had brothers and sisters. He wanted to know whether there really was dust under her couch. He wanted to trace her jaw with his hands and press his thighs against hers and ask her in whispers, in her ear, and watch her curls spring back as he pulled them. Was it forging an illusion of intimacy with her because they shared pain and succor and breathing space once a week? Looking at her face streaked by streetlights, he could not believe that it was so. They watched each other too carefully.

She liked him. Maybe even as much as he liked her. He had a chance with her. That was all he needed to know.

She opened her mouth as if to say something, but the rain that had threatened all night came down around them like streamers at a New Year's party. She shook her head.

Ask me, he thought. *Tell me something. Keep talking to me.*

But she started to back away and he had to, too. Here, on the street, with her edges becoming soft and wet, he knew that he could not stay. He had to be content with calling out good night.

Chapter Four

"You and Scott Santos," Helen said. "Spill it."

They were drinking fancy juice drinks and eating tofu scrambles at Breakfast Bar. It had been Sarah's turn to pick a brunch place, obviously. Petra stared at her nearly empty glass. The Kale Mary tasted tangy, salty, and delicious, but it had been expensive, especially considering it didn't contain any alcohol. Absently, Petra grabbed the rest of the spelt and olive focaccia from the breadbasket and wondered if it would be gauche to ask their waitress for more. None of the other patrons looked like they ate bread.

"You didn't agree to go out with him again, did you?" Sarah said. She pushed back her short, black hair.

Petra shuddered. "Of course not. I was, as usual, aggressive and uncool. He was, as usual, gorgeous and obnoxious. I almost lost my temper and punched him. He triumphed and smoldered. End of story."

"Why did you even talk to him? Helen, why didn't you stop her?"

"Helen was occupied," Petra said, shooting her friend a sharp glance. Sarah and Helen had been at odds lately, but neither seemed willing to explain why. "And I needed the patients. He pretended not to recall our fling, then he reluctantly agreed to kick a few my way, and then tried to pass off some sob story about how he envied me for opening up a solo practice."

Peppery Sarah leaned back. "It sounds like it went well," she said. "You accomplished what you set out for that evening. I don't know why you always put a negative spin on things that seem to be fine."

"He found me too combative."

"He actually looked interested when I came up," Helen said, not looking up from beneath the brown fringe of her bangs.

"I guess that's true. He was also saying we should consider another go at it."

"He found you hot and he agreed to refer patients. Sounds like you won on both counts," Sarah said.

Put that way, it did make the evening seem better than she thought.

"I also talked to Aditi Singh—"

"She's nice," Helen said. They had done their neurology residencies together.

Sarah glared at her.

"She is," Petra said, looking curiously at the two of them. "Plus, I caught Lee McDermott before he left."

"All in all, it sounds like you did well," Sarah said.

"Then why did Santos act like he didn't remember that we'd gone out? Not that I care about him in particular, but it is pretty galling for him to pretend that I'm not memorable when clearly, I was."

"He was messing with you, Petey," said Sarah. "You have to admit, you see why he did it. You make it so much fun by getting sputtery. It sounds like his recall was pretty much perfect."

Helen nodded and ran her long fingers absently up her drink. In med school she'd taken Petra in when her friend couldn't find anyone to rent her a place. They had shared the one-room apartment for almost a year. With anyone else, it might have been hell, but Helen supplied silly paperbacks and cookies when Petra needed comfort and she let Petra clean – or not clean – in her own way. And because they were both studying and in different rotations, they didn't have that much opportunity to get on each other's nerves. Also, Helen could have slept through the Big Bang and not have noticed the universe forming around her. It was one of the foremost considerations when choosing a roommate, Petra had since decided. If the practice went under and she had to rent out her living room to a bunch of co-eds, she would make sure to find out if they were easy sleepers.

"It's hard to put yourself out there and ask people to think of you," Helen was saying, "especially when you're not used to getting attention. But it doesn't mean that they think you're weak or failing. It's just all part of the system. They'll expect you to send them patients with suspected diabetes, or irregular heartbeats. It's like getting professors to write recommendations, or asking people to be your references."

"I hated doing that."

"But everyone does it and everyone needs it done. For instance, did you mind it when I asked you for a letter when I was buying a condo?" Helen asked.

"No. It was easy because you're a perfect person to live with."

"Exactly. So you shouldn't worry about asking people to recommend you. It's how the world goes round."

"Speaking of, did you get some of your patients to write reviews?" Sarah asked.

"One of my patients told me he'd do it, but I haven't seen anything," Petra said, picking at her tofu.

Ian Zamora. Last night, he had been warm and kind. At least, that was the illusion he gave. For a moment, she even thought there had been a pull of attraction between them. It hadn't been the first time, either. Sometimes, she sensed that his stoicism during injections had just as much to do with her hands smoothing the curve of his arm as it did with the pain. She often caught him looking at her and his skin pinkened under the intimacy of her exploring fingers.

Or maybe that was just his reaction to the shots.

Still, their conversation last night was revelatory. Not that she wanted anything to happen – not that anything could *ever* happen – but after a night of steamrolling and sucking up, it felt nice to have a quiet, personal conversation with someone who didn't seem to be inspecting her for weakness.

In the morning light, however, she was not sure what had taken place. It helped that he had a slow smile that a woman could easily find herself falling for. He talked a good game, Ian Zamora, but he shouldn't be trusted.

She also found herself disappointed in him for having failed to produce a review. She had checked. Somewhat obsessively. And it wasn't because she thought that he should be thinking of her as much as she seemed to think of him. It was beyond the feeling of desperation she felt for her practice. She felt almost betrayed by him, as if he had promised her something more than a careless paragraph on a website, and she were more than his doctor. He *had* said he understood the importance of a review. He even implied that it might not be entirely favorable. But when it came down to it, he had written nothing, and she was now taking his memory lapse far too personally.

She shook her head. She must have been imagining the tension between them last night. From now on, she should keep her distance. She'd administer the shots, tend to his itches, and send him on his way. She would be the perfect, polite robot professional. Inner Hippocrates gave her a "You go, girl!" cheer. If she encountered Ian Zamora on the street, she would remind herself that her white coat shielded her from private questions and revelations.

She certainly did *not* have a crush on him.

"Helen," she said, feeling punchy again, "you and Mike Lockhart last night – what was that all about?"

–

Sarah's tips seemed to be working, or maybe it was just dumb luck. Petra picked up a handful of new patients near the end of the month. She was still in the hole, but at least she wasn't losing money as quickly as before. She stared at her bottom line again and glanced away from the big red numbers on her computer screen. There was just enough time to phone her mother. Petra preferred to discharge her filial duties from the safety of her office. It was a good way of limiting the amount of time she spent talking to Lisa Lale. She could always say that she had a patient.

Lisa answered on the first ring. "How's business?" she asked.

"It's great," Petra said brightly. "I had some referrals, and even though we don't get a ton of ragweed in these parts, I snagged a few sneezers."

"Will that be enough? You know, new small businesses go under at a rate of eighty-five percent per year."

Petra quelled her rising panic by trying to sound logical. "What does that even mean, Mom?"

"It means you should be very careful with what you do with that money your father left you. Don't go spending it all on encyclopedias."

"Mom, I was ten years old the last time that happened." Petra would have given anything for her mother to be the kind who bragged about the fact that she was a doctor. But apparently to boast was to anger the gods. "How's Ellie?" Petra asked. Her half-sister was in her first year at the University of Washington. She was Petra's favorite way of deflecting attention from herself. In a perfect world, Ellie would have been a hell-raiser. Instead, she was polite and had very earnest ambitions of going into city planning. Ellie was tall and blonde, like Lisa. It was hard to believe they were from the same family.

"She says she's doing well, but you know with the hook-up culture and the binge drinking the college kids do, I wonder how she really is. I read that some dorms have stripper poles on every floor."

"Your daughter who wears a #BANMEN T-shirt to bed every night? I doubt she's interested in subjecting herself to the male gaze. Besides, I thought she was still dating Jenna. They're both sensible kids."

"I just don't understand you millennials sometimes."

"Look, if Ellie didn't excuse herself to throw up in the middle of your last phone call, then she's probably doing fine," Petra said, glancing at her clock.

"All the same, I think I'll send her some AA pamphlets," Lisa said.

"Maybe a few extra for Jenna, and some that they can leave around the dorm."

It was funny – with Lisa, Petra found herself in the unusual position of acting like an optimist. She was suddenly ready to spout all sorts of nuggets from greeting cards and motivational posters. *Have a little faith! What's the worst that can happen?* It wasn't that Lisa was trying to criticize her children, Petra knew, but she worried about them so much that she lost all confidence in their ability to take care of themselves. The fact that her own mother trusted no one, least of all herself, made Petra reluctant to admit that anything was wrong in her own life. Petra's father's desertion had hit Lisa hard. She never changed her name, not even when she married Ellie's dad. Lisa always claimed that she'd never seen it coming. But for Petra, he had always been detached, if cheery. He never spoke of his parents – Petra met her stern Indian grandmother just once – or his heritage, or his childhood, saying he didn't like sad stories. One day, Nik Lale was a happy-go-lucky manager. The next day, he was gone. Petra remembered arguments, though. Fights under hissed breath. Angry thumps of belongings thrown into boxes and the sound of her father's car starting late at night. Her father had certainly made preparations to leave. Petra liked clomping around the house in his black leather shoes, and those were gone on the day her mother started crying in earnest. His bottle of aftershave and the cassette tapes he listened to had also disappeared. Even the Raffi Christmas album was gone. When she was older, Petra liked to think he'd taken it because listening to it would remind him of her. But most likely, he had just made a hasty sweep, and grabbed it with all of the others.

Ellie's father had at least stuck around to be a father after his divorce from Lisa. He was Nik's opposite, in many ways. He was somber but mild. He owned a small bookkeeping business and restored old homes. Ellie's father was kind enough to include Petra on trips to the amusement park, or buy her presents at Christmas, but Petra kept herself detached. She wasn't part of *that* family. She didn't even look like them.

Petra heard the door of the outer office open. It was time for Ian Zamora's appointment.

–

The breakup with Danielle had been pretty terrible. She was still calling him. She asked him to escort her to a corporate dinner. Even if they'd still been going out, he would probably have found an excuse to skip it.

It was his own fault for drawing it out. His guilt allowed Danielle to convince him to take her to the newly opened Carioca. The lights were dim and João Gilberto crooned romantic nothings to various *mais lindas* in the background. It gave Danielle exactly the wrong idea. Worse, Ian knew the chef and that night, Juan felt he had something to prove. Before they ordered dinner, he sent them a plate of scallops with green onion aioli, then a pink shrimp sorbet, then a tiny black bean soup. What was supposed to be a quick, casual meal stretched into an endless evening. Danielle kept a running commentary on each dish as it appeared, taking pictures and posting to her Twitter account. He got the feeling that if he broke up with her while she was posting, she'd have a photo of him captioned and hashtagged and would be fielding comments about his perfidy. So he waited.

After the meal, Juan insisted they tour the kitchen. While Danielle squealed over some cleverly shaped mousses, Juan told Ian the latest filthy jokes. Ian's

Portuguese was rusty, but he dredged up a few phrases. Juan laughed at him and told him he'd never hold on to a woman that way.

Ian ended up blurting it out in the car as he dropped Danielle off. She sat there turning it over, parsing his words, and scrunching her brows as if she couldn't understand him. She didn't cry, but she was close.

He knew he wasn't the worst person in the world. But he had raised her hopes and pretended to be a man with staying power. He made it worse sitting in the car with her telling her it wasn't her fault. By the end of the evening, Ian was so exhausted that he returned home and fell asleep on his couch with his clothes on and every single light in his apartment blazing.

Now, Ian sat in what he now thought of as his chair and looked around Petra Lale's office. A few minor changes had taken place. There was a box of tissues on the square coffee table, a fresh selection of magazines, and – she had listened to him – a water cooler in the corner. Still no receptionist, he noted, although a different J.R.R. Tolkien paperback lay on the desk.

Petra now ushered him into her office as soon as he arrived, questioned him genially about the size and quality of his reactions last week, then swabbed his arm with alcohol and gave him new shots. She barely talked to him. Clearly, she had things running more smoothly. This should have pleased him. But he admitted that he felt disappointed with the polish she had acquired. Or maybe he wished that she spent more time with him. She was always polite and attentive, but she never referred to their encounter on the street. She seemed reserved, remote, clinical.

He sighed and sat back in his chair in the waiting room. The kid was here again.

"Hey," Ian said, rubbing his tender arm.

The kid nodded back, looking up from his iPhone.

"Not going to call your girlfriend?" he asked, after staring at Ian for a moment.

Well.

"I don't have one anymore."

The kid gave a long, contemplative snort. "Are you at least porking women on the regular?"

"*Excuse me?*"

"You do know what that is, don't you?"

"Of course I— Jesus, *how old are you?*"

"Twelve. But I read a lot. I know all about it, too."

"No, I really don't think you do. And I'm not about to say anything more."

Kevin sighed, but continued to stare expectantly at Ian. "Will you at least tell me what it's like?" Kevin asked.

Ian glanced around desperately for something with which he could kill himself. Water cooler? Too awkward. Tolkien paperback? Too slow. *Us Weekly*? Too soft. Luckily, Kevin began making his odd choking noise and Dr. Lale strode into the room. "More post-nasal drip?" she asked.

Kevin nodded and batted his eyes at Petra. She chucked his chin, and Ian experienced an electric wave of jealousy, not for the way she touched the kid, Ian told himself, but for the ease that she clearly felt around Kevin. Besides, what was she doing, patting him? He was twelve, not four. Clearly, the kid enjoyed it too much.

Petra ushered Ian into her office to check on his reactions. He had wised up for his appointment today, and he was wearing a short-sleeved polo shirt. With a quick twitch of the cuffs, he exposed the big red bumps where Doc Lale had stuck her needles. She hissed in sympathy and at the sound of her breath near his ear, he felt himself tense again. She touched the hot skin of his shoulder. He wanted to lean against her slight frame, rub his cheek against her. He was almost dizzy with want. Was he having some sort of aberrant reaction to the shot? He thought of Kevin's elegant term: porking. *Thanks to Kevin, I'm going to associate sex with breakfast sausage for the rest of my life.*

"These are some big reactions," Dr. Lale murmured, interrupting his thoughts. "You did take your pill before the appointment, right?" She was shaking her head. "We'll leave you at the same level next week. You aren't allergic to a lot of things, but when your body decides on a target, it really hones in."

His glance fell on her lips just then. He might have groaned.

Doc was still examining him, concerned. "Are you all right?" she asked. "You look a little hot – I mean, warm. Is your throat feeling itchy?"

She pressed her fingers to his neck and he coughed.

"No, no, I really am okay," he said. "I just, I just was confused by something." He groped desperately for something to say. "I was talking to Kevin in the waiting room. I— uh, I'd forgotten what that age was like."

"Oh?"

Try not to think of sex. Try not to think of sex, he told himself. But he didn't know how to change course. "Boys are strange," he blurted.

It was hard to believe that Petra Lale found him glib and charming.

She laughed. He hadn't heard her beautiful laugh in a long time. "They're pretty gross," she agreed. "It's a medical fact."

She turned again and made a note on her iPhone. As she updated his chart, he watched the curve of her neck. A curl stuck up wildly behind her ear and he wanted to tug it gently. In addition to lusting after her, he *liked* her. It wasn't enough that she had eyes like glinting crystals and her fingers were smooth and tipped with round, unvarnished nails. But she was sweet about weird Kevin, too, and when she laughed, she threw her whole body into it. It was as if she had the same struggle. Suddenly, her voice was cool. "Same time next week?" she asked.

He nodded. Clearly, it was time to leave. And yet, he found himself hesitating. "Things seem to be going well around here. Nice water cooler, by the way. How's the practice going?"

The wall of reserve around her deepened. She barely looked up at him. "It's a work in progress," she said neutrally. "Thanks for asking."

He cast around for something to say. "I was supposed to have written a review for you. I haven't forgotten."

"How scrupulous of you," she muttered.

How could he tell her that he'd started to write it a few times? He had written one overly formal paragraph, another that made him sound smitten. He pictured Petra reading both and he felt embarrassed. He knew he had to come up with one after giving her a condescending and pompous speech about the importance of reviews. Now, he couldn't write it because he didn't want her to think less of him.

She got up and started to rearrange the little bottles of allergens in her refrigerator. Then she conceded, "Listen, it's not an epic poem. If you can't find anything to say about the practice or the doctoring, at least you could say... that it's easy to get an appointment. I shouldn't have put you on the spot."

"No, I didn't mean—" He gathered his thoughts. "I'm not saying that I couldn't find anything good about your skills. I keep coming week after week, don't I? I don't do time in your waiting room just so I can chat with Kevin. I do like watching you with him, though. He thinks you're great and you are. Maybe he even has a little crush on you."

She unbent a little at that. She obviously didn't mind if Kevin had a thing for her. Maybe Ian's reaction was normal, too.

He went on. "You obviously really care about your patients. Besides, a lot of the bumps have been smoothed out. The place looks less, uh, empty. You're right on schedule. You still need a receptionist, though."

Then he stopped before he could sound like more of an asshole.

She finally laughed, much to his relief, and looked at him from under her lashes. "Bossy, aren't you? I see why you went into business for yourself. I'm working on the other problems. I've increased Joanie's hours, but I can't have anyone in full-time yet because—" She paused and admitted softly, "Well, I guess I hinted to you that night, I really can't afford it." She shook her head. "I really, really shouldn't be talking to you about this."

He let out a breath. She remembered that night, too. And something about her troubled eyes told him that she remembered the red undercurrent of attraction and vulnerability that had run through their conversation. It made him feel terrible that she suddenly seemed hunted. But it also made him feel triumphant and warm.

"Come over to Field for dinner sometime this week," he said, ducking nearer to her. "On me. Bring... that friend of yours who likes carbs."

"It's tempting, but I can't accept gifts from patients."

"It's not a gift. If you bring that friend – or boyfriend, of course – and get them hooked on our food—"

"You mean, more hooked than Helen already is."

"Then, I'll consider it fair payment."

A pause.

"It's just dinner," Ian added, letting his voice grow warm and dark.

He watched the slow blink of her beautiful eyes. The short lashes fanned against her cheek.

She glanced at him then looked away quickly. "Helen will be freebasing from the bread basket by the end of the evening."

"I look forward to seeing that. What do you say? C'mon, don't think too hard about it."

"Don't think too hard because the proposal doesn't make any sense? Or don't think about it because I need to stop thinking?"

"Yes."

She grinned. "For once in my life, I promise, I won't think."

Chapter Five

"I love that place," Helen gasped.

"So you think this is okay? This is really not an exceptionally ethically questionable move on my part?"

"Hell, no. When should we go? I'm free Thursday."

In retrospect, promising Helen fresh butter and warm breads was not the best way to get an honest, well-considered answer. Petra knew her friend was already mentally rifling through her wardrobe, trying to figure out which were her loosest pants. Knowing Helen's judgment was impaired made Petra even more reluctant to check about her greater, and more serious ethical violation: it seemed very possible that she might have a teeny, tiny crush on Ian Zamora, her patient, a man who put his life in her hands every week.

She lacked moral fiber. She was the ethical equivalent of a Twinkie.

"You're such a great doctor," Helen enthused. "You may not have quantity, but the quality of your patients is unquestionable. Are you sure you want to bring me? Wait, forget I said that. This place would be wasted on Sarah. She'd choose the vegetable plate and order half of it boxed up before it even reached the table."

"You know, a recent study from the Mayo Clinic links a high-carb diet to early dementia."

"Lies, dirty, dirty lies. I'll see you Thursday."

As it turned out, one of Helen's patients needed emergency surgery. Sarah couldn't come because she was going to a lecture on micro-lending with a multilingual economist. Sarah probably preferred that to a date with a hot breadbasket, anyway.

Petra smoothed down her green dress. She tried on a scarf and decided to leave it off. On one hand, she hated having a cold neck. On the other, she didn't want her accessory to end up in the salad. As a concession to comfort, she decided on a pair of big wedges. Life was too short to be hobbled by pointy shoes.

She would probably be alone for most of the evening, Petra told herself. She eyed herself in the full-length mirror, unsure if it was worse to be dressed badly and alone, or dressed well enough that it seemed like she'd been stood up. If the allergist thing didn't pan out, she thought wryly, she could write a book on etiquette for the dateless, since she was putting in all the research already.

Petra stuffed the scarf in her purse and added a pair of earrings, in case she needed a wardrobe change halfway through dinner. She leafed through her wallet. She checked her phone. She decided to take the roundabout way to the restaurant to calm her nerves.

She was not going just because she was looking forward to seeing Ian, she told herself. He probably wouldn't even be there. Or if he was there, he'd probably just say hello.

At precisely seven o'clock, after having walked around the block five times, Petra presented herself to the hostess, who promptly showed her to a seat.

By degrees, her anxiety began to abate. The hostess, although slinky, was relaxed and curious. She introduced herself as Lilah; clearly she wanted to know more about Ian's special guest. Around Petra, people were laughing and drinking wine. Lilah nestled Petra into a quiet corner, partly concealed by a spray of ferns. A waiter brought out a glass of Chardonnay and a delicious gem of a stuffed mushroom and placed a menu in front of her. The room was warm and it glowed with the light from a row of hurricane lamps. She admired the tin ceiling over the wide, polished bar, the muted sounds of silverware clinking on dishes.

Soon, she felt herself even more soothed by a velvety lamb stew. She was glad that she hadn't had to make conversation or be forced to share bites of her dinner. Her waiter would have to scrape her out of the chair like a melted caramel.

I should treat myself more often, she thought drowsily, even though technically she had not paid for this dinner. In her mind, she planned solo excursions for tapas in a smoky bar, filled with gorgeous Spanish men. She should go hiking. She should travel to Tibet and meditate, pal around with Sherpas. Today, a restaurant: tomorrow, the world. She would also learn to pull money from hats. She tipped her glass back for a deep swallow.

This was how Ian found her as he strode into the room, seeking her gaze. She almost snorted the contents of her wineglass. Her pulse zoomed to life again. She was ridiculous, she thought. He stopped at a few tables to say hello. Everyone responded to him, and he laughed and chatted. But it seemed that his warmth was all for her. She reminded herself it was an illusion. All the people he spoke to probably felt exactly that way. She watched him as he came within the last few tables near her, and she put down her glass and wiped her palms on her thighs.

Then he was in front of her. Her chest gave a squeeze. He hesitated a moment. He sat down.

"Enjoying your meal? How has everything been?"

"Better than a massage," she said. "Better than violins."

What? She was not drunk. She looked at him out of the corner of her eye, but her extraocular muscles weren't meant for these kinds of acrobatics.

"Better than a birthday with a chocolate cake, balloons, and a petting zoo," she added hastily.

"Now I'll know exactly what to get you when you turn thirty-two."

He remembered. They smiled at each other goofily for a minute and the room seemed to still.

"You've got to try the butterscotch pudding," Ian said finally. "Nina, our pastry chef, has a great touch."

"This has been so wonderful, thank you. And thank your staff for me. Really, I'm stuffed."

"You're going to skip dessert, aren't you?"

In truth, she'd been looking forward to it all night. She hesitated. "Butterscotch," she said, "and pudding. I don't know how I feel about either of those things. On the other hand, I definitely always enjoy chocolate in almost any form."

Ian sat forward. "Nina's cake is wonderful, but you can get chocolate desserts anywhere. The butterscotch pudding at Field, however, is in its own category."

"On the contrary, Ian Zamora, clearly you've spent too much time in upscale restaurants because I'm here to let you know that you can get butterscotch pudding almost anywhere. As I recall, it's the flavor that you buy when the grocery store has run out of vanilla. When you do make it, you wonder why you even bothered with dessert because no one wants to finish this weird sweet, sludgy stuff."

Ian grinned. He leaned forward. "Petra Lale, MD, obviously you've never had good butterscotch before, and by that, I mean real butterscotch that tastes rich and thick and is fragrant with vanilla and brown sugar, not to mention the garnish of bourbon-laced whipped cream. Nina has to lock it down in our freezers when she makes it because staff are always dipping their fingers in the bowl."

Petra glared. He was making her want things that she should not want to enjoy. "This isn't part of the famed upsell, is it?"

A laugh. "No. It's because it really is wonderful."

Ian signaled to the waiter and within minutes, he set a bowl quivering with thick, blond custard, white dollops of bourbon cream, and two perfect raspberries in front of Petra. Petra looked up to see Ian watching her closely.

"Please don't tell me that you're going to sit there and stare at me while I eat," Petra said.

"I might interject a comment or two."

"Won't you at least share it with me?"

"Nope," he said.

She swirled her spoon in and took a bite, and another, and another.

"I'd almost think you were trying to seduce me," she murmured.

She glanced up. His face seemed frozen.

Oh God, what had she said? "Erm, what I mean is, I think you enjoyed being right about the pudding," Petra said. "It's simple and wonderful, and delicious. There's really no other word for it except delicious."

She was trying to sound normal and perky, but her voice was strained and she couldn't look at him. The terror in his face was only magnified by the fact that perhaps *she* had been trying to rouse *him*. Flirtation had whispered across her mind while she had been eating – no, not just flirtation, but lust. She had pulled the spoon out of her mouth slowly. She had licked it. She wanted to check his reaction and now she knew. He wasn't interested. Worse, she should never have been trying to interest him.

She placed the offending silverware beside the half-empty bowl. Her hands were trembling slightly. No wonder she'd never considered being a surgeon. She'd probably slice herself before the operation got underway.

"I should probably get back to work," Ian said.

He looked a little glassy-eyed.

"I should probably let you," she said.

Ian didn't move. "Petra," he said.

She could feel her heart pounding wildly. She squeezed her thighs tightly together. Her breath came fast. Ian's face was close to hers. His eyes were so dark.

Lilah chose that moment to come to the table. "I hate to interrupt," she said.

Ian and Petra practically jumped up at once. Ian put his hand wildly through his hair. "A problem out front? In the kitchen? Gerry wants to yell at me?"

"Uh, yeah," Lilah said.

"I'm on it."

He put out his hand and Petra took it. "This was really wonderful," she said. "Thank you."

He shook his head. Petra didn't know what that meant. Within seconds, he was gone.

Lilah and Petra watched him go. Lilah said, "I've never seen him sit down with anyone before. Did you know his family or something?"

Petra's face burned. She didn't want to reveal her relationship to him, especially because of the speculative look that had appeared in Lilah's eye. "We— we're more recent acquaintances than that."

Inside her head, a bearded Hippocrates muttered an oath.

—

She hadn't said anything terrible, she thought as she sat in her apartment, still in her coat. It was just a little phrase, a harmless sentence – *I'd almost think you were trying to seduce me* – and it had really been about the admittedly delicious butterscotch. But it was enough, wasn't it? Ian had gotten wind of her crush and she had made him – her patient, one of her few regular patients – uncomfortable. Petra didn't remember how she'd managed to drag herself out of the restaurant and back to her apartment that night. The rest of the week passed in a shameful red haze. She didn't remember looking at her schedule and noting that Ian Zamora had canceled his appointment for that coming week, and that he had not rescheduled with her receptionist.

She did, however, notice that someone had written a five-star review of her on DocStars.com, and she thought that maybe it was Ian.

> Petra Lale is an excellent, competent doctor, but more than that, she's a human being who clearly cares about the welfare of her patients. She's honest, she remembers one's allergies, and recalls the details of her patients' medical history. She even knows which arm the patient prefers to use for shots and she administers them with a delicate touch. In the brief time I have known her, she has

worked hard to improve her practice. She has
been kind and funny.

It was a pleasure being treated by her.

It was terrible. It was stilted and insincere and she didn't
feel competent. She closed the page.

Chapter Six

"Kevin," Petra said, "we need to talk about boundaries."

Kevin gave his snort, which Petra took as assent.

"I let people talk on their cellphones in the office because, let's face it, you have to wait a long time in here with nothing to do. But I think maybe some of the newer patients don't love it when you comment on their conversations."

Kevin nodded.

"So help me out, Kevin. I need patients. Just try not to say anything much."

"But I can still listen."

"Yes, you can still listen."

Spring-like weather, and subsequent pollen counts, had brought steady dribbles of new patients to the office. Joanie was now installed behind the desk full-time, and she had moved on to the oeuvre of Joyce Carol Oates. Petra considered this a vote of confidence in the future of the practice. Sarah's cousin, meanwhile, had designed a new website for the practice, which included pictures of goldenrod swaying in the background, looking artistic, and to Petra's mind, slightly ominous. They were, after all, itchy-eye and sneezy-nose inducing menaces. She wasn't above a little stealth marketing. The designer had also included a staff page with a fuzzy picture of Petra and a simple bio, and a glossy headshot of a pensive-looking

Joanie. Joanie had included information from her acting portfolio. Sarah's cousin also suggested a blog or a Twitter feed, but Petra decided to hold off for now. The website also included forms allowing people to schedule appointments online and a page of quotable testimonials. Ian Zamora's review was one of them. Petra did not look at that page. Five months had passed since he'd stopped coming in for immunotherapy. She had moved on.

Kevin sighed. "I can't help it if I have a lot of questions for people."

"What kinds of questions do you have?"

"Questions about *ladies*, Doctor."

Petra looked swiftly at the outer door. Maybe coming out here to chat with Kevin had been a bad idea, but she had wanted to talk to him in his domain. Considering how much time he spent in her waiting room, it was indeed his.

Who were these ladies, anyway? Was there more than one possibility? For *Kevin*?

"Is there an adult who you can go to with these questions? Your dad, maybe?"

Kevin snorted, out of disgust, rather than due to respiratory distress.

"A guidance counselor? Favorite teacher? Maybe a clergyman? Godparents? Your uncles or aunts?"

Kevin rolled his eyes. She had never received the eye roll from him. She felt vaguely hurt. Still, she had a duty. "As your physician, I can always try to answer questions you might have."

"You're great, Doc, but see, you're also a *lady*."

Well, at least Kevin had noticed.

"That means my advice will be more accurate," she persisted, albeit half-heartedly.

"When's the last time you hooked up with someone, Doc?"

She sucked in a breath. Sometimes Kevin seemed utterly and dorkily clueless. Then, he'd suddenly zing her with such perception that her teeth nearly rattled. "We're talking about you, Kevin."

"It's okay, I'd like to hear more about you. Maybe I can learn from your mistakes and you can benefit from my war stories. We'd give each other romantic advice."

"It wouldn't be appropriate, Kevin."

"You say that a lot now, that things are *inappropriate*."

"Well, that's because I need to set professional boundaries." Petra stood up. "Kevin, I hope you find someone to talk to about these things. I can't reciprocate, because I am your doctor, but I'm a good listener and I'm always looking out for you."

She ushered him into her office and checked his welts. He pulled the sleeves of his sweatshirt down again before she could give him some cream. The shirt was too big for him and the material flapped around him like a pair of wings. He looked like a sad condor. "Thanks, Dr. Lale," he mumbled, jamming his hat on his head. "You know," he said, "you could always put a TV in the waiting room. That would distract me a lot."

He clattered out.

Petra sighed and updated Kevin's record. She called on her inner Hippocrates to tell her that she had handled Kevin correctly, but received little consolation from his soothing murmur.

She checked the clock. She was overdue for a phone call with her mom. She held her head and dialed slowly. Lisa answered on the first ring. "How's business?"

"You sound chipper," Petra said. "What's up? Any distant relatives dying or on their deathbeds? Neighbors mistreating their animals? Sisters of mine cocking up in school?"

A pause. "Petra, you sound a little mean lately."

"Maybe today I just sound the way I usually feel, Mom."

"What's wrong? Is it that practice of yours? You're going under, aren't you? Should I call Uncle Jeremy?"

"It's fine. Birch and alder allergy season is beginning. You should go and hug a tree for me."

Her mother wasn't deterred. "It isn't some boy is it?"

"It is definitely not a man. Remember Lisa Lale's number one edict from on high? Men are not to be trusted to make a woman happy."

"I have never said that."

"I don't have my Portable Lisa Lale with me, so it's not an exact quotation, but I think I'm familiar with a number of variations on this theme."

"Well, I shouldn't have ever said anything like that."

Uh-oh. Petra could only remember hearing that tone a few times in her life. "Mom, do you have something to tell me?"

A pause.

"I've started seeing someone. Actually, I didn't want to tell you, because I wasn't sure how it was going. We started dating almost six months ago."

Petra closed her eyes.

"He's a psychiatrist. Of course, it's still early in the relationship. I don't know how he feels about me yet. I'm no spring chicken, you know," she said with an attempt at a light laugh. "I'm trying to be realistic. After all, we've both been through divorces, although his ex-wife sounds

68

like a truly selfish person. She left him with an elderly dog who had to be put down and the closets haven't been cleaned out in years. So many pantsuits. And she told their kids he would foot the bills for their phones."

Petra murmured incoherently and shuffled papers on her desk. Her mother was dating? She was so confused.

"But it's true, we've only been seeing each other for a short amount of time. I want to be realistic about this. We don't agree on a lot of political issues. Israel is a big sticking point. And he seems to think that it's okay to just throw everything in the trash: batteries, glue guns, old shirts, hairspray—"

"I don't even want to know how you know this."

"It's troubling, isn't it? But I don't think it's the sign of some deeper problem. He's probably just lazy."

At a different time, Lisa Lale would have argued that laziness *was* a deeper problem, Petra wanted to point out. But her mother was still talking.

"I was lonely, Petey. The hallway to my bedroom just echoes. I walk past your room and your sister's and the doors are closed. They were always closed before, when you lived here, but now I know you two aren't behind them. So, I went and I met a man online. I know it sounds so prurient, Petra, but it wasn't one of those no-strings-attached things where we met for anonymous sex with paper bags over our heads—"

"Jesus, Mom!"

"I didn't give him my last name or my phone number at first. I met him in a public place and I didn't even let him so much as hold my hand until the end of the evening. But it felt so good just to talk with someone who was interesting and male and who was interested in me. I didn't care if he was in it only for sex."

"Mom."

"Men aren't that fussy, Petra. That's something I did learn from marriage. Well, maybe they've got the right idea. Maybe I shouldn't be so picky, either. Maybe I shouldn't expect anything. I sound old and crazed and desperate, don't I? I sound lonely. I swear, I never thought I'd end up like this, Petra. But sometimes, it is very hard. He has been very kind to me," she added.

Petra finally spoke. "What's his name?"

"It's Jim. Jim Morrison. He showed me his driver's license. I guess his name is actually James."

Lisa laughed awkwardly, and so did Petra.

"Well, Mom," Petra said, after a moment. "You snagged a rock star." Her stomach felt sour. "I have to go now," she added. "Just... take care of yourself, okay? And be careful that he doesn't see your credit card statements. And your bank statements. Don't give him your social security number."

God, she sounded like her mother.

"Come visit," Lisa said. "Maybe you can meet him."

Joanie buzzed to tell her that her next patient had arrived. The rest of the afternoon passed in a pleasantly busy way, but as Petra cleared papers off her desk and pulled out her bags to go grocery shopping, she felt unsettled.

Her mother had her nascent, imperfect relationship. Kevin had a few ladies he was eying. She didn't have anyone to look forward to. She was lonely.

As she locked the office, she traced her fingers along the name stenciled in the door. Petra Lale, MD. Even outside the office doors, she would not be allowed to forget what she was, she realized with sudden anger. But what was she if she were not a physician? She had taken pride in her profession, in the fact that she healed people. She couldn't dance. She was a lousy dresser. She couldn't make small talk. At this one thing, this one important thing, she had been good, and she was grateful that she was good at it.

Until she met Ian Zamora.

As Kevin noted, she was also *a lady*. Unfortunately, her female parts and her doctor parts had fought. And now she was lonely. Beyond that, she was also possibly an ethically compromised person. After all, she had drooled over a patient who was giving her free food. If he thought she'd been harassing him, he could have had her license suspended.

Despite all of this, she still did think of him. She dreamed of his hand reaching for hers across the table of a restaurant. She wondered what he looked like without his glasses, what his hair looked like first thing in the morning. She wondered how his legs would feel against hers. She could almost imagine his warm rapid pulse, his mouth, a leisurely tongue. In dreams, he tasted like bourbon and cream.

She was allowed to dream about him, wasn't she?

In the grocery store, she leaned her forehead against the cool door of the frozen food section. Originally, she had planned to eat lima beans, her version of comfort food, and watch *Nova*. But now, that sounded pathetic.

Petra pulled herself upright. Nothing had happened, after all. She hadn't compromised herself with a patient. She hadn't lost her license. Her practice hadn't gone under. She had only hurt her heart, just a little. Her friends were awesome. She was going to be fine.

She put the lima beans back.

There was only one thing to do on a night like this. She dialed Sarah.

Ian fiddled with his tie. It was unlike him to be nervous, but on this evening, his life was about to change. He scrutinized himself in the mirror, then patted his neck again. No one would be looking at him, anyway.

The secret was to treat it like any other party, he thought. Never mind that it was a gathering of people who mattered to him, never mind that taking this step could ruin him. *Stop being such a pessimist*, he told himself. *This is a happy occasion*.

He could hear his staff rushing past his office getting ready for the big night. He pulled out his phone and checked his lists again. Flowers, delivered. Photographer, already snapping away.

"You look like you're going to throw up," Gerry said, wandering in.

"Aren't you supposed to be working on the food?"

"This is Marcia's night to shine. I'm supposed to look benevolent, yet sexy." He struck a pose with his hand on his new goatee. "How's that?"

"Do you think we'll have enough of the Willamette Valley Pinot tonight?"

"Not the way I've been drinking it. You should try some."

Ian started to make his way up the stairs. Gerry followed.

"It's just friends, family, loved ones, and food bloggers," Gerry said. "They're all just people who adore us – or want to see us fail miserably. Some days I'm not sure which."

They strode past the kitchen and opened the doors. A roar greeted them.

Stream was open.

For the last five months, Ian had worked almost nonstop. Whenever life kicked him in the gut, this is what he did. This time, he'd been given a one-two punch. As a result, Stream was born.

He had gone to Gerry with the idea for a bar that served local wines and beer. The place would have a menu of mostly small plates. Better still, a space opened up a few doors down from Field. They'd acquired licenses and building permits through a combination of charm, bribery, browbeating, and persistence. They hired a chef and developed a menu. Ian recruited some serious wine and beer geeks to man the bar and sling drinks. They bricked. They installed wainscoting. They fired two contractors. At some point, they stopped speaking to each other over the expense of copper pipes and fittings. But Gerry was still in charge of the kitchen at Field, and he couldn't be over at the new space all the time, so Ian put in even more hours. He started spending the night in his office again. He sacked one last contractor and took on the final renovations himself while juggling the paperwork, and the day-to-day operations of Field. Near the end of it all, he was ready to get down on his knees to blow on the newly poured concrete floor if it would have made it dry faster. The night before the soft open, he stayed up until dawn polishing the pewter on the old light fixtures they'd bought from a firehouse. He was on his own strict deadline. After all, he didn't have to answer to anyone about his time.

He didn't let himself stop to think because whenever he let himself be idle for a moment, his mind careened immediately toward Petra Lale. That night when she came to Field, he had almost lunged across the table to eat her for dessert. She said, *I'd almost think you were trying to seduce me*, and he had realized that that was exactly what he had been doing. He had been staring at her mouth, encouraging her to stroke the silverware with her tongue. He would've sucked on the pudding smeared over her ascetic lips. He would have taken her in front of everyone at his restaurant.

He'd been creepy.

For a moment, he'd convinced himself that she was as attracted to him as he was to her. He'd seen the pink of her cheeks and the widening of those beautiful eyes. He canceled his appointment for that week, thinking of how he could find a way to ask her out away from her office. And then she'd sent the letter. *Dear Ian Zamora*, it said. *This is to inform you that I can no longer function as your physician. As you might be aware, you failed to reschedule your last two immunotherapy appointments...*

It went on to say that she would continue to provide emergency care for thirty days and recommended that he find another physician. Her signature, in bright blue ink, looked a little smudged. The small disorder on a pristine, impersonal letter was so Petra, and for some reason it hurt something inside him.

He had *really* fucked up a lot of things that night she had visited Field. Maybe she had flirted with him a little bit. Maybe she had even found out more about his personal life than he wanted anyone to know. She had distanced herself even before that night. She stayed professional and tried her best to be a good doctor. He knew vaguely that there were rules against dating patients. Even in the butterscotch-induced haze, he sensed that she held herself back, as if she were telling herself that she should not respond. But he had spooked her enough to send him away even though she needed patients. She could not have gotten rid of him without struggling with her decision. He had been fired as a patient because his doctor had noticed that he had practically gotten a hard-on watching her eat dessert.

And yet, five months later, he still thought of the brightness of her face, her slim shoulders and legs, and the laugh that seemed bigger than she was. He enjoyed his time with her, this despite the fact that he almost never left her without bleeding. He missed the pleasure of her hand sliding across his skin. He missed her breath on his shoulder. He sometimes thought about her fingers massaging cream into his arm.

So he'd thrown himself into his work once again. He'd given himself even more to do. Now that Stream was open, he was afraid that he would have to go back to hating himself.

The bar's opening crowd pushed around him. He put on a lazy grin and shook hands. He declined wine and set about talking to his guests. Wait staff, bearing trays of tiny lamb chops and shrimp chips and hamachi, passed by. He grabbed a tray himself and pressed food and drink on people. He fielded compliments about the exposed copper pipes. Someone spilled a drink and he wiped it up unobtrusively. Despite the fact that he was on alert and too warm, he managed to feel proud about the floor. He may have talked a little bit too long and enthusiastically about the beauties of poured concrete.

Gerry was off in a dark corner, talking to a petite brunette. He was no help at all. Lilah, at least, was moving around the room smiling, pressing kisses on cheeks, and directing the wait staff. He had chosen well, elevating her to manager of Stream. Plus, it got her out of Gerry's orbit.

By most standards, the night would have to be deemed a reasonable success. The team behind the bar seemed solid. No brawls had erupted. No one seemed plastered. The crab cakes had been a little dry; they probably would not make it onto the menu. Staff had been slow picking up dirty glasses, but everyone was drinking quickly tonight. By the time they really opened, they'd have a few things hammered out. He pecked out a stream of reminders on his iPhone.

He was about to slip into the kitchen, when he cast one last glance around the room. Under the sconces near the door, he saw her. Her hair burned so bright under the lamplight that he could feel the warmth of it reach his chest.

Petra.

He heard a crash.

Chapter Seven

"I don't believe in allergies," the man who claimed to be the chef was saying. "Some things make me itch and sneeze, but I don't believe in making them more important than they are by acknowledging them."

Petra took a big gulp of her wine. Good thing it was delicious.

"People are always saying, *I can't have shellfish. I can't have strawberries. Those noodles can't touch the sauce, because I'm sensitive to gluten.* Let me tell you, gluten is the shit. All that chewy, springy stuff in your mouth? It satisfies your stomach and it makes your soul happy."

It was a beautiful room, too, she thought, looking around, and the invitation had come at a perfect time. Sarah said something garbled about her multilingual economist and a party. That was enough for Petra to go home and throw on a dress. She didn't know the reason for the celebration, she didn't know anyone who'd be there, she didn't know the name of the place — it was so new that there wasn't even a sign over the door — and that was glorious. She quaked for a moment when she realized that it occupied the same stretch of buildings as Ian Zamora's restaurant, Field. She had assiduously avoided the street for months. But tonight, she was determined to be different. What did it matter to her if he was a few doors down from her tonight? They wouldn't be breathing the same air, or keeping the same company. Even if they were, she was over it. She hadn't really and truly crossed any lines; it only felt like she'd done more because she wanted it to be more. If anything, he was the one who ought to be guilty. He had turned his piercing brown eyes on her despite the fact that he was almost engaged.

Besides, he was probably busy at Field. She was safe.

So, now she was standing in a room with a lot of beautiful, hip people. Men in slim pants with artistically arranged beards stood beside women wearing jeans and silky tops, or slinky, off-the-shoulder cocktail frocks. She was glad she had put on a dress she'd bought on eBay. It gave her boobs, and because it gave her boobs, she had never worn it. Tonight, by God, she was ready to own her cleavage. She felt a sense of triumph that was only diluted by the incessant buzzing of Insult Chef, allergy-skeptic.

Insult Chef swirled his wine. "Every day, there's always some clown who's asking, *Oh, can I have the salmon, except salmon makes my tongue itchy, so could I have chicken instead? And I can't have the herb gremolata because garlic gives me hives, so could I have a tomato sauce instead? And can I have potatoes instead of carrots just because I'm an asshole?* And then, I'm just like, hey, why don't you save your money and go to KFC and get yourself a bucket of chicken?"

"What's a gremolata?" Petra asked. She liked the word. It was almost worth sticking around for the explanation.

"It's herbs, chopped so fine that they're almost a sauce. Usually we use a bit of lemon zest and parsley—"

"And garlic."

"You were listening. That's rare in a doctor."

"How am I going to inject you with snake oil if I don't keep my ears open?"

"Good point."

78

Insult Chef's eyes searched her face and he moved in a little closer.

Petra took a large step back. She bumped into the wall. "Maybe you do believe in allergies, but you just hate people who lie about them."

"No. Everybody lies about allergies. Even the allergies that don't affect me. Can't pat a bunny? What a jerk. Can't sniff the flowers? What a weakling. Can't be around dust? Well, either break out the vacuum or break up with me."

"You're a prize."

"What? I love bunnies and flowers and people who clean for me."

Petra put a hand on her hip. "Does this work for you?"

Insult Chef waggled his eyebrows and edged even closer. "Let's just say, I'm still testing the recipe."

He wasn't a bad-looking guy. Some women probably found his swaggering irresistible. But Petra laughed at him. "Aren't there any twenty-year-olds you can try this on? I mean, come on. Trying to egg me on so that I argue with you? That would imply that I care what you think of me, when all of my really profound feelings are reserved for this excellent wine that you're serving. So, if you really are the chef here, make yourself useful and get me another glass."

"I do admire you, you know," said the chef. "You're capitalizing on people's weaknesses. Can't fault you on that. It's like the whole thing I do with food trends. I can't stand that weird foam shit. I think it's stupid. But people see the words, and they buy it up. So we put it on the menu." Petra raised her eyebrows. Insult Chef took the hint. "Was that the Pinot Gris you were drinking?"

As soon as he lost himself in the crowd, Sarah swooped in. "Were you just laughing with that guy?"

"*At* him, Sarah. I was laughing *at* him. He told me I was a charlatan. I told him to bring me more wine."

"Look at you, Miss Sparky. I remember a time when you would have caved. Or gotten really depressed at the kind of losers who would try to pick you up, as if it reflected on you."

"That time has passed. I'm a new me. I've left all my mistakes behind. This was a great idea, Sarah. I need to go out and talk to people. This is a great room," Petra said enthusiastically.

It was a great room. Its honey-colored wood panels would look as beautiful in sunlight as they did now, under lamps and candles. It reminded her of Field in some ways, she thought reluctantly, because apparently Field was her ideal. It had the same cozy nooks and sexy corner booths. But there was something clean and spare about it, even when filled with people. It was not what one expected from a bar. She turned slowly, admiring the place, and her gaze focused suddenly on a dark head in the crowd.

Ian.

"I have to go."

"What?" Sarah said.

There was no time for an explanation. Petra put her head down and steamrolled her way toward the door. She grabbed her coat.

Then she heard a crash. Someone began yelling for a doctor.

Sarah reached her first, but Petra took in the woman's swelling lips, her labored breathing, and the EpiPen clutched in her fist. She had probably been trying to make it to the bathroom when the reaction overtook her. While Sarah checked for other injuries, Petra bundled her coat and Sarah's together and elevated the patient's feet.

Out of the corner of her eye, she noticed that Ian and the hostess were calming the crowd and gently pushing them away from Sarah and Petra. He was so good with people, she thought with a degree of envy, before turning back to the patient.

With Sarah holding the woman steady, Petra raised her arm and plunged the adrenaline into the woman's thigh. Someone screamed.

–

Much later, after they watched the ambulance drive away, Sarah pulled Petra aside.

"Want to tell me what that was about?" Sarah asked.

"We helped a woman who was having anaphylaxis?"

"Not that, you dope. The way you planned to bolt before that woman collapsed? The looks that Hottie McManager gave you when we were waiting for the ambulance? The way you refused to glance at him? I've never seen someone work so hard to avoid meeting someone's eyes. If I didn't know you better, I'd swear that you developed a sudden fascination with my boobs."

Petra's dress was wrinkled, and her palms and knees felt sticky. She didn't even want to think about how her camel coat looked after it had spent time on the floor. She hated that hard, concrete floor. And she certainly did not want to discuss Ian Zamora with Sarah or her date, the multilingual economist. But Sarah was following her home. And Aarno smiled benignly, as usual. All the languages of Europe lay at the tip of his tongue, and all he ever did was grin.

As if reading her mind, Sarah turned to Aarno and murmured in his ear. He frowned and shook his head.

She pushed him away. "We'll be fine. Petra's apartment is right here. *Näkemiin*, Aarno."

He kissed Sarah, and she and Petra watched Aarno lumber silently into the night.

"How's that going? Are you sure he's an economist, because it looks like he could be a member of the Finnish mafia."

"Let's not change the subject," Sarah said crisply.

She grabbed Petra's arm and held on tight until the whole sordid story spilled out in dribs and drabs.

"I just didn't want you to think I was a terrible doctor," Petra said, finally.

They were at her apartment. She was drinking a glass of water, and she had changed into sweats. Sarah wore one of Petra's old nightgowns, which was too short for her, and she had wrapped an afghan around her legs.

"Having a crush on a patient is definitely a no-no, but I guess you didn't cross any real ethical lines with him," Sarah said. "Yet."

"He's a former patient," Petra argued faintly. "Former patients are a gray area for the American Medical Association."

Sarah ignored her. "Well, he clearly seemed to be very *focused* on you."

"You really think? No, you know, never mind. Let's not even talk about whether he was attracted to me, because it doesn't matter. I am never seeing him again. Even though his businesses are in my neighborhood. And he lives close by and my vow is completely unrealistic."

"Well, he *was* a dish, I mean, if you like the smoldering brown eyes and lean, athletic type."

"And his smile, his smile could kill you. And his arms, you didn't get to see them close up. Or touch them."

Sarah held up her hand. "Ho-kay, slippery slope, Petra."

"It was more than that, though, Sarah. I got emotionally involved. We talked a lot, maybe more than we should have. And even when we didn't talk, there was an undercurrent. Or maybe I just wanted there to be something. It's easy for us to imagine we really know things about patients."

"That's because we do. We know where they hurt most. And that's why it's unethical to date them, even when they're no longer your patients," Sarah said.

"We know physical things about them, but what do we know about the kind of people they are? Different patients have different styles when they get their shots. Some of them sort of huff and puff their way through. Some of them squeeze their eyes shut. Some of them just can't take their eyes away from the sight of it going into their arm. Or they can't hold still for more than two seconds. They flinch.

"Ian would look at me – not my hands, not the syringe. He'd hold still and watch my face. It's like you said, he was very focused on me. And then when I was done and I wiped the blood off, he'd glance away and nod and thank me as if nothing had happened, as if he hadn't been studying me."

He'd watched her with something akin to desire, she thought. Sometimes, she could hear him swallow. She could feel his breath.

She crossed her legs and cleared her throat. "Plus, he talked to me, he really talked to me a few times. Anyway, it made me feel – I don't know – powerful. Fascinating."

"Of course he makes you feel powerful," Sarah said. "You were injecting him with substances. You were healing him."

"Yeah," Petra said, deflated. "That's probably it, isn't it?" She turned away from Sarah. "I did the wrong thing, didn't I?"

Sarah slid even further down the couch. "What do you want me to say, Petey? Do you want permission to go after him? Because you know how I feel about the tricky ethics of doctor–patient relationships. I'm not saying a medical board would come down on you, but you don't want that kind of attention, especially so early in your career. And worse, you just don't want to go down that road ethically – bending rules here, and nipping there. Better to just keep it clean and well defined. I know you think you liked him, but there are other people in this world with fewer complications who can make you feel just as good." She touched Petra's hand. "You should probably forget about him. Maybe go online to find a date."

Petra shook her head. But she agreed. "Well, how about you, Sarah? Why are you bothering with Aarno if all you want is man candy? Why do you date the professors and multilingual economists if you're in it just for the screwing?"

"I like smart men. But I'm smart about it."

Chapter Eight

"Well, that wasn't the worst opening in history," Gerry said, sitting at the bar.

Ian slouched deep in a red banquette. His shirt was unbuttoned and sloppy. He felt like his body would never move again. He felt ossified. "How so?" he asked, his voice barely emerging from his chest.

"We didn't have any trouble with drunks. Nothing like a medical emergency to sober everyone up. Plus, Sally Kerns didn't die. How lucky were we that there were two doctors in the house, one of whom happened to be your former allergist?" Gerry paused.

Ian stayed very still.

"What I don't understand," Gerry added, gathering steam, "is a food blogger who goes through life not being able to eat certain foods. I don't believe in allergies, as I was telling your attractive little allergist. My working theory is that the little doctor might actually be a mesmerist. You know, she has those exotic eyes that can go all crazy, and she hypnotized Sally into thinking that her throat and face would swell up. And then they did. You, of course, would have been the next victim, judging from the way you stared at her."

Ian clenched his fists but didn't make a sound.

"Also on the plus side, we can strike the prawn chips fried in peanut oil from the menu. Not local and they seem like a bad luck item."

Still no response.

Gerry sighed. "You don't even care, do you?"

Ian shook his head.

"You want to tell me what this is about?" Gerry toyed with his drink. He had switched from wine to Diet Coke after everyone left. It was Gerry's secret shame. "Of all the locavore gin joints in all the towns in all the world, she has to walk into mine."

"Maybe I stopped listening to you because you stopped making sense."

"I'm narrating your thoughts. Am I halfway right?"

No response.

"Clearly, you have a thing for the pixie doctor. You weren't exactly staring subtly at her. Is that the lady you were seeing when you dumped that lawyer? Were you scratching the allergist's itch? Was she making house calls? Giving you thorough checkups?"

Ian stood up slowly and deliberately.

"So you are actually listening. Because I was thinking that what I needed tonight was a punch in the jaw." Gerry kept his voice steady, although he had gone very still. "It would be like the cherry in my drink."

They regarded each other warily.

"Nothing happened," Ian said.

Gerry shook his head. "You like her. Why'd you stop seeing her?"

"Because we weren't 'seeing' each other at all. We weren't dating. She was my doctor and I made things weird between us when she tried to keep it professional."

Gerry nodded.

The lights were out, except for the one above the bar. Ian reached under and pulled out a bottle of decidedly non-local Scotch. He dropped back into his seat.

"You could ask the woman out. Clearly, you'd like to do that."

"Gerry, sometimes your clueless bro act goes from funny to scary. She fired me as a patient because she didn't want me around." Ian poured himself a few fingers.

"Doctors can do that?"

"Can and did."

"Really, Ian, I don't get the feeling that this thing stayed one-sided. I mean, I talked to her and I knew she wasn't interested in me. I was hoping I'd wear her down. With you, yeah, she likes you."

Ian shook his head.

"And you like her. I've never seen you like this before. You were going to deck me."

Ian smiled for the first time that night. "Gerry, we get into fights about mollusks and plumbing and sourdough bread—"

"I can't believe you don't like sourdough."

"My point is, you're one very annoying shit."

"I think the only reason you haven't talked to her is because you like her too much and it scares the hell out of you. You know, it's difficult being friends with you. You don't exactly give anything of yourself. You don't confide. Even with the business, you keep most of it to yourself. I'm grateful that you leave me alone to be a genius cook, but it wouldn't kill me to learn about the financial side, for instance, make it more of a partnership in reality."

Ian looked around his empty bar. He wondered how Petra had come to be in the crowd. Had she come on purpose, knowing that she would see him? Would she

87

have talked to him if the night proceeded differently? She tried to avoid him when she spotted him, though. If it hadn't been for Sally Kerns, he might not have caught his former doctor at all. After the ambulance went away, she eluded him. He didn't get to thank her or offer to get her coat cleaned. She didn't let him ask how she had been doing. He even wanted to ask about Kevin.

But she had looked at him, when she thought he wasn't watching, and she hadn't seemed scared of him. He didn't know what it was and he didn't have time to analyze it when she practically sprinted away with her friends. While he stood in the cold night, wondering if his eyes – if his gut – was tricking him, Gerry and Lilah had taken care of the rest of the crowd. When he walked in, Gerry was making a speech. His words made everyone laugh, probably at Ian's expense. Ian didn't care.

"Do you think we'll be ready for an official opening next week?" Gerry asked. "Or should we wait, see if we can actually kill someone first? That would be a coup."

Ian finished his drink. "For our first course, shrimp dusted with bee pollen, bound together with a coating of peanut butter. Have someone stand by with epinephrine. Start a new trend in injectable dining."

"That could actually work."

"I'll start drafting plans tomorrow. I need a new project."

He took Gerry's glass.

"Go home, sleep in a proper bed," Gerry called, as Ian headed to the kitchen. "Call her tomorrow. Just try. The worst she can do is take out a restraining order."

–

Petra tried to forget the previous night, but the universe had other plans for her. By morning, Sally Kerns had written a breathless (hah!) account of her anaphylactic reaction on her blog. She'd found Petra's number and asked her to contribute a few tips about dealing with food allergies. Petra suggested a list of warning signs to look for and Sally added a link to Petra's website.

The blog post had only been up for a couple hours and it had already brought in a few telephone inquiries. Petra was happy to book them. Something good had to come out of it.

Between appointments, she decided to check on her mom, but the phone rang and rang. When it finally clicked over to voicemail, Petra left a message, then hung up. Odd, she thought. Lisa always picked up. Petra called her sister.

"Maybe she's out with Jim Morrison, lighting her fire," Ellie chortled.

"I don't know what's grosser – that thought, or your pun."

"One of us was going to bust it out soon enough. Mom's a big girl, you don't have to worry about her."

"I'm not worried about her. I'm just worried *for* her."

"Here we go," Ellie said.

Petra could almost hear the eye roll.

"What do you mean by that?"

"I mean that you egg each other on. Who's going to go bankrupt? What can possibly go wrong in the world? Who can win the negativity sweepstakes? And then you both insist you're fine."

"That is not what we do. If anything, she's the one who's always telling me not to trust anyone."

"And you do it right back. Remember a couple of years ago, when she wanted to crochet handbags and sell them online? You unearthed some newspaper article about how only two percent of sellers make their living that way. And some even lose money from shipping and dissatisfied customers."

"I don't know if it was as low as two percent."

"She's retired, Petey. It's not as if she wanted to make a ton of money from it."

"She just had all these stars in her eyes."

"And you had to discuss it to death with each other. Over multiple phone calls."

"She wanted to buy a ton of yarn. She had her eye on a huge lot. She could have crocheted cozies for every tea set in China."

"Then why not just persuade her to buy less? Why tell her to scuttle the whole idea? You're more alike than you think. You're both so pessimistic and scared to do anything. Then, when you can't stand all that self-recrimination and blame, you close your eyes, jump in, and do something impulsive. There's no happy medium for you."

Ellie was an annoying brat. But Petra didn't have a good reply to that, so she changed the subject. "Have you met him?"

"He's fine."

"What does that mean? How long ago did you meet him?"

"I met him months ago. She's just dating him. He has all his teeth. He didn't kick the cat, or Mom. Leave her alone."

"She is worrying about it. She's having a fucking melt-down over it."

"Don't throw plutonium on the reactor, then. Don't forget, I've seen you two in action. Pretty soon, a minor foul becomes a bonfire. You throw insults and doubts on top of one other and by the time you're done, the little man is toast. I don't know what's worse, the idea that the only men who could be interested in you are horrible, or the one where you two think you're both deserving of so little." Ellie's voice shook a little.

"But Ellie, it's just that she decides she's lonely and she makes bad choices that she knows are bad choices. I try to look out for her. Maybe I play devil's advocate, or maybe I try to make her see something she missed…"

Ellie was silent.

Petra tried again. "You don't blame me for your dad—"

"No."

A pause. Petra held her breath.

"You were a teenager and they were both adults. You weren't helpful, Petey, but you didn't cause their trouble."

"Ellie."

"But you're not a teenager now, and Mom puts more stock in your opinion than you think."

"Please, the woman questions every single move I make. She—"

"She listens to you, Petra. You think you're talking to dead air, but Mom is sensitive. She remembers everything you say. And believe me, she's proud of you, even if she has no idea how to show it except by frantically trying to make sure you don't disappoint her, or yourself."

Petra held her head and put her elbows on her desk. She never realized that Ellie felt this way.

"Just leave it," Ellie was saying. "Even if she takes some wrong turns, she's stronger now."

Petra swallowed. "How is your dad, anyway?"

"He's good. He came up for a visit last weekend. Took me out for a fancy dinner and gave me money for laundry."

Petra felt a stab of guilt. "He's a nice guy."

"I'll tell him you said so."

Petra nodded, even though she knew her sister couldn't see her. The light on her phone was blinking. She had another patient. She took a deep breath. "Okay, sweetie, I have to go. But I love you. And if you want to come visit, just let me know. Your dad isn't the only one who can take you for a fancy dinner."

"Score," said her sister, sounding normal again. "I promise I won't hit you up for laundry quarters. Although if you could convince your gyno friend, Sarah, to come up sometime and give a talk at the Women's Center..."

"Ugh. She'd love that. Don't feed her ego."

"Just see what you can do."

—

Listening to Gerry was a bad idea, Ian thought as he stood looking up the stairs to Petra's office. For all Ian knew, the discharge letter could really be the prelude to a restraining order. It had been so long and he had no idea where he stood with her. Did her strenuous refusal to acknowledge him mean that he still affected her, in some way? If she'd been utterly indifferent, she would have at least said hello.

Right?

He remembered that she had told him she felt socially awkward at all times. She certainly didn't look like a geek last night. She had been bold and decisive when treating Sally Kerns. Even now, he could remember how she held her arm up for a few seconds before plunging the needle in Sally's thigh. Petra's bicep had bulged a little and the neck of the dress tightened across her chest. He'd gotten turned on by seeing her in action.

Yeah, maybe he was a creep.

He had to make a decision. Was he going to wait down here like a groupie, or would he go up and try to talk to her, in her office, where she had cases full of sharp, pointy needles? Not that he thought she would try to harm him, but he probably shouldn't startle her.

Maybe he should send her an email.

He took out his phone and a small figure nearly stumbled into him. "Kevin?"

Kevin squinted up at him. "Oh. Hey. I thought you stopped coming."

"I did. But…" He couldn't think of an excuse for being there. "Is this your day for an appointment?"

Kevin shrugged. "I thought I'd come to hang out. She's busier now, but she lets me do that sometimes. She won't get a TV, though. Why are you here? I thought needles made you cry, so that's why you quit coming to appointments."

"No. Is that what Dr. Lale said?"

Kevin shrugged again. "She never tells me anything anymore." He added, "Actually, I know you didn't cry. I could hear you flirting with her through the office door." He hitched his book bag higher on his shoulder.

Ian didn't know how to answer that. He also didn't want to go up to talk to Petra knowing Kevin would hear every word. Especially because he wasn't sure what he was going to say. He tucked his phone back in his pocket and turned to leave.

"Maybe you can help me with this," Kevin asked. "How do you get a sophisticated woman to go out with you?"

Ian stopped. He looked around. He was on the street in front of the office of his crush, about to run away because he was wary of scaring her. "I am not the best person to ask for romantic advice," Ian said.

"I know. But at least you had a girlfriend, even if you didn't know what to do with her." Kevin wrinkled his nose at the memory. "All I need are guidelines, maybe some sort of flowchart. Like, if she won't even talk to you, but just kind of looks through you when you go up to her and say hi, what should you do? Should you get her flowers? Or should you work her friends, first?"

"If she doesn't respond to a friendly greeting, then you should just leave her alone."

"Even if she's hot."

"Yes."

Kevin took out his phone and made some notes. "Okay, this is good information. Now, say she does say hi, but in a sort of vague way that indicates that maybe she's just being polite. Do you bust out the flowers then?"

"Aren't you allergic to most flowers?"

"I make them out of tissue paper."

"And you're still making that sound you make with your throat and nose?"

"I'm trying to clear my postnasal drip."

"Maybe you shouldn't talk about postnasal drip."

"See?" Kevin brightened. "This is important for me to know."

Ian felt like he was getting off message. "But really, if you can talk to the girl easily, and if she makes you laugh and you want to just spend time with her, then she's probably great and you're fine and you don't need my help."

"Yes, but I want to bag a hot woman. There are several in my middle school who will speak to me. I'll settle for any one of them."

Had Ian ever been like that? He winced. He *had*, not even that long ago. Who was he to ask out Petra Lale? He was just a horny kid who had glimpsed something that he couldn't have.

And then, she stepped out onto the sidewalk and stopped right in front of him and he wanted everything all over again because he was a greedy little fucker.

Neither of them spoke for a moment. Kevin, however, watched the two of them curiously. Petra's face looked frozen in between a glare and a smile. She was also turning pink.

Ian rubbed his head. He said the one thing that he could safely say. "I wanted to thank you for what you did last night."

"What did she do?" Kevin asked eagerly.

"She saved someone's life. A woman was having a bad allergic reaction, and Dr. Lale injected her and stayed with her until the ambulance came."

Petra was shaking her head but she seemed maybe faintly pleased?

He kept his voice neutral. "Let me invite you to Stream, again. At the very least, you deserve a drink for preventing someone from dying on our floor. I'm pretty sure you staved off bad publicity and even more terrible karma."

Petra put her handbag between them like a shield. Ian eyed it, wondering if she was going to pull Mace out of it or call 911. Possibly both. Maybe having Kevin around as a witness was a good thing for both of them.

The kid hopped around excitedly. "Can I come? Can I bring a lady?"

"You have a girlfriend? Already?" Petra asked. She seemed temporarily distracted, even a little stricken.

"Not yet. Ian is teaching me how to get with sophisticated women."

Fuck.

"Is he now?" she asked.

She hoisted her purse higher. Christ, her bag was huge. Forget Mace. He'd never survive if she struck him with all of those chains and leather straps.

He tried another tack. Turning to Kevin, he said, "You can have sodas, and maybe you'd like the mini pork sliders and some other dishes."

"Do the sliders have wheat? I'm allergic to wheat. And I can't have soda."

"You can take off the bun and just eat the pork. Or maybe we can find something else for you. Spinach dumplings?"

Petra and Kevin shook their heads.

"Polenta, cheddar, and scallion croquettes?"

They shook their heads again.

"We'll find something. And maybe we can have lemonade on hand. Lemonade is okay, right?"

"Yes," Kevin said. "But not with mint."

"Are you allergic to mint?"

"No, I just don't like it."

Ian thought of delivering a lecture about how the kid couldn't afford to be fussy, given his limited options, but Petra held up her hand. "Kevin, Mr. Zamora, this is a very nice offer, but I can't actually come with you."

"Why not?"

She addressed Kevin. "I can't date a patient, or double date with one."

"Actually, it's not a date," Ian said.

"Right," she drawled. Nonetheless, she was blushing and stealing glances at him.

Ian felt a surge of hope. *I might not get Maced*, he thought giddily. His shoulders relaxed a fraction.

"Like I said, it's a thank you. And a sort of apology."

She seemed wary. At least she was looking at him.

"I'd like to take care of your dry cleaning bill, if you'll let me. Your coat and dress probably got dirty last night. It was a beautiful dress."

"I've never seen you in a dress, Doc," Kevin said.

"It was red, and it looked silky, very soft." He had wanted to run his hands over it.

As if she had heard his thoughts, her eyelids fluttered closed. *Yes!*

Then they snapped open. "The blogger, Sally Kerns, contacted me today. I wouldn't worry." Petra turned away. "She doesn't blame you and she's not going to pan your place. I don't have any influence over her, anyway."

"Ian's just trying to thank you, Doc."

"Look, Ian— Mr. Zamora, you can't take Kevin to a bar, even if you're the owner. Kevin, what would your father say?"

"He won't mind, especially if there's a doctor there. What if you have to save my life?"

"You're right, Kev," Ian said. "Doctor, you'll have to come in an official capacity."

Petra glowered but Ian turned to Kevin. "You and your lady friend can give me detailed notes on what you think of the place. It'll give you something to talk about."

"I always have something interesting to talk about," Kevin said.

Petra coughed. It might have been to cover up a laugh.

They moved aside to let some other people past on the sidewalk.

"You should also wear a suit," Ian added.

"I hate suits."

"Sophisticated women like men who look polished and smell good and make an effort."

Kevin turned to Petra.

"I'd love to see you in a jacket and tie," she said, with an evil glint in her eye.

She was taking her revenge on both of them. Ian liked that.

"Don't worry, you'll look sharp, Kevin," Ian said. "It'll be a private, pre-opening dinner. We'll have candles, nice music. The staff will hang on your every word. The lady will be impressed."

Ian put his arm around Kevin's shoulders. He glanced back at Petra. "Six o'clock tomorrow. I trust you know the address."

Chapter Nine

Outmaneuvered, Petra fumed, surveying her living room.
Just what did Ian Zamora want with her anyway?

Who cares? her hormones screamed.

She grabbed her headphones and her running shoes
and set off toward the waterfront path. It was still chilly
and rain threatened. Her eyes watered in the cold air. But
pushing against the wind and wet suited her mood today.

He wasn't her patient anymore, was he? It had been
months since the last time she'd seen him. And sure, Sarah
had warned her not to complicate things, but what harm
was there in having a small drink with him, and with
Kevin as a chaperone? The man was grateful.

Franz Ferdinand shouted out from Petra's headphones,
asking if she "wanted to."

"Yes!" she yelled, running faster.

She didn't have to be instantly suspicious of everyone
who seemed to enjoy her company, she thought. And she
had done some real doctoring that night.

Pausing to stretch her tight hamstrings, she texted
Helen.

I am awesome! she wrote.

You are awesome, too! she added, as an afterthought.

She started to jog slowly again.

Just stay cool, she told herself. Even if he really liked
her, even if he asked her out, she wouldn't be able to go

out with him. She should enjoy some wine she'd never normally be able to afford, ogle Ian just a little bit before she never got to see him again.

She jogged a little faster and stared out at the water. "How many miles do you run?" a guy shouted, catching up to her.

"I don't know," she yelled back.

She decelerated even more to let him pass, but he matched her pace.

She smiled, more of a baring of teeth in the cold wind, to encourage him to move on. He grinned back. What was she going to have to do, slap him on the butt?

"You have good turnover," he yelled. "I've been watching you for the last mile."

He'd been watching her... footwork. Great.

"Yours seems awesome, too!" she shouted back.

There didn't seem to be a lot to say, but Foot Man loped along beside her.

She had been out of the loop for so long. Was he actually trying to pick her up?

She assessed him. Nice running gear. No *eau de homeless* about him. She couldn't appraise his hair color – rain and sweat had dampened and darkened it – but she'd guess it was a shade of brown. At least it wasn't pulled into a ratty ponytail. Bone structure and muscle structure looked good. Eye color, again, difficult to tell, but at least she couldn't see any jaundice.

There's more than one way for me to keep my distance, she thought.

-

She had brought a date.

He had planned to talk to her, charm her. He planned for interruptions from Kevin and Lilah, and possibly Gerry. He was prepared for an uphill struggle.

He had not planned on her bringing a man.

At least she had the sense to look slightly ashamed of herself. She also looked great. He wondered if she had worn the silky blouse and slim jeans to impress the young one she'd brought.

"I'm sorry, I didn't catch your name," Ian said.

"Marsalis."

"Right. Marsalis."

The fucker.

–

Ian's knee brushed Petra's. She tightened her hand around a water glass and willed herself to keep still. It was hard to know how successful she was. Her skin tingled.

Ian appeared unaffected, as if the touch had been an accident.

The staff began bringing out little plates and while everyone exclaimed over the food, Petra compared the men surreptitiously. Marsalis wore skinny jeans and a soft tee printed with sparrows and vines. He had another bird tattooed on his arm. He probably had a thorough knowledge of indie bands. But there was something unformed about his features. He was soft in the cheeks and around the chin. Even the way he mouthed his vowels and consonants seemed mushy. He was probably a couple of years younger than she was. She put her chin up. She could handle it.

She turned to Ian. He wore his usual button-down and jeans. His clothes were softer, a little broken in. She could imagine his thigh muscles, flexing underneath the denim, as he sat forward and explained each dish to Kevin and his date, Penny. He blinked and Petra watched his long eyelashes brush against his cheek.

She shouldn't be noticing Ian's lashes, or picturing the rippling that went on under his clothing. Marsalis was here, and he was buff, and he had a tattoo. (Of course, the ink probably increased the likelihood that he had hepatitis C, but she decided to ignore that for now.) Overall, Marsalis probably lent her some kind of hotness cred due to his youth and hipness.

But Ian was endlessly fascinating, despite the fact that she knew so much about him. She knew how old he was. She knew that he'd had his appendix out, and that his father had died of melanoma, and that his eyes widened and he sucked his cheeks in lightly when he felt pain. She knew that his touch set her skin fizzing.

She wondered how he looked when he came.

He met her eyes and lifted an eyebrow, as if he knew what she had just been thinking. She couldn't look away. Lust arced between them. He edged closer to her and his knee brushed hers again. His thigh felt hard.

Foul, foul! screamed inner Hippocrates. Somewhere he had obtained a ref's whistle and he blew it until his little toga strained.

She bumped away quickly and ended up closer to Marsalis. Stupid red leather seats.

Kevin announced that he would tell the tale of how he'd managed to get his father to throw up the night before.

"This isn't table talk, Kevin," Petra said automatically.

"I don't mind," said Penny eagerly.

Marsalis and Ian shrugged at the same time. Petra darted a quick glance at Ian and saw him looking at her from under his lashes. She glared.

Fine. Kevin's anecdote would probably curb any desire she felt to curl her fingers in Ian's collar and lick his lip. She should be encouraging the kid to gross them out.

"I wanted to make a go-cart," Kevin said eagerly, "but my dad wouldn't let me. So I decided to make a milk carton raft instead."

"You can't have milk," Petra said right away.

"I just needed the containers. My dad uses milk in his coffee."

"That's what you get from this, that he can't have milk?" Ian said to Petra. "How about the fact that he's making a *raft*?"

Antagonism, and something else, shimmered between them, again. Petra's hand tightened into a fist.

Kevin ignored them both. "So my dad came home last night, and was, like" – he did a high-pitched voice – "*What is that smell?* And I reminded him that my olfactory sense was gone." He used the word "olfactory" with pride. Penny gave him a sigh that sounded suspiciously adoring and Petra loved her. "And Dad was like, *It smells like something is rotting in the guest bedroom.*"

"Hoo boy," Marsalis said.

Ian regarded him stonily.

"Please tell me you rinsed the milk cartons," Petra said.

"I *thought* I had. Anyway, when I opened the door, Dad practically fell backward. And then I dragged the raft over to show him, and he threw up on it." Kevin looked pleased.

"All that work," Marsalis said sympathetically.

"Don't encourage him," Petra and Ian said together.

Kevin smirked.

Ian turned to Marsalis and said, "So, *Marsalis*, how did you and Petra meet?"

Asshole, Petra thought. *Stupid, annoying, sexy, smug, goddamn thigh-rubbing asshole.*

"We were out running along the Greenway trail," Petra interjected tightly.

Ian didn't even look her way. He and Marsalis seemed to engage in a kind of male telepathy that, if heard aloud, probably sounded like grunting and chest beating. Another plate came and Penny dug into clams and breadcrumbs. At least someone was enjoying the evening. Petra let out her breath slowly.

"Do you live around here, too?" Kevin asked.

"Yeah," said Marsalis. "It's a great nabe. I share a place with a few other guys."

"A few?" Ian asked.

"Five or six. It's sort of a floating number. We live in a loft. Open space, you know."

"Cool," said Kevin. "Do you do any multiplayer games together?"

"We all go off to our corners for Empire, and we yell at each other."

"What if you want to get alone with a girl?" Kevin asked.

Petra kicked him. The white oak table was hiding a multitude of sins tonight.

Marsalis smiled lazily. "It's cool. We understand when someone needs privacy."

Ian's eyes glinted in the candlelight. "And what do you do for a living, Marsalis?"

"I take a few classes at Willamette."

Petra's mind stuttered. *How old—?*

"How old are you?" Kevin asked.

Petra couldn't kick him again. She was his doctor, and she was pretty sure that *First, do no harm* covered bruising. "You don't have to answer that," Petra said.

Marsalis grinned lazily. He reached over and put his arm around Petra. She winced and tried to cover it with a cough. She couldn't help herself.

Ian, to his credit, did not smirk.

It was a school night, so Penny's mother came by to pick them up at eight. Kevin gave the servers and Ian and chef Marcia a tiny bow. Penny, taking her cues from Kevin, performed a curtsy and echoed his words. Kevin held the car door open for Penny.

Now, it was just Petra and the boys left.

Awkward.

"Well," said Petra.

"Well," said Ian.

"Can I walk you back home?" Marsalis asked, slinging an arm around Petra and kissing her on the cheek.

But it was too late for Petra. Inner Hippocrates was wringing his hands.

Ian interrupted. "Actually, Marsalis, Petra and I have some business to discuss. Why don't you head on out alone? The night is young."

And so are you, Petra thought, looking sadly at Marsalis.

Marsalis nodded. He looked amused, as if older women often used him for the purposes of making their elderly lovers jealous. He shrugged into his leather jacket and ambled off. Ian and Petra watched him and waved, like a pair of doting grandparents. His shapely rear end disappeared behind a corner.

"Don't say anything," Petra said, holding up her hand. "I'm already trying to imagine myself explaining the statutory rape charges to a medical board."

"He didn't get to say how old he was," Ian noted.

"The less I know, the better," Petra said.

—

Ian pursed his lips and he saw that she clenched both of her fists. Still no polish on those fingernails. He gestured to the bar and she sat down. He reached up, nabbed two wineglasses, and poured them each some red. "Is it really worth all this trouble to get rid of me?" he asked.

"Is it really worth all this trouble to pursue me?"

He looked her directly in the eye. "It is," he said.

She shot him one long, hard look, and he met her eye, almost found himself pulling her toward him. But he couldn't touch her, not yet.

"It's complicated," she said, finally. "There are other major circumstances. But a big issue is that you were my patient and it would be unethical. The American Medical Association considers it misconduct when doctors carry on with patients, with good reason, and except in special cases, the AMA frowns on relationships with doctors even after the patient is no longer a patient. Their guideline says doctors and patients should wait at least six months after the patient ceases to be a patient. In Great Britain, relations are banned outright. Maybe it sounds like quibbling to you, but I've sunk so much of my life into this practice. My savings, my degree, my reputation. I just can't risk any trouble so close to the beginning of my career."

Petra fiddled with the stem of her glass.

"I don't want to make problems for you, but if what you tell me is accurate, no one — not even the American

Medical Association – can hold your actions against you. I came on to you. You stayed professional. That's my story. Plus, I'm no longer in your care and I haven't been for almost six months. You made sure of that. Did you write the letter because I made you uncomfortable in any way? Because I'm sorry if I did, but you and I know that there's more to it than that."

His gaze searched hers again. It was her turn to look uneasy. "No, I was protecting myself in case you thought I sent the wrong signals."

Ian was pleased about that one.

"And what signals were those?" he asked, giving her a dark look.

"No. No, you were my *patient*. There should have been nothing. Radio static. Cone of silence."

"I never quite understood what's so terrible about a doctor dating a patient."

"Of course it's terrible. You come to me because you're sick and vulnerable and in pain. I'm supposed to help you not take advantage of your weakness."

"But I don't feel exploited. I came in to your office because I get sniffly around cats. It's a minor inconvenience, which, as you pointed out, would be helped if I stopped hanging around felines. I'm not dying. It's not like you would be putting a clown nose on me and posting pictures of it while I'm lying in a coma."

"Minor inconveniences turn into life-threatening events every day. You're still under my care technically – and really, forever. Unless you've found a new physician, I am your allergist. What if you have a reaction to something else one day, and you end up in that coma?"

"Really, you'd do the clown nose thing?"

"Big red shoes and a squirty flower. And naked pictures, of course."

As soon as the words were out of her mouth, she stuck out her chin, as if she already knew what he was thinking and needed to stop it. "My point is that I need to be able to treat you and be objective if you stop breathing and go to the hospital. You also have to feel comfortable to come to me and speak honestly. That's more likely to happen if you don't think that I might exploit you."

"But I stopped being your patient. You even backed it up with a letter. And I feel comfortable coming to you. And I like speaking to you."

She looked guilty, then hurt. That hurt him.

"I sent you that letter because I couldn't be a competent doctor for you, because I was afraid that I'd let my feelings cross the line. I hate the fact that I couldn't be your physician. What am I if I'm not good?"

"You are."

"Well, you have feelings for me, so your word doesn't count for much."

They looked at each other. She was right. It wasn't just that she smelled nice and he enjoyed the shape of her legs and ass encased in those jeans. He liked her because of who she was, and she had always tried to be a good person. He wasn't sure he had liked anyone quite this way before.

"Let's look at objective measures, then. I felt better. Kevin has improved."

Actually, he wasn't sure how Kevin was with his allergies, but he couldn't possibly be worse. Ian did feel guilty, though. He hated that he'd caused her to second-guess her abilities.

"We could try to equalize the playing field. Tell me about your medical history."

She stood up.

"Don't mock me," she said quietly. "You may think that I just hand out nasal sprays and I'm not someone who treats cancer or operates on the valves of your heart. These aren't just scruples. Something unexpected could happen to you. Look at Sally Kerns. Her doc still isn't sure what made her react that night. Don't trivialize what I do."

"I'm sorry." He stepped a little closer. "I'm not mocking you. I'm serious. I think I should learn as much about you as you know about me."

She was furious and horny and her temples throbbed because no matter how much she was trying to control the situation, the reins seemed to slip out of her grasp. And he knew it.

"Are you going to take my blood pressure?"

"I'll trust you on that. How is it?"

"It's fine."

It probably wasn't. She could feel her heart drumming in her ears.

"Is there anything significant in the family history?"

"I don't know."

He raised an eyebrow and she felt herself growing defensive. "I mean, no. Although I don't know much about my dad's side."

"That's fine. I've already learned so much. Do you smoke, drink, do drugs?"

"Does boxed wine count?"

He was crowding her closer to the bar. And she was letting him. "Pervert," he said, almost in her ear. "Are you sexually active?"

"No."

But I'd like to be.

She sat down on a barstool. Hard. "Are you sexually active?" she asked.

"No," he said.

"But you had a girlfriend?" she persisted.

"That ended months ago," Ian said.

"Why?"

"I met you."

Danger, danger. Was this somehow her fault? He denied it, but had she been giving him signals? She had a crush on him and she'd tried to keep it tamped down for the sake of her practice and her sanity. But he knew and he'd come for her anyway. *What's the harm?* her hormones whispered. *He's not your patient anymore.*

The pause was enough for him to seize control again.

"Let's get back on track. What are your allergies?"

"I'm fine with aspirin and penicillin."

"So you're an allergist with no allergies."

"Well, that question usually just means drugs. But I react to dust and cats."

"They match mine."

"Then clearly we belong together," Petra said.

She bit her lip and glanced up to see him smiling that half smile.

"So, any other information you need?" she asked. "Insurance card?"

"I need to examine your arms."

"What?"

But she knew what he meant. She looked down at the blouse she'd worn and tugged at the sleeves. As she rolled them over her elbows, the silk seams stretched. The openings squeezed her upper arms unattractively. "This is not the right outfit for this sort of thing," Petra grumbled.

"Hey, now you know how I felt."

"You knew coming in that I'd be sticking you. I didn't know till ten minutes ago that you'd get the urge to play doctor."

He traced up her bare skin and the arm bulge caused by her tight cuff. *Armfin top*, Petra said to herself. *Muffarm top. This is very definitely not sexy at all.* But his nails continued to graze the curve of her elbow, and then he gently pushed two fingers under the edge of her sleeve and traced under her deltoid to the ridge of her latissimus dorsi. She felt a little breathless. The Latin wasn't helping.

"Well, that's done," he said, huskily. "Now I just have stick you with a bunch of needles."

His warm fingers still moved under her clothing.

"Not a chance," she said. Her own voice was a little hoarse.

He dipped his head down and she closed her eyes. She had slid partway down the stool and his other hand had reached her waist brace her. He was near enough that she could feel his breath on her nape, so close she could almost feel his lips brushing against her. One of his knees touched the back of her leg. And he was tall, so tall that his body enveloped hers. She felt electrified.

It was an awkward position to maintain.

She shook his hand out of her clothing and almost fell off the stool.

"Well," she said, standing up, "I should probably get going."

She did not meet his eyes.

"I'll walk you home."

"Don't you have a restaurant to run or something?"

"They'll muddle through."

He held up her coat and buttoned her up snugly. The walk was silent, but too short. They stopped in front of her building.

"Thank you. For another dinner. And I'm sorry about Kevin and Penny. And Marsalis."

"Next time, we'll try just the two of us."

"I don't think there should be a next time."

"I disagree," he said.

Then he kissed her.

Chapter Ten

He hadn't given her any warning, so his lips hit the corner of her mouth and her astonished eyes were still open. They froze, faces mashed together asymmetrically. His glasses were smudged and askew. Petra had stuck her arms out when he grabbed her and they were still flapping in the air.

She began to laugh.

"I can't believe that I had you built up in my mind as some sort of sex god."

His arms were still around her and he could feel the vibrations from her giggles all the way up and down his body. The exhalations of her laughter blew over his face. He felt silly, embarrassed, turned on, and crazed, all at once.

"Maybe this is stupendous and you have no idea what good is," he said gruffly.

"You *missed*. How can you be any good if you can't even aim properly?"

He kissed her sloppy and lopsided on the other side of her mouth and she laughed again.

He made a move as if to kiss her mouth, then he bit her chin very gently. Her eyes fluttered shut. He started backing her into the side of her apartment building and he smoothed his lips over the point of her jaw, over the smooth cheekbone. Her fingers pressed restlessly against him and he squeezed the thick fabric of her camel coat wishing that he could find the narrow hips underneath. Her skin had felt like butterfly wings. He licked the corner of her eye and nosed her gently. He pretended to go for her mouth, then kissed her ear and her throat.

She sighed. And like that, she let him go and pushed away from him.

"Nice seeing you again," she said hoarsely.

She disappeared behind the door.

–

Inner Hippocrates was strangely silent as Petra stood in front of her mailbox and willed herself to calm down. He'd probably fainted dead away when Ian started his sacrilegious examination of her arms.

Maybe it was okay because she hadn't kissed him full on the lips. Maybe it was okay if there was no tongue involved. Maybe she could go through a whole relationship with Ian, including sharing forks, nakedness, and DVR remotes, as long as they didn't kiss.

Loophole! Loophole! her hormones chanted.

She trundled herself up to her apartment. She felt elated and miserable at the same time. Was this the kind of confusion that came from lust and bad decisions? Had she given in irrevocably to impulse? Was she turning into her mother – a neurotic, worried creature whose pent-up itches led to terrible boyfriends and husbands?

The answer, of course, was no. The husbands and boyfriends had their good points. And Petra had shut Ian down, after all. She could practically see him panting against the glass as she'd closed the door.

She caught a glimpse of herself in the hall mirror. A warm haze surrounded her. Same curly hair, same thin nose, but everything about her seemed duskier and dewier. Her skin felt sensitive. She was still slightly breathless. If she hadn't known what it was, she'd think she were having an allergic reaction. A man with soft lips and dexterous hands had put himself against her and tunneled his fingers under her clothing. His eyes came alive when he saw her and he groaned when she left him. He wanted her. She definitely wanted him. It felt wonderful and delicious and corrupt.

And she had put a stop to it and done the right thing. She should be proud of her self-control.

She fell onto her couch, kicked her shoes to the floor, and shimmied out of her coat. As she did, her phone fell out of her pocket. She had a message from Helen.

Were you drunk texting me yesterday evening?

No, Petra thumbed back.

A few minutes later, a reply pinged back.

OK. I agree we're both awesome.

–

Ian felt terrible. He felt restless. He felt energized. He felt wonderful. He was all over the place.

He didn't even have her number.

Ian briefly considered heading back to Field after seeing Petra home. He imagined getting his mind off of the press of her small body by totaling receipts, glaring at his employees, and drying piles of white dishes. For some reason, that didn't appeal. He had split another full day between Field and Stream. He decided to return to his apartment and have a shower. He carted an armful of mail upstairs, dropped it on the mantel, and looked around at his apartment.

He had only brought girlfriends here a couple of times, and then, it was usually only a stop to pick up a shirt that didn't smell like a deep fryer, or to change into sneakers. He wondered if any of those ex-girlfriends had even sat on the couch. He seemed to remember offering someone a glass of water, and not finding any clean cups.

What was Petra's apartment like? Would he be invited in? She still knew much more about him than he knew about her. He had planned to draw her out with questions, but instead of taking his time, he'd shoved his fingers under her blouse. Of course, he'd only managed to feel up her arm. It was a nice arm.

He made his way to the shower, dropping clothes and shoes along the way. He looked in the mirror at his bare chest and shoulders. The bones stuck out more than they used to. He had lost weight over the last couple of months and it made him look older. Had she noticed? Of course she had. Her bright glance missed nothing; when it sparked over his body he wanted to crush her to him to see if he would burn up.

He had it bad.

He took a cool shower and emerged rubbing a towel in his hair. He surveyed his apartment. He thought about hiring a cleaning lady, but he always reasoned that there was nothing to clean with no one actually living at his apartment. Boy, he was wrong. He picked up an armful of discarded clothing and stood in his living room. A leather couch, a glass coffee table. A TV that he had never bothered to attach properly to the wall. And the dust. How did a place manage to accumulate dust when no one stayed there? He swiped absently at the surface of his coffee table. It made him sneeze. No wonder he hated it here.

For the first time in a long time, he found himself wandering around his apartment, opening cabinets and peering behind doors. The interior of his linen closet didn't look familiar. He hardly remembered if there was anything in his refrigerator. What did he even have to offer Petra if she stayed there overnight? Sure, he had scoffed at Marsalis's roommates and loft earlier. The kid probably skateboarded around his loft with his college buddies and had a bathroom with no door. But could Ian argue that this emptiness was any better? Did he have any clean cups? Could he offer Petra anything to drink? At his businesses, he could present three different kinds of water. But his businesses weren't his life. He had never planned his life around work. That had been his father's way, and despite the fact that Ian had loved the man, he didn't want to be anything like him.

He walked into the living room and picked up, one by one, the rocks his dad had helped him collect. The collection was almost all he had of his parents, aside from his photographs. He knew that his mother's silver wedding band was somewhere. It had some sort of filigree, but no stones. He didn't want reminders of their terrible marriage. Even before his mother died, his father, a mining geologist, had carted his family to towns around the world. Luckily, Ian picked up languages fairly well, and he played soccer, smiled easily, and ate everything people put in front of him. This guaranteed that he made friends in Australia and Chile and the other places that Tomás Zamora had dragged them.

His mother had not adjusted as well.

He was restless and he had to do something. He was after a woman who refused to date him, even though she liked him. She had her principles. He was supposed to respect them, because he liked her, and he trusted her to know what was best.

But he wasn't really her patient anymore.

The only way he could really stop being her patient was if he started being someone else's.

Dammit. As if he'd already begun, his arm started to itch.

But he had never shied away from work. He started gathering his dirty laundry and wiping down the empty surfaces.

His time with Petra wouldn't end this way.

He had a new project.

—

"I thought we agreed that you wouldn't see him again," Sarah said.

"I didn't actually see him. I had a date with someone else."

"But you ended up wrapping your lips around Ian's."

"Those parts didn't really touch."

Well, they had a little, at the corners. The very sensitive corners. And there had been *the hands*. She rubbed her thighs with her sweaty palms and shifted a little in the back seat of the car.

"There's a word for what you're doing here," Helen said. "It's called equivocation."

"I think the word is bullshitting," Sarah stated flatly.

"Do you get your mothers to push by terrifying them? Because let me tell you, you are making my ass tense up," Helen said.

"I don't terrify pregnant women," Sarah said, gripping the wheel more firmly. "I don't terrify anyone."

Petra surreptitiously tightened her seat belt.

They were headed to a wedding. Sarah always insisted on taking her car because that meant she could drive. Helen brought a Rand McNally road atlas and argued with the GPS as if it were a real person. This, of course, made Sarah nuts, and it caused her to adhere even more strictly to the speed limit than Helen could stand.

Two more hours until Seattle, Petra thought.

She slid further down into the back seat. At least they were at each other's throats rather than hers. She felt no need to be involved in discussions about her love life, her lack thereof, or that gray no woman's land which she now inhabited.

"I have never, ever in my life been attracted to a patient," Sarah said.

Helen snorted. "First of all, you are a heterosexual obstetrician, so no kidding your patients don't buzz you. Second, never? Like, not even when you were doing your clerkships? There were no smoldering delinquents with hungry eyes during your psych rotation? No cute dads dandling cherubic children on their knees—"

"Technically, those aren't patients," Petra couldn't help interrupting.

"No nerdy-yet-cute scientists with chemical burns to their fingers? No sweaty Muay Thai boxers with possible concussions?"

Jesus, what had Helen's ER rotations been like?

"No hunky foreign diplomats with mysterious fevers? No square-jawed soldiers with PTSD? No stoic fire-fighters?"

Sarah pressed her lips together.

"A-ha! I knew it!"

Petra breathed a sigh of relief, partly because Sarah had admitted it, and partly because the litany of imaginary males was making the car seem unbearably warm.

"That does *not* count. I treated him for, like, five minutes in the ER and the chief resident was breathing down my neck the whole time."

"So you like to be watched while you commit moral crimes in your heart," Helen said, poker-faced.

"Shut up! Shut up! Why am I even friends with you?"

Right on schedule, Petra thought. Last time, it had been over Justin Timberlake, and the time before, argument erupted over the composition of the Supreme Court. In another half an hour, they'd forgive each other and start singing show tunes at the top of their lungs. It was hard to decide what was worse.

"My point is, Sarah, it happens. We're human. Sometimes, we become attracted to our patients."

"When were you ever swayed by a patient?" Sarah asked. "Petra told us and I spilled. Now it's your turn."

"I'm called on consults in the ER all the time. It's entirely possible that I've dated someone I've looked at. I don't remember everyone."

"Seeing as you haven't gone out with anyone since Terrible Mike, I don't see how that would be possible," Petra said.

Sarah and Helen ignored her. "My dad was one of two GPs in our town," Helen said. "My mother came in for a tetanus shot because she'd stepped on a rusty nail while visiting a friend. My dad ran into her again at the grocery store, and then at church later that week. They got married two weeks later. Should my dad's license have been revoked?"

Sarah sped up and changed lanes. She looked uncomfortable but stubborn. "It's a nice story, but the reason we do have these rules in place is to protect patients. A woman who has just been diagnosed with stage III breast cancer is vulnerable. A depressed man with suicidal thoughts is at risk. Some terrible person, some horrible doctor, could come in and make that cancer patient think he's God. An unscrupulous shrink could cause a total emotional crash."

Helen shook her head. "The question is, Sarah, do you think my dad is horrible? He gave my mom, who didn't even live in town, a tetanus shot. And after they got married, he'd check her throat when she was sick, and he even delivered my brother. Technically, he was practicing medicine on her. She was his patient. Was that unethical? Was he exploiting her?"

She turned in her seat now. "Do you think Petra is horrible, Sarah? She gave Ian some allergy shots and then she discharged him from her practice when she was sure that she couldn't be objective anymore. Are those the actions of an immoral doctor?"

Sarah's shoulders were practically at her ears. "I don't like relativism, Helen."

"We treat people on a case-by-case basis, Sarah. Ethical dilemmas are judged that way."

"We help people using treatments that have been proven effective to large populations, *Helen*. It's the foundation of evidence-based practice. We don't use a drug or discard a treatment protocol, or abandon principles, just because that seems to work for one person, or, in your case, one marriage."

The silence was ripe.

"Do you think you're doing anything wrong, Petra?" Helen asked.

"I can't tell right now," Petra said, her eyes darting between her friends. From the vehemence behind the discussions, she had the feeling that this was not about her at all. "I don't think I've exploited him at this point, but who can tell down the road? And then part of me is worried that if I let this slip by reasoning that I'm not doing any harm, that maybe I'll let other things pass by. And that maybe this is the beginning of me being a terrible doctor."

"Exactly," said Sarah. "It's a slippery slope. And if you date him, my friend, then you have stepped into the skis yourself and pushed yourself down that hill. Not to mention that it might harm your practice if he decides that you've done something wrong."

"I don't think he'd be vengeful."

"Would you go out with him if he asked you?" Helen said.

"I don't know," Petra replied honestly.

"I wish you'd just go to the wedding and find someone to sleep with and forget about him," Sarah said.

Helen whirled her head. "Why is that always the solution with you, Sarah? Need to unwind because your job sucks? Find a giant Finnish boyfriend and sleep with him instead of talking."

"What exactly are you saying to me, Helen? Spell it out and use precise terms so that I won't interpret it any which way."

"What I'm saying is that your solution to our problems is stupid and narrow, rather like your blanket condemnation of Petra's situation."

"And you're saying you're perfectly fine with it. That Petra can just go and blithely screw the man and there will never ever be any fallout."

"No. I'm saying that she should approach with caution, but it's hardly impossible."

"Well, isn't that enlightened of you. Or maybe that's just what I'd expect from someone so morally flexible that they feel they can cheat on Terrible Mike, and then trash talk him to her friends."

Silence.

"What?" Petra said. She looked at her friends. "Helen?"

Helen could not meet Petra's eyes.

Sarah pulled into a gas station. Silence enveloped them all as she turned the engine off.

It seemed there would be no show tunes today.

Chapter Eleven

"Trivia night," Ian said.

When Petra didn't answer – how could she? – he added, "It's to benefit the restoration of the Morgan factory building. I'm a local businessperson. You're a local doctor. Between your knowledge of medicine and Serbian inventors, mine of wine and rocks, we'd probably kick ass. Plus, you can network."

"You're hanging around outside my office again," Petra said, buttoning up her coat tightly.

She pretended that she was looking in her bag for something. But her insides were quivering. Ian Zamora was standing in the rain, waiting for her. And he looked very good wet.

"Well, I don't actually want to go into your office, because someone might think I'm a patient and we can't have that. And I don't have your home phone number, so I've resorted to haunting the block. I'm thinking of opening a sidewalk cafe here this summer. Coffee, pastries, maybe a violinist."

"It rains 364 days of the year here. In case you haven't noticed, you're getting soaked."

Petra started to walk. Ian fell in step beside her. He wore a hooded navy fleece that fit his shoulders nicely. In the rain, his jeans had molded to his thighs. She was so fascinated by his quadriceps that she almost tripped. She shook her head.

"I shouldn't have socialized with you and Kevin that night," Petra said.

"I invited Kevin. You just happened to be there."

Petra sighed. "I don't think we should date, Ian."

"It's not a date. It's a fundraiser. Plus, you'll find out all the good neighborhood gossip."

"You could pass that on to me when you see me."

"Does that mean you want to see me outside of these completely serendipitous meetings we keep having?"

Petra stopped. She had planned to go home, but she didn't want Ian following her there, because she might invite him upstairs. God knows where that would lead. Well, she knew where it would lead, because she had already started trying to remember what underwear she had on.

She wondered what kind of underwear he wore.

She shivered. He noticed and made a gesture like he was going to put his arm around her and she jumped away. He noticed that, too.

"Let me at least get you a cup of coffee or something."

He steered her to a cafe and she asked for a chamomile tea. He got the espresso.

"I had a horrible weekend," she said, cupping the mug. "Because of you and this situation, my friends had a terrible fight. Physicians are opinionated buggers. We make our living by telling people what they should do with their lives. It got very personal and now Sarah, the one you met at the restaurant, is holding something my friend Helen did against her. Helen isn't talking. Sarah thinks we ganged up against her. It's ugly."

"I don't know if I got everything, but it sounds like they already had something going on before I showed up."

"I guess," Petra said dully.

She was too tired to argue. It had been hard to relax in the hotel room she shared with Helen and Sarah that weekend. Instead of helping each other with their hair and makeup and playing silly synth-pop on their iPods, they had all retreated to corners of the room and struggled quietly with zippers and brushes and mascara wands. Of course, she hadn't slept that night, and last night hadn't been much better. Now, the thought of fighting Ian – or fighting her own desire for him – held little appeal.

"I know you feel terrible, but maybe that's why you should come out with me. It's a Monday. What could possibly happen on a Monday?"

That is how Petra found herself in Maloney's, still wearing her sensible office shoes and her ugly, tweedy office pants, sharing a basket of fries with her former patient and screaming out answers at the top of her lungs.

The three-dollar cover, which Ian paid, got them cans of Pabst Blue Ribbon and a two-top near the emcee. The highlight of the game was when Petra knew the slang for vagina popularized by *Grey's Anatomy*. Actually, the highlight was when Ian kissed her after she screamed, "Vajayjay," and she let him. She felt that familiar thrum of recklessness, fueled by alcohol, sex, and intellectual arrogance. He tasted beery and greasy and sweet and sour from the fries and ketchup. He tasted like all the best kinds of bad things that could happen in life.

Plus, Sarah was an asshole, sometimes. Helen, too.

Who could blame her for kissing Ian? Ian, who hovered over her, looking a little mussed, a little sweaty, staring at her as if she were the most amazing person in the universe.

It was hard to stay focused after that.

They didn't win. They didn't even come close.

–

Maybe he was taking advantage of the fact that the beer had put a flush in her cheeks. Or that she was laughing so hard at him that she could hardly stand up. She was adorable, with her hair wet and her face shiny from the rain. He had been telling her about the time he had driven across country with a college friend. They had a bet to see who could eat McDonald's the longest. For every breakfast, lunch, dinner, and snack, the only thing they could have was McDonald's. And water.

"It was a pretty easy bet for both of us," Ian was saying. "We got to Boston, our destination, and neither of us had given in. We finally decided to call it a draw. We stopped in a rest area, both of us allowed to get whatever we wanted. Mateo came back with a giant bag of Taco Bell and I had a bucket of KFC. Just to spite each other. Each year, we send each other McDonald's gift cards on our birthdays. At Christmas, we send each other the used ones. Proof that we've been exercising our cards. He's a cardiologist, by the way."

"And you own a muckity-muck restaurant. I wonder if I could hold this over you," Petra mused.

"You'll have to do a lot better than that. I think our kitchen staff has a direct line to Domino's," Ian said.

"I guess a Bat Signal-type light would not be discreet."

"It wouldn't work well on rainy evenings like this."

It had gotten colder. It seemed a terrible night to be alone. As they approached her building, they became quiet.

He followed her inside her building. Even though they hadn't touched, it was as if his nerves were tethered to hers. Every time she moved, every time she looked at him, or stretched her neck, or wet her lips, he felt it. He could hear her breath coming, fast and deep.

She opened her door and stood aside to let him in.

Slowly, she unbuttoned her coat. He unzipped his jacket and held his breath. Still not a word from her.

He took the wet outerwear and hung it on the rack. He still hadn't put his hands on her. They hadn't moved from beyond the hallway. She had not even turned on a light.

She reached a tentative hand toward him and put one, two, three fingers on his chest.

It was enough. He wrapped his arm around her waist and lifted her to him. His heart pounding in his veins, he pushed her down the hall until they almost fell over the arm of a couch.

He tugged her down on him.

He had wondered about the inside of her apartment, but now he was in it, he paid it no attention. He was mostly focused on her wild mouth, her tongue, her waist, and her bottom, which flexed against his palms as he pulled her closer and closer to him.

She had unbuttoned his shirt and was sliding her hands through the coarse hair of his chest. She dragged her nails along his ribs and he hissed against her mouth. They drew back and looked at each other, both breathing hard by now.

She unbuttoned her shirt. Her skin flashed in the darkness and she wore a soft cotton bra. He licked his way down her neck and into the shallows of her cleavage. She bent and nipped him, tooth against collarbone. Urgency and pleasure stabbed at him. He couldn't form words. Something had changed for her, and he didn't want to think of what it might be, because if he defined it, they might stop, and he didn't want to, not now.

Her fingers started on his zipper. His cock jerked high, higher in response and he heard himself whimper. Her hand wrapped around him and he thought he would go mad. He was fumbling with her bra now and kissing her sloppily. Too many arms were in the way, trying to accomplish too many things. His pants were halfway down, his shirt hanging from his shoulders. His glasses were smudged. Her blouse rustled to the floor, and she tilted her hips to let him work on the button of her pants and ran her hands up his chest again, sliding his shirt off, and... she stopped.

She touched the burning bumps on his arms.

"What's this?" she said, even though she already knew.

He licked his lips. His tongue felt swollen and thick.

"I decided that since you'd always consider me under your care, I found someone else to be my doctor so you could do this with a clear conscience."

"You've started getting shots again."

She got out of his lap and sat at the far end of the couch. She crossed her arms over her chest.

This was not a good sign.

"Who is it?" she asked shakily.

He swallowed and tried very hard to think. He couldn't remember his own name right now. "It's Jatinder Singh. I take it he hasn't contacted you for my records yet."

"Jatinder Singh."

Her voice sounded flat. "Did you say anything about why you weren't seeing me anymore?" she asked.

He shook his head. He shifted uncomfortably. He was still half dressed and fully cocked. Words and thoughts were very difficult. "I wanted you to have a clear conscience because I know that's important to you," he said slowly. "Even though, for the record, I don't feel exploited and I never did."

She was so far away and he was starting to get cold. But if he pulled his pants up now, then they would stay up for the rest of the night, and he didn't want that.

"What are you thinking?" he asked.

"Why are you even getting shots again? You don't have a cat. Okay, so there's dust all around us. It's just I'm muddled. At the beginning of the evening, I wasn't even going to go out with you. Now, I'm not even wearing a shirt and you're seeing another allergist. I mean, officially I'm pro shots, but I feel like I've lost a patient."

He pulled up his pants.

"You did lose one – or rather, you terminated the relationship with a letter," he said, with more than a touch of frustration. "We can't have it both ways. If we want to do this, and believe me, I want to do this, you can't be my allergist, you can't think of yourself as my allergist."

She covered her face now, which left her breasts clear. He didn't let himself stare at them – much. His voice turned pleading. "I thought I'd make it easy and clear. I hit on a way to make sure that you understand, and everyone else understands, that you are most definitely not my doctor, that someone else is. *I am in another physician's care.* Nothing spells it out better than getting shots from someone else."

She shook her head. "I know you did this for me. But I still kind of hate it."

She hated it. She wanted to be his doctor more than she wanted to have a relationship with him.

He zipped his pants, rebuttoned his shirt, and adjusted his glasses. He put on his jacket and stood still for a moment to let his dick calm down, to let her change her mind. She was still frowning, not at him, but at some spot beyond him.

He left without a word.

Chapter Twelve

Kevin found him at Stream.

"I should be asking you for advice," Ian said, unloading crates of wine from a dolly. "First time around, and you find Penny. She's a great girl."

"She wasn't my first choice," Kevin said, sitting on a pile of boxes. "Talk to me, man to man, about ladies."

"Make yourself useful. Start opening these," Ian said, handing Kevin a box-cutter. "Kevin, if I help you with this, you're going to have to promise not to be an asshole."

"Ass-hole," Kevin repeated gleefully.

He flicked the blade up and down.

"Oh, please. You're not two years old. You've heard the word asshole before and you've used it." He looked down. "Don't tell me you're allergic to cardboard."

"It's just that no one's ever given me a box-cutter before."

Ian didn't know whether he felt scornful or alarmed. By the time he was twelve, he had used a Swiss Army knife to cut apart the wire fence of a chicken coop and he had gouged his initials in all the trees in Brazil. Maybe he had just been poorly supervised.

"Penny's a cute girl. But she's not a challenge, you know. She likes me and I like her. Easy pickin's."

"First of all, Kevin, don't be disrespectful of Penny – or of women, or of people, period. Plus, do you really want to go out with someone who hates your guts? I thought the point was that no one would date you. Or did you actually mean to say that no one you were interested in would consider you?"

"She's using me, too, you know. She doesn't like me in that way at all, I think. She just wants to say she got with a guy."

Kevin opened a box and peered inside. "Nothing here but wine," he said.

"Start putting them in these racks," Ian said.

Kevin slid them in slowly, as if every bottle were too heavy for him to handle.

Hanging out with Kevin made Ian think of Petra. Hell, everything made Ian think of Petra. Rain, odd facts, zippered pants, itchy arms, couches, tables – everything made a separate image flash in his mind. He should not think of her, but he was apparently like Kevin. He was fascinated with what was difficult and prickly and distant. He hadn't been interested in anyone else since he met Petra. Worse, now he knew how she looked when she was overjoyed and flushed and triumphant. She'd nipped him and licked him and he'd caught a glimpse of her small, perfect chest. Now, he knew how her eyes glowed in a darkened room and how her sweat tasted. She was salty and delicious.

But he couldn't go out with the woman again.

"I need to be suave. I need to figure out how to do romantic gestures," Kevin said. "How do you do that?"

Don't get allergy shots from another doctor and assume things will go your way. Don't be a presumptuous douche.

"Not everyone can get away with gestures. Try being quirky. It's probably your best bet."

"No one ever said, *I quirked her panties off.*"

Ian shuddered. He was out of his depth. He wished once more that he could talk to Petra and he knew it was the wrong thought to have.

"Then at the very least, try to be kind," Ian said.

Kevin looked disgusted with him. Ian felt a little disgusted with himself.

–

There was no one, Petra thought, scrolling through the contacts in her phone. Sarah and Helen were out of the question. Her mother was definitely not a candidate, and she was probably hanging out with Jim Morrison, anyway. As for her sister, Ellie, well, their age difference meant that they had never giggled or confided in one another that way. Although, if it came down to it, Petra suspected that Ellie knew far more than her older sister did about men.

When it came down to it, Petra had screwed up. Again.

If she were standing strong on her principles, she should never have gone out with Ian, kissed him, invited him back to her apartment, and straddled him shirtless. If, however, she were intent on seducing him, she should never have leapt off of him and practically accused him of cheating on her with another allergist. That was just confusing.

She felt bad for him. He had been trying: the man had gotten shots for her even though he didn't necessarily need them. But for some reason, feeling those bumps on his arms had made her angry and scared, even while her lust raged on. She felt out of control and she hated it. She remembered how hurt and frustrated he looked as he pulled his shirt back over his beautiful chest. He had done something for her that he thought would please her, or at least make her more at peace with herself. She had no such serenity. So many ambivalent and oddly defined responses coursed through her. Her mind was going in circles.

Regret. That was the only coherent feeling, punching through all others. She wanted a second chance. Things would have turned out different. But now, there was nothing she could do about it.

She decided to go for a run to clear her mind. It was late, but she wouldn't go for long.

The course took her through the streets of her neighborhood, past the small park she loved, past people strolling and laughing in the cold, clear night.

He had done something for her because he respected her feelings. But did he want too much in return? He was getting shots so that she'd feel okay about their relationship. Was it too much too soon?

It didn't feel like too much too soon.

Either way, he probably didn't care now.

She jogged slowly and carefully and tried to clear her mind. On the sidewalk, a group of people stood outside a restaurant after dinner saying their goodbyes. She avoided Ian's businesses. She cruised past the weathered brick warehouse buildings, past the new towers, and past glass and steel apartments, jerking her head enviously at the lighted windows, imagining people inside, laughing, talking side by side. And of course, while she was sightseeing through her own neighborhood, she nearly ran into him.

–

He watched her warily as she slowed down. Not that she had been running all that quickly. If he were a sensible person, he should have stepped back and let her keep going. As usual, whenever he came within three feet of her, he wanted to close the space between them until their bodies were merged.

He stayed where he was and jammed his hands in his pockets.

"Nice night," she said, after a pause.

"Yes. Not a cloud in the sky."

Another pause. "You're not at work."

"No, I just came back."

He reminded himself that she was the one who was supposed to explain things to him. But she looked messy and lustrous-eyed and all he could think about was the fact that he'd seen her half-naked. The streetlights picked up the sheen of her running tights and he tried not to look at her legs, the crescent of her bottom.

He had cupped that gorgeous ass last night.

"It's getting cold out here, for me, at least. Would you like to come up?"

She nodded. "I've always wanted to see the inside of one of these fancy buildings," she said, as he pushed the elevator button.

"I like it," he lied.

He opened the door to his apartment and they both blinked in the flare of light.

"It's... clean," Petra said.

"I hired someone recently to take care of the..."

"Dust."

"Yes, dust."

"It's okay to say dust in front of me," Petra said.

"I was just afraid I'd trigger some sort of outsize reaction if I referred to my..."

"Allergies. You can say that in front of me, too."

137

"Okay," said Ian. He still looked a little tense. "Would you like some water? Or something else? Wine?"

"Water would be great. Tap is fine."

—

She winced at herself. Under the wind jacket, she wore a quick-dry T-shirt, which was shiny in all the wrong places. And there were her running tights, striped with reflectors that could probably be seen from space. At least, if he tried something with her, he wouldn't miss this time. Not that she thought he would try anything with her. Then again, she was in his apartment, so maybe she was forgiven.

She shouldn't count on it.

He handed her a glass. They sat down on his black leather couch. It was an awful couch. It squeaked when she settled on it.

"I should apologize," she said.

He appeared to think about this.

She started again. "You should know something about me," she said. "I can't stand being the bad guy. Everywhere you look here, from every angle, I've done something terrible to you. I've been a bad doctor. I may have made a pass at you. I certainly had many thoughts and dreams about you while you were my patient. And then you got shots because of me and I didn't appreciate the gesture."

"I shouldn't have expected it," he said quietly. "I didn't ask you. I made assumptions and I'm sorry."

"I wish we could begin again," she said helplessly. "I wish I could get a clean start on everything."

"We can't change the circumstances under which we met," he said.

They had both apologized, but it wasn't exactly encouraging. Not that she blamed him. He put down his own glass of water and turned his gaze on her. His chest was lean and strong under the crisp shirt. She wanted to run her hands from his cuffs, up his biceps. She wanted to sit in his lap and bite his chin. She was drawn to him, and he to her. It would always be like this between them, she realized. It frightened her that it would work – the attraction could work – between them, even when the rest of it seemed to be a disaster.

She took the easy way out. She closed her eyes and leaned over and gave him a small, soft kiss. She put her forehead against his.

She heard him say, "I've decided that the best thing about having you in my apartment is that you can't kick me out."

He reached and pulled her toward him, putting his hands under her shirt.

He kissed her until she felt sparks snapping under her eyelids and a rush of warmth between her thighs. She squirmed. And then she started to think, again.

"I want to do this," she gasped, as he pulled her shirt up and off. "I really, really do. But maybe not just right now."

"Why not?"

He kissed her again. Then he kissed her chin.

"Sports bras are not sexy," she whispered.

"I find them quite compelling," he whispered back.

His eyes wandered over her chest.

"They smoosh everything together," she said.

"Lucky bra," he said. He ran his hand against the smooth fabric.

"And then there's the name. Bra. It's such a weird sound."

He pulled back a little, but his fingers remained occupied. "Are you trying to talk me out of this?" he asked, sliding his thumbs under her tights. He drew the waistband down under her and pulled them off with a snap, casting them to a remote corner of the room.

She winced in arousal and embarrassment. She smelled like sweat. She was damp and her legs were probably stuck to his leather couch. She'd make an awful sound when she tried to rise. Maybe if she moaned loudly enough, he wouldn't hear it. He ran his hands over her calves and knees and thighs. She sucked in a breath. Yep, making a lot of noise wouldn't be a problem if he kept this up.

"I don't think you're going to be able to talk your way out of this one," he murmured.

She groaned again as she felt his fingers tunnel under her buttocks. He hauled himself up and her with him, her skin stinging, almost ripping from the couch, making her eyes smart. She grabbed his shoulders and bit his neck against the pain. Her legs wound around his waist and he stumbled up and toward his room.

"God," he said, throwing her on the bed. "You're going to kill me. We're going to kill each other. It's going to be great."

He pulled off his shirt and Petra bounded up to her knees. She was tingling and frantic. She ran her fingers roughly over the planes and angles of his chest, down his ribs, and pushed around to his firm ass. She drew him down so that he too was kneeling on the bed. They sucked on each other's lips and slid their tongues together. She rubbed herself against him urgently, but there were still too many layers between them. He slid his big palms into

140

her underwear and shoved it down to her knees, then he started to pull up the tight bra. He got it up over her breasts and to her upper arms, where it stayed stuck.

She wriggled, her movements on top and below bound by her stupid underclothes.

He laughed softly.

"Oh, come on," she panted.

She was still trying to move her arms, but instead of helping her, he stood up and began to unzip his jeans. She watched for a moment, her achiness and frustration mounting almost to a point that was unbearable, then she began to struggle even more with her Lycra bindings. She had almost gotten the bra past her face, when she felt him grab her waist and wrap his lips over a nipple. All muscle control fled, and she lurched and would have fallen, if he hadn't been there to spread her on the mattress, his hot mouth never leaving her.

She was blindfolded by the sports bra and almost sobbing with frustration. Between her legs, she felt a throbbing fist of want. Her thighs struggled now, rubbing along his coarse dark hair, along his cock, as she tried to make any movement that would bring him closer to her. Finally, he raised his head and helped her pull off the bra. She kicked off her underwear. And as he looked in her wild eyes, he flicked her clit back and forth with his thumb and pushed his fingers into her slickness and she came almost at once, her legs spreading, her heels digging into the bed.

He groaned, and kissed her and reached over to his nightstand.

"It's a good thing that happened, because I warn you, it's been a while, so this probably won't last very long," he said. "I'll do better next time."

"Famous last words," Petra said giddily. "Wait, you're leaving your glasses on?"

"I want to see everything," he said.

"Oh. That's… that's kind of hot."

He gave a mysterious half smile and it made her shiver. She watched avidly as he pulled a condom on. Then he kissed her and pushed in, and the feeling was almost too much for her overloaded senses. Her pussy was still pulsing from her orgasm, so she concentrated on breathing. His eyes narrowed and his hair flopped. She reached up to push it back and she could hear his groans. She loved his groans. Her body was becoming taut again, just listening and watching as he panted and slid, so she dragged his head down for a kiss. "I'm going to make you come," she whispered fiercely.

That did it for him.

He crashed into her wildly until her teeth started to click and then he fell on top of her and she felt his pleasing weight pressed into her chest and stomach, on her pelvis, and along her legs. He breathed her name.

After a while, he shifted himself onto his elbows and mouthed her neck, her chin. "Are you good?"

His glasses were smudged and slightly askew.

"I'm good. Are you good?"

"I'm good. I'm very good."

It was true.

Chapter Thirteen

She was swearing, wearing only a pair of underpants, and searching for something in his room. He put on his glasses and checked his clock. Six eighteen. He groaned.

But then she turned and he saw her dainty breasts, which he suddenly got the urge to prod with his index finger, her belly button, the quivering curve of her stomach.

"Good morning," he said.

"Damn," she muttered, not meeting his eyes. "Where is that stupid bra?"

Petra Lale was not a morning person, he thought, adding to his store of knowledge about her. He pictured the way she had leaned over his counter while she ate cereal in the middle of the night and how her legs had stuck out from the covers when she finally fell asleep. She would not escape so easily.

"I thought you hated the jog bra."

"I do," she said, getting on her hands and knees. She looked under the bed and then under the night table. He edged over to her side and stroked her waggling rump.

"What?" he said, when her head popped up. "I'm encouraging you."

She made a noise and kept looking.

"Do you regret last night?" he asked.

"No," she said.

She did not, he noticed, ask him.

Finally she gave up and stood, her gaze still roving the room.

He threw aside the covers and rolled over onto his back. She went quiet and very still. Her eyes crept to his groin. "You should put that away," she muttered.

"I was planning on it," he said, grinning.

She tried to hide a smile and bent over to shake the sheets that he had vacated.

"C'mon, your turn. Drop those panties."

"I hate the word *panties*," she groused, putting one hand on a hip.

The grumbling should have been a turnoff, but even though she stood there, frowning about his word choice, she was naked, except for the aforementioned underpants, and her legs were apart, and she was so unself-conscious, so supremely herself, that it made his dick hard. Harder.

"What do I have to do to get them off?" he asked, watching her.

That half smile again. She turned and he couldn't see her breasts. Too bad. On the other hand, he now had a better view of her ass. "Think of a new word for ladies' undergarments," she said. "A good one, a fierce one. Then popularize it."

"What counts as popular?"

"An entry in the Oxford English Dictionary?"

"Wow, you really kick it old school. Would you settle for an Urban Dictionary entry?"

She frowned at him, or at least she tried. Her eyes glinted and she gave him another saucy look. He hooked his leg under her and tumbled her to the bed.

"Oh, well," he said, pushing the scrap of underwear aside, "I can fuck you without taking them off."

He didn't let her go until he had fed her a piece of toast and coffee. He was annoyingly cheerful. She had to admit that she felt the laughter bubbling its way madly in her chest, too. It was a little bit like hysteria, but with less potential for tears and screaming involved. Maybe it was happiness. Whatever it was, she was fighting it with all she had.

She had to give up on finding her bra. Ian watched as she pulled her tee back on. The slippery, quick-dry material rubbed and molded against her nipples immediately, causing him to smirk. She pulled on the tights, self-conscious and turned-on again, and found her socks and shoes and jacket.

"I'll walk you home," he said, standing beside her in his hallway. He was still naked, and drinking coffee. It was a good look for him.

"It's early. I'll be okay. This is a safe neighborhood. Plus, most criminals ply their trade late at night rather than early in the morning."

"You're quite the little Miss Sunshine, aren't you?" he murmured, kissing her hair.

She barely escaped.

She only had two appointments that morning, but the drug rep came in and tried to entertain her with stories. She couldn't pay attention. He gave her a pen and piles of samples, and instead of wondering idly how much she'd get if she sold it all on eBay, she considered sending Joanie home early. Not that Ian would be free tonight. Maybe he would. Petra didn't really care.

There was that effervescence in her chest again. Maybe it was gastroesophageal reflux.

In the afternoon, one of her patients went to the hospital for asthma. It was across town and she didn't have privileges there yet, but she went in to see Rose Marie and sat down with her mother to reassure her. She called the girl's pediatrician. Rose Marie was fine, though. She was discharged soon afterward, and they made an appointment for follow-up the next day. Petra made a note to check how often the girl was using her inhaler.

Then, it was five already.

She shucked off the white coat and called a goodbye to the receptionist. She checked her phone, determined to ignore all calls from Ian for the rest of the evening. Not that he had telephoned.

She wondered what he was doing.

She would not swing by Stream like a crush-struck teen.

Instead, she went to the grocery store and bought a package of frozen lima beans and some lemons and oranges and box of butter, and she sat down and tried to read the *Journal of the American Medical Association* while eating a bowlful of lima beans.

Her phone rang.

"You didn't support me," Helen said. "You didn't help me out. You think I'm a horrible person. Like Sarah."

"That's not true. I was just so confused at the time. And you know Sarah. She can be challenging. She takes arguments too far. Actually, you both do."

"I just started talking, and it was like I couldn't stop."

"Neither could she."

A pause.

"Not so awesome now, am I?" Helen asked.

"It was a stupid thing to say. Affirmation should never be filler. You know I really love you, don't you?"

"I know. I hate the false enthusiasm, though. I hate faking it to make it."

"I hate when people say, *A pretty girl like you should smile.*"

"People who tell me to smile need to fuck off. Especially men. What is that?"

Petra put her empty bowl in the sink and rinsed it.

"What did you have for dinner?" Helen asked.

"Lima beans."

"The single vegetable dinner. I remember it well."

Petra put the bowl in the dish rack. Behind it were three identical bowls. This was her life.

"Maybe you can tell me what happened," Petra said.

"I'd rather talk about you."

"Okay," Petra said carefully. She took a deep breath. "I think we might be seeing each other."

She didn't have to say who. Helen had already figured it out. Now that Petra had said it aloud for the first time, it seemed strange and exciting and still wrong. She wanted to take her confession and stuff it back into her mouth. She wanted to savor it quietly. She was seeing him. She had sex with a beautiful man. He was funny and smart and he had gorgeous shoulders and a delicious mouth, and he liked to touch her in wonderful ways.

"It's fun," Petra said.

"Fun?" Helen said. "Fun? We went through hand-wringing and a nearly lethal debate on ethics so you could have a few laughs and tickles?"

"That wasn't the right word."

"So try harder. What's he like? I never got to meet him. Make me feel less miserable by telling me how pretty he is and what an amazing, generous kisser he is. Or maybe make fun of him so that I can laugh."

Petra was quiet for a bit. "I ran into him last night," she said.

Repeatedly. Pleasurably. With my naked body parts, she thought.

"Good."

Petra squirmed.

"And we… talked. And I really like him."

"I knew that."

Petra had almost nothing else to say. She knew she was disappointing Helen with her reticence. She could have gone into details. She could have described kisses and positions. She really should have said something more.

But it was private. And he'd been the subject of that horrible argument and a part of her still wondered if she was doing the right thing, allowing herself to get involved with him.

"Sarah got to meet him, didn't she?" Helen asked.

"Not exactly. She just saw him and he might have thanked her for helping with the patient we worked on at the bar opening."

Another silence. "She asked you, and not me, to go to that opening, even though she knows I love Field."

"I think she said you were busy."

"I wasn't. No, she just doesn't want to be alone with me lately. Because of the thing I did. Because of Mike."

"Are you sure you don't want to talk about it?"

"I'm sure." Helen's voice was flat again.

"Hey," Petra said. "I'm not disappointed in you or mad, or whatever. I was just surprised to hear it. And maybe now I'm worried about you."

"I'm okay," Helen said, softly.

After Petra hung up the phone, she wondered why she avoided Helen. She felt strange, as if she had to split her loyalty equally. But Sarah remained stubborn and unmoving, and would probably stick it out until Petra and Helen made some sort of concession.

Except that Petra didn't have all the information. If anything, Sarah and Helen were keeping things from her.

Her friends were frustrating. She couldn't talk to them. She desperately wanted to be able to talk to them.

Mostly, she hoped that Ian would call.

Chapter Fourteen

"Knickers," said Ian as soon as she picked up. "What if I call your underpants knickers? Like the Brits."

She was lying in bed in a Curious George T-shirt. She had been trying to sleep for half an hour, at least. It was a relief to hear his voice.

"Nicker. Isn't that the sound that a horse makes?"

"So that's a no?"

She sighed. "I like horses. I was one of those girls who liked ponies. I read all of those *Misty of Chincoteague* books, and *Black Beauty*. I didn't know how to ride. The desire for horses is some sort of symbol of sublimated sexuality, they say, because all you want is a big animal between your legs."

"So knickers is a resounding yes? Because it's sounding better and better to me."

"I'm not sure."

"You have a deeply ambivalent relationship with your undergarments."

"Apparently, I have deeply ambivalent relationships with everyone," she sighed.

"Not me, I hope."

"Of course not," Petra said a little too quickly.

He paused. "I guess stud-monkey is a fairly straightforward description of what I am to you," he said lightly.

She tried to keep it easy, too. "It sounds like you've been talking to Kevin."

"As a matter of fact, I have."

He was walking. She could hear wind. "Are you outside?"

"Yes, in the rain. I can see my building. I'll be in my lobby in a minute."

She waited and the background noise cleared. In her mind, she followed him into the elevator and down the long hallway into his apartment.

"You're good with kids. Kev really likes you," she said.

"Good might be a stretch. Kevin seeks me out and I just sort of listen to him talk with my mouth hanging open in shock."

"Same," Petra said. "Although he does remind me a bit of myself when I was that age."

She shifted on the mattress and closed her eyes.

He must have heard the creaking. "You must be tired. I'm sorry I called so late. I wanted to hear your voice. I wasn't thinking."

"No," she said, "talk to me. I love talking in the dark."

She could almost hear him smile. "I didn't know that about you."

"I guess we didn't talk much. Last night."

He swallowed and she almost laughed. She toyed with the hem of her T-shirt. "What are you doing?" she asked. She heard water running.

"I'm rinsing out the glasses. I bought new ones recently and now I have to make sure that they're clean."

"Your life is never-ending drudgery."

"I wouldn't say that," he said. He seemed to move the phone closer to his mouth. "So, are you wearing knickers?"

She shivered. "I've got on plaid boxers and a T-shirt. I've had the shirt since I was a teenager."

He absorbed that information in silence.

"I'm trying to imagine you as a teenager," he said, finally. "So far, you've got curls, the brain of Kevin, and a very thin T-shirt."

"Oh," said Petra, "you wouldn't have liked me."

"How do you know?"

"You seem like you would have been, you know, popular. You were probably one of those effortless guys who ran track and sunk baskets and was smart in school but managed to stay humble. You probably made friends easily. I'll bet the girls loved you."

"I played football – or soccer as you call it," he said. "But we moved around all over the world. I was always the foreign kid. My dad's work took us to a few different continents. And then my mother died and I went away to college—"

"Where?"

"U San Francisco. My dad stayed abroad, and my mom's family lives near the Oregon–California border. USF was close enough, but not too close. It was a bit of a culture shock after all that time in South America. I was more comfortable speaking and thinking in Spanish, at that point, so I started out feeling isolated. English was my mother's language. I felt like a child – I was a child – whenever I spoke it. I trained myself to get used to it, especially when I got here. I watched a lot of movies." He cleared his throat. "A lot of romantic comedies. A *lot* of them. Then when I moved here, well, I guess you already know that Portland is pretty white. But like you, I've got that ambiguously ethnic thing, and I worked to blend in.

153

Maybe it worked too well. The guys in the kitchen say I have an American accent when I speak Spanish now."

"Oh," said Petra, again. She didn't know what to say.

"I'm sorry. This is the unsexiest phone sex I've attempted," Ian said. "I guess when you start off talking about horses and move on to race and dead mothers, you're taking a risk."

"Phone sex, is that what we're doing?"

"You can decide," he said easily.

"You make it sound simple."

"Everything is simple."

—

The next few weeks were a whirl. When they got together, they pounced on each other. On evenings when Ian had too many disasters to oversee, he would text her late to see if she was awake. She always was. She would call him and they would settle down to talk while he got ready for bed. They kept different hours but they managed to find each other, nonetheless. Sometimes she met him at Stream and witnessed his deft, easy way with strangers and regulars. She watched how women, in particular, responded to him, and it made her gut clench. But he saved his huge, eye-crinkling, jagged-toothed smile for her and she knew that her answering smile was just as bright. When he came to her, he slid his palm over her back and used his height and head like an umbrella, shielding her from the raucous laughter of the room. She felt a pang about adjusting her schedule to fit his late nights but he woke far earlier than he usually did in the mornings to see her off to work. They stayed at his place most of the time. He had more space. His apartment was cleaner and newer.

Being with Ian was like being on break. She didn't fret about her paperwork, even though she knew she should. She didn't worry about the sad little balance in her checking account. She didn't worry about her friends.

And that was part of the problem. She couldn't afford to forget about her practice and the rift with Sarah and Helen. Ian was making noises about letting go of some of his responsibilities at Field and Stream while she needed to concentrate more on hers.

When she was alone and the waiting room was empty, she almost resented him. It was easy for him. He had money. He had people clamoring for his services. He hadn't lost his friends and entered shaky ethical ground in order to date her. But that wasn't his fault, was it?

At some point, Petra realized that she had also lost track of her mother. Which was a relief, actually, now that Petra thought about it.

She managed to forget, that is, until Lisa showed up in Petra's waiting room, unannounced, with a blondish, graying gentleman in tow.

"Mom," she said, not quite able to keep the trepidation from her voice. She looked at the man, who had to be Jim Morrison. Lisa was holding his arm and he was gazing at her placidly.

"We decided to drive up for the day to see you. We have some news!"

Petra tried to usher them into her office, but her mother inspected the outer room with concern. Shelly Kelly and Kevin sat there, waiting out their reactions.

"I have a couple of minutes. Why don't we come in here for more privacy?" Petra said.

"Darling," her mother said, looking around. "Shouldn't you see to your patients?"

Lisa had never called Petra "darling" in her life.

"It's fine," Petra said. Lisa swept in. Petra had never seen her mother looking like this. She was wearing a boxy lemon-yellow suit. It made her look like a cough lozenge.

"This is Dr. Jim Morrison. Jim, this is Petra, my daughter, the allergist."

Lisa waved toward Petra causing a ring on her right hand to sparkle. A gigantic, ugly, yellow diamond.

Her mother was getting married. Lisa had known the man for, like, a month — or at least, she'd only told Petra about Jim Morrison a short while ago. Then again, it hadn't taken much for Petra to become moony over Ian.

"Are you sure it's okay to keep people out there?" her mother repeated anxiously.

"They're waiting out their reactions, Mom," Petra said.

She tried to project an aura of calm and ruthless clinical acumen. She motioned them into chairs and sat behind her desk.

"It's so nice to finally meet you, Petra," Jim Morrison said. "Lisa is so proud of you."

He was bulky, but not stout. His hair was thinning, but not entirely gone. He had very smooth skin and his eyes were gray and sharp. There was a bit of a challenge in them. She wondered what else Lisa had said about her.

"This may seem very sudden to you," Lisa began.

Petra held up her palm. "You're both adults, you know your own minds."

Jim Morrison took in her upraised hand.

"Lisa Morrison has a nice ring to it, doesn't it?" Jim asked mildly. He asked everything mildly. He probably joked with grocery store cashiers, talked about the weather, and ordered the assassination of high-ranking European diplomats without raising his tepid voice.

"We're so happy," Lisa said, clutching his other arm.

Petra lowered her hand.

"So, you're taking his name? A woman who kept her first husband's name, and refused to take her second husband's even though he was the father of her other daughter?"

A nervous glance.

"We haven't agreed on that part yet," Lisa said.

"You could change it back to your maiden name. Since you'll be getting the name-change papers with the marriage certificate and all," Petra suggested.

"I'm sensing a bit of reluctance on your part for your mother to give herself over fully, Petra," Jim said.

"She doesn't have to give herself over fully," Petra said tightly. "Besides, she's the one who doesn't want to take your name. I thought I was suggesting something diplomatic, you know, that didn't favor the other two husbands."

"Well, your mother and I have tabled the discussion on her reaction for another time," Jim said. "This is new for all of us, after all. I want your mother to make a full commitment to me and I need you to make her feel supported in her decision to marry. Maybe your vote would make her feel validated and loved."

Petra gritted her teeth. He made it sound like he was asking for the most reasonable thing in the world, when really, he was a complete stranger who had turned her mother into an equally strange person. A weird, yellow-garbed woman who called her "darling."

"That's a nice thought," she said, trying to sound as placid and monotonous as he did. "Why don't you change your name to Lale, then, as a reciprocal gesture? Maybe it would be a nice break for you, not having to suffer all those Doors jokes."

"Petra!"

"Now, Lisa. Petra was sympathizing," Jim Morrison said. "She didn't actually make a joke, she just referred to the acclaimed rock group and how awkward my name has been for me. Although, to tell you the truth, I find it useful as an icebreaker. When people joke about me, that means that I can find a way to make them friendly."

Like taming a feral cat, Petra thought.

"We wanted to take you out to lunch, Petra. To celebrate."

Her mother was going to choke from the tension.

"I really have to examine Mrs. Kelly's reactions. You know how it is with patients, Jim."

"But this is a special occasion!" her mother said.

"You did show up unexpectedly," Petra pointed out.

"Dinner, then?"

"I'm afraid I have plans," Petra said pleasantly. "I'll see what I can do to change them."

Fat chance, she thought.

Petra ushered them out and brought Shelly Kelly in.

Shelly was fine, but that didn't stop Petra from poring over her patient's arms like they contained a secret code. She ate trail mix from her desk drawer rather than go outside to get lunch, on the chance that Lisa and Jim were nearby. She didn't want to have them delay their lunch, make her eat a club sandwich, and listen to them coo over how happy they were.

She might have felt a pang over the fact that they had driven all this way to see her and tell her the news in person.

She also might have felt guilty for having neglected her mother – neglected her practice, neglected everything – because she had been mooning over Ian. And now Lisa was in the clutches of one of those soft-voiced, baby-skinned men who petted cats and ordered the destruction of the world on a whim. Or maybe he wasn't evil, but her mother certainly wasn't acting like herself.

Her phone call to Ellie went to voicemail.

Luckily, no phone calls came. Just as well. Three more patients showed up that afternoon.

If only her mother could have seen that.

Chapter Fifteen

They were side by side in a u-shaped booth in an old diner. Ian had insisted that they leave the neighborhood for once, and he promised her a restaurant with black and white milkshakes and waitresses with beehive hairdos. It was comforting, eating hamburgers and being called "hon" by a woman in a pink uniform. It was especially comforting because Ian was massaging her shoulders as she sipped her drink.

"I don't see how my sister can be so cavalier about this. He's awful. She's changing everything about herself. She was wearing a yellow suit, for god's sake, and she had a weird urine-colored diamond on her finger, set in gold. It was like a buttercup drank too much Goldschläger and threw up all over her."

"Yellow diamonds can be valuable," Ian said into her tense shoulder.

He had good hands, with calluses on the fingers. Maybe he played guitar or piano. There was so little she knew about him, and yet so much.

Lisa and Jim had called again before dinnertime, but Petra repeated her excuses. Jim seemed happy to drive back to Astoria early. She could hear him in the background calling for Lisa, then practically revving the car engine. It was too early to have them meet Ian anyway. If she had it her way, Jim certainly would never meet Ian at all. How would she even introduce them: *Mom, Stepdad-to-be, meet my former patient. We recently started screwing, but I've had the hots for him for months.*

She supposed she could find a more tactful way of phrasing it, but she didn't want Jim Morrison to detect even a whiff of guilt on her. She had to hide her weakness.

Not that he was the enemy.

"She has a history of making bad decisions, romantically," Petra said. "This will be her third marriage."

"She's impulsive?"

"The opposite, really," Petra said. "She's careful and she doesn't date. And then, it's like a dam develops a hole and the water breaks through. She realizes she's lonely, she finds someone, but then, she has doubts, she dithers and criticizes. Of course, the whole time, she'll never stop with the questions and second-guessing until the marriage is trash. At least that's how it was with Ellie's dad. I guess I didn't hear quite as much about it this time because she didn't share the news as soon."

"How was it with your dad? Was she the same way?"

"She did question his decisions often. But he let her down again and again. He wasn't honest about things like money."

"Did you see him after he left?"

"Once or twice. He moved to California and left me the funds that I used to start the practice. And I know I should be furious with him for other things, though. There's so much I don't know about him, about what I am. His family background, his life. He was of Indian descent. But Lisa was never comfortable talking about my dad and racial stuff and it used to make me anxious, although talking with Sarah and Helen – and now you – helps. Helen is Hapa and Sarah's of Chinese descent.

162

They're much more at ease with it than I am. I suppose I could have tried to find out more about my dad, but I was too busy studying and working and being horrible to my mom. My mom was the one who was around for me to be angry at."

Tilting her neck, she looked at Ian's dark head with a mixture of fear and tenderness. He worked his fingers over her scapulae and pressed his thumbs deep down into her infraspinatus fascia. She inhaled sharply.

"Did your dad ever want to get married again?" she asked.

His mouth was at her ear again. "If he did, he didn't get the chance to tell me. My father was a good parent when he was around. Told stories, taught me how to build fires and what to do if I ever got trapped in a mineshaft after a collapse. But he probably wasn't the most reliable husband."

–

He hesitated, wondering how much to tell her, especially now that she had confided some of the details of her own childhood. He didn't share easily and he could tell that she was preoccupied. Her eyes roamed the diner, as if she expected the four horsemen of the apocalypse to ride in and stop at their table.

At the same time, he was reveling in the intimacy of it. They alone together, in an over bright room full of strangers. Her hair curled into his cheek and his hands moved across her shoulders and back, and she was confiding in him things that she had probably never told anyone. Willie Nelson crooned in the background. Ian loved her secrets. He and she were more alike than she knew.

She turned to him, her eyes questioning.

"Up until now, I thought your parents had some sort of ideal marriage," she said lightly.

"They stayed together, yes," he said. "But that's all."

If his father hadn't been there, his mother would have been entirely alone. But if they hadn't been on strange continents, his mother would never have felt so lonely. Terry Zamora wasn't the type who learned to say thank you in a language other than English, or make friends with the womenfolk at the town well, or to learn to bargain for vegetables in marketplaces. She had grown up in a small town in Oregon and Tomás Zamora had swept in and swept her away and Ian had been born shortly afterwards.

What Ian remembered most about his mother was the incessant cleaning. In the kitchens of the rented houses they lived in, she would be on chairs, scrubbing the walls until they were white, or her head would be in cabinets or under beds while she dusted and mopped. If she couldn't control the world outside her house, at least she would be in perfect control of the environment within. Or die trying. A few of the places they lived boasted gigantic insects or snakes. He remembered finding her huddled on a table one day, hiding from a water bug that had crawled into the middle of the living room to die. He remembered another time: a huge storm caused all the mangos to fall from the tree in their yard onto their tin roof. His mother had grabbed him from his bed and forced him to hide under the arched doorway. He wasn't sure what she thought was happening: Someone was stomping on the roof? Someone was throwing bricks at their home? His father was out that night and didn't return until morning. He found his wife and child, asleep on the floor.

He did remember that, on a return trip to the States, his mother had begged to be left behind with Ian. Ian wasn't so sure he wanted to do the same. His cousins were all older, and he couldn't get away with sneaking into a movie or skipping school to go swimming in a pond, not in a town filled with his relatives and busybody neighbors. What surprised Ian was how his mother was when she returned to her family, how confident and powerful she suddenly became. The woman who was too cowed to buy a pound of fish from the docks could now scold a grown man on the street for parking too far away from the curb. She could joke with a shopkeeper about the price of a winter coat, and she could venture out of her parents' house to throw snowballs at her nieces and nephews.

At the time, Ian wasn't sure he liked it. He was fourteen and growing into independence.

His father had mowed his mother down again. He made promises. He was exuberant and charming. But eventually, he disappeared, like he always did, and left his wife and child to fend for themselves in a strange country. His mother complained bitterly that she did not understand why he insisted they come if he was just going to leave them again.

Maybe she had been drinking, maybe she had taking nips for years. Ian was never sure. After the accident, he stopped traveling with his father. His father let him make his own decision. Maybe Tom Zamora felt guilty about how his wife had passed away. He had almost not come to the funeral. Ian went back to Oregon to his mother's family and he went to school. And much later, even Tom came back to die.

Slivers of sadness and hatred laced his thoughts about his parents. Petra was right: their fathers had gotten off easy. Their mothers hadn't been perfect, but at least they'd been around to face their children.

Petra's hand crept up to his cheek. "Where did you go?" she asked.

Ian roused himself. "I was thinking that there are things we never know about people's marriages, even when you're the product of that marriage."

"Hmm, that's true," said Petra pensively. "Although it doesn't stop you — by which I mean me — from forming opinions."

He had to smile at that.

He toyed with her hair. "We should go," he said.

If their first weeks together had been a refuge, a delirious oasis, then tonight, they fucked with the full awareness of all the failures that had gone before them. He was careful with her face, her shoulders, her hips, her hair. He traced the contours of her lips and the undersides of her breasts.

He didn't want to forget this feeling, this wonder and reverence that he felt with her.

He kissed the soft round of her belly and felt her curl her hips up. Her hands were in his hair, pulling and rubbing. He moved lower, grazing his stubble against her thighs, making her shift and sigh. He moved his thumbs along the long inner muscle and traced a line between her legs. He felt her tense under him.

She had pushed her shoulders into the pillow and her neck arched up. Her body twitched with barely restrained impatience. He smiled and gave it another long stroke. It bloomed wet and gleaming under his fingers.

She spread herself wider. He put his mouth on her and licked her nub again and again. She thrashed restlessly and muttered another encouraging expletive. He reached up one hand to toy with her nipple and encountered her fingers there, already busily at work. He rested his chin on her mound and watched. It was a beautiful sight. But she bumped him impatiently, urging him to go on. He buried his chuckle in her and mouthed her clit again. Her lower body clenched and flexed as he worried his fingers in and out of her. In another few moments she cried out and his chest flooded with feeling again.

Petra raised her head and regarded him with glazed eyes. "Come up here," she mumbled.

Her body was still giving little shivers and twitches. He kissed his way briskly up her torso and smiled when he reached her lips.

She grinned lazily at him and smoothed a languid hand down his body. He entered her heavily, intending to savor her. She seemed to sense the mood he was in and despite the fact that she had been worried earlier, and that she was probably exhausted, she murmured savagely in his ear and trailed her fingers along his back and rear. She looked at him like she would never forget the feeling, and he felt the pull of her, deep in his gut, in his groin, in his soul, and he felt himself ready to burst.

Had he ever felt this way about anyone before? He could hear her almost sobbing in his ear, her body convulsing around him again, her arms pulling him into her, and she jolted wildly. His body thundered forward, he couldn't think, he could only feel, and he knew he had never felt this before. He had never felt this much fear, this much tenderness, this much happiness. And whether it came from him or from her, he was not sure. The feeling mingled like their sweat and the smell of their sex. It was impossible to know where one thing started and the other stopped. He closed his eyes and fell on her, almost slowly, and they rolled to their sides, still panting, their mouths pressing desperately together. His eyes met hers, questioning, and he tried to nod and skimmed her cheek and neck with his lips again. She needed some sort of reassurance and he wanted to agree to whatever she asked. Finally, he kissed her again and pulled away to dispose of the condom. She laughed shakily.

"Hi," she whispered, still searching his eyes.

"Hello to you," he whispered back, holding her face.

–

Petra woke up in Ian's bed again and checked his clock. It was almost seven. She stifled a sigh and contemplated sliding out. But if she did that, then, of course, that would mean that she would have to begin her day. And if she began her day, then, she would have to remember that her mother had turned into a canary and was getting married to Dr. Evil, her best friends were barely speaking to each other or her, and she probably only had two, maybe three patients to tide her through the hours.

She turned herself in Ian's arms to study him. His brow seemed a little furrowed, even in sleep. She reached up to smooth it and found herself running her index finger along his straight nose, across his lips, and along his strong jaw. He was beautiful. His body was just as beautiful. She had to stop her finger from moving still lower, under the sheet.

Last night, she thought he had seemed sympathetic, yet distant and sad. But when they had come into the bedroom, something about the hush of their clothes falling, the way he held her and looked at her, seemed to say he was telling her something. He was trying to communicate something important.

Or maybe it was just lust.

She pulled herself up and padded to the bathroom. The apartment was cold and she wished she had a warm robe or quilt to huddle with. Maybe she would bring one next time. She found her toothbrush. She washed her face and wished he had some moisturizer. She changed the toilet paper roll, wiped down the counter, pulled his thin, black comb through her hair, and stopped.

What was she doing?

She was already becoming domestic: planning to bring a robe and face cream, storing a toothbrush, cleaning. She had no idea where he was or what he was thinking. He had told her yes, last night, and she had felt better, for some reason. But she had not even asked a question. They had never talked about the relationship. She was letting the promise in his gleaming eyes distract her from her problems at the office. She sat on the toilet seat and pressed her hands to her cheeks. It would be fine. She could work harder, spend less time with him. Except. Except, part of her didn't want to shuffle papers and make phone calls and try to rustle up more patients. It was easier to just fall for him and ignore the niggling voice in her head that said she was a bad physician who'd abandoned her principles and couldn't keep her practice afloat.

It was ridiculous. They had really only been together two, three, maybe four weeks. She knew he had a loud, squeaky leather couch, and that he had traveled all over the world. She didn't know what his favorite colors were, or if he liked to read, or what kind of music he listened to. She had never met his friends, unless she counted Gerry, the man who didn't believe that allergies existed. She preferred to believe that Gerry did not exist.

Petra almost burst out of the bathroom, but he was still sleeping. It seemed a pity to wake him when she knew he would have a long day. It was a Friday. Surely, the worst restaurant and bar day had to be a Friday.

She stood over him, naked and cold.

Without his glasses, he was almost a stranger. He was a stranger. She wasn't sure of him. She wasn't sure of herself.

Chapter Sixteen

"How long have you known?" Petra asked, pacing her office. She didn't have to worry about shouting, because she had no patients. Again. Joanie was out for lunch.

Petra's sister cleared her throat. "They drove up on Monday and took me out to dinner at Nigiri."

"You sold your approval for a fancy dinner?"

"Hamachi and yellowtail. It was delicious. Besides, I didn't sell any approval. They don't need our consent. Last time I checked, our mother was of age. What are you telling me? You held out for dinner and the down payment on a house?"

"They didn't even stop to see me, really," Petra said, aware that she was whining.

She sat down at her desk and sprang up again.

"Weren't you working?" Ellie asked.

"I'm starting to think that Mom chose a time when I'd be busy."

Although, given how she'd mentioned that she didn't have many patients, maybe her mother had thought to find her alone. She did not share this information with her sister.

"It doesn't matter," Petra continued, aware that she was now sounding like she was five years old. She was glad there was no one about to witness it. "It was a short visit. They wanted to shop, presumably for more pastel suits for

Mom. They're going for the Secretary of State look, from what I can tell. She's even transformed the way she talks for him."

"Was it really going that well for her before she met Jim Morrison?"

"It was okay, Ellie."

"How would you know?"

"What do you want me to do? Dance a hornpipe? Throw them a party? I'm supposed to tell her how I feel, aren't I?"

"No, actually you don't have to. She already knows. This is none of your business. It's not like she has any money he can take away from her. It's not like he can leave her knocked up. So he's a little condescending. But she can handle him. Just try to trust her, the way you're always asking her to do the same with you."

"She could get hurt."

"*Argh*, just stop it. Stop bossing people around, stop thinking you know better than anyone. You're such a doctor."

A pause.

"I should drive out to see them this weekend," Petra resolved. "Can you meet me there? I'm not doing this alone."

Ellie made a noise and hung up the phone. Apparently, Petra *would* have to do this alone.

It wasn't that she hadn't heard her sister's message. A detached part of herself realized that she should leave her mother be. But that wasn't how Petra operated. She had to scratch at it and worry it and roll it around her head.

She tried to think objectively about the whole thing. Evidence pointed to Jim Morrison being a jerk, especially his heavy-handed pissing contest with Petra yesterday. But it really wasn't her business. Had her mother seemed at ease with Jim Morrison? Had Jim Morrison tried to make her feel better? Had they once shared any glimmers of the eye, had they made little signals to each other, little touches on the elbow? Had there been a caress down the back?

Were they the way she was with Ian?

Not that things were perfect with Ian.

All morning she had been prowling, ever since she'd woken up, in fact. She stood at her desk and paged through her computer. She had promised to call Kevin's pediatrician to update her on Kevin's progress. She had also made a note to talk to Moira Shane about seeing a gastroenterologist to investigate her persistent cough.

Petra sat in her desk chair. People were telling each other to trust their instincts. She believed in her ability to read symptoms and come up with possible diagnoses, but she always went with evidence first. Helen and Sarah claimed to be good judges of character. Petra had no idea what that meant. Her instincts only gave her information about sleep, food, and sex.

When they had sex, she had no doubts about her feelings for him. It was only after, when she had time to consider things, that she wondered what she was doing getting involved with someone when she had so many worries – when he was the catalyst of so many of her problems.

She shook her head. She didn't resent him. It wasn't his fault. But she did have to approach this with a brain unfogged by lust or tender affection.

Oh, shit, she thought. Tender affection? Where had that come from?

As if she had conjured him up, she heard her phone beep.

I missed you this morning.

She would not smile. There was no one to witness it, but she would not be weak.

She wrote back, *You were sleeping so well.*

It seemed best not to let him know that she had been freaking out and tearing around his room like a frenzied, naked (but quiet) hyena, eager to leave him and his firm deltoids and soft hair and sad, sleeping smile far behind. She had actually run from his apartment, albeit with her shoes off, so that she wouldn't disturb him.

Sometimes, she really loved hiding behind texting.

Doing anything Sunday? he wrote. *It's a slower day. Thought we could be lazy together.*

A pause. Another line. *Take a drive somewhere?*

Temptation coursed through her. That sounded fun. She hadn't gotten around much since the ill-fated wedding. *Invited myself to Astoria to visit my mom,* she thumbed back reluctantly. She added, *And Jim Morrison.*

Would she ever be able to call him Jim, she wondered, without tacking on his last name? Even while texting, she felt compelled to add it.

Overnight? Ian wrote back.

Gah. No. Sis can't make it. Will just rent a car and drive.

In the next minute, he called her.

"I could come with you," he suggested. "We could take my car. This could be our outing."

"Why would you want to do that? It won't be fun. Besides, won't you be busy? Aren't weekends big for you?"

They weren't big for her. She'd added Saturday hours in an effort to drum up business. So far, no takers.

"Lilah and Gerry can cover for me. Gerry wants to learn more about management. We could walk along the shore. I haven't been to the shore in a long time."

She felt herself sliding under the influence of his voice. But she really had to concentrate on surveillance of Jim Morrison and his nefarious plans. And she didn't want to be worried that Ian would think she was being mean to her mother.

"We could go up on Saturday night," Ian continued. "Spend the night in a bed and breakfast. I can get someone to recommend a place to me, or if your mom knows somewhere that would be great."

It sounded so appealing. Of course, there was still marriage and the Jim Morrison issue to get over. And the fact that she would be introducing Ian to them.

They didn't have to know how she and Ian met.

He was lovely. How could her mother disapprove of a kind, smiling man with deep brown eyes, who ran a successful business? There had to be something wrong with him, of course, but maybe his charm would lull Lisa into forgetting to find fault with him. Just like his charm had lulled Petra.

"Do you not want me to come?" he asked. "You don't want me to meet your mother?"

"I just—"

Some of it was true. She did not want her mother finding anything wrong with Ian and asking Petra if she had time for relationships when her practice was in peril.

"I want you to come. It's just not the best circumstances. I'm just afraid that you will see Jim Morrison and Lisa and run screaming. Or that you'll see us fight or that she'll try to tell me something about you that makes

175

me sad. It's one thing to tell you about my problems. It's another for you to witness them."

"What could she say about me that would make you sad?"

"I don't know," she lied.

Ian said, "I don't think there's anything that she could say about you that would make me run away. Why don't I come and make this easier for you? I could make the whole trip different."

"You would make the whole trip different," she said, sincerely. "And maybe I don't want to feel good, maybe I don't want you along, making me feel better about everything, making everything seem so easy." She laughed uncomfortably. "What I'm saying is, you won't see me at my best."

"Who says I have to?"

Chapter Seventeen

"Pantalettes," he said.

They had pulled out onto Highway 30.

She had been quiet all the way out of the city and now she was gazing out the window at the winter landscape. It wasn't the best time of year to take a drive. The trees looked scrubby and sparse and the sky and roads and land seemed gray in the remnants of the evening light. At least traffic hadn't been bad.

Had he pushed too hard to come with her? He glanced at her profile, the curved cheek, the sardonic lips, curved even now, the little pointed chin that he loved to kiss. He could practically hear her thinking. Not that she was always like that. In bed, she let her guard down. The more they talked and had sex, the more they slept together, the more she just let herself be. Obviously, he needed to spend more time with her. Which suited him just fine.

But right now, he needed to distract her.

"Pantalettes," she repeated, frowning. "Not a bad replacement for the female-underpants-word-that-shall-not-be-named, but I think in reality, pantalettes are actually more like bloomers. They're long and lacy."

"How about bloomers?" he asked.

"Too poufy. I thought you were supposed to invent a new word. It's not fair to take an old word and make it mean something different."

"People do it all the time. Besides, those weren't the rules," he said. "You never said anything about reclaiming and recycling. It wouldn't be very Portland of me if I didn't at least try." He put his hand on his heart and adopted an expression of woebegone earnestness mixed with condescension.

She laughed. He loved that laugh.

She was looking at him again, her eyes traveling up his jeans and shirt, across his arms and neck until he practically felt her on his lips. How did she do that? Had she taken some sort of course in medical school that made her able to envision every sinew and bone and nerve on a body?

"Let's pull over and make out like horny teenagers," he suggested. When she demurred, he added, "Why not? We're not in a hurry."

"We're barely on the road. We've got another hour before we get to the inn."

"We could stop in a motel. Maybe one with a mirror on the ceiling," he said, trying to push her farther.

"Are you always this classy with the ladies?"

"You haven't lived until you've felt the friction of your bare bottom on a polyester bedspread."

She held her breathing in check, he could tell. Her nimble mind was turning over the possibilities. "And I suppose you have?" she asked.

"I'm just trying to expand our horizons here," he said.

-

Petra felt close to giving in. Her eyes skimmed over his jeans. She was making him crazy, and that made her delighted and insane. If she reached over and—

Sarah, with her infinite good timing, chose this moment to call.

"I've got tickets to the ballet tonight. I wanted to see if you were up for it."

Not a word about the fight. This was Sarah's style. Although, frankly, Petra was surprised that Sarah had been the one to call first.

"I'm driving up to Astoria."

"You should have told me. I'd have gone up with you."

"I'm fine."

Sarah waited a beat. "You're with Helen, aren't you?"

Petra sighed. "No, I'm not. And besides, Helen loves the ballet. Why don't you ask her?"

"I can't. Not after what I said to her. It's like trash talk came out of my mouth and it's hanging above my head permanently like a series of thought balloons. Helen's never going to be able to look at me without seeing them and I'm never going to be able to look at her without seeing her seeing them."

"Sarah."

"Who are you with, then? Are you with him? You know, whatever, Pete, whatever. Obviously, you have to take Helen's side on this whole thing, because you always do. I'm left looking like the hard ass because I said what needed to be said. So you and Helen and your various male friends can have your fun and damn all the consequences. Just don't get judge-y when I do my thing."

"*Sarah.*"

Petra looked at the screen. Disconnected.

Ian glanced her way. "Trouble?" he asked.

Petra pursed her lips. "It's nothing." She sighed. "Why am I starting to feel like perpetual-crisis woman?"

"Maybe you care too much."

She rolled her eyes.

"I'm not saying that's a bad thing. In fact, maybe it's something I like about you. You're in a profession where you take care of people. I like seeing you in action, although I'm sorry that it seems to be tearing you apart lately. Maybe I've spent my life not caring enough."

He checked over his shoulder and pulled smoothly in front of an SUV that had been hogging the road.

"Tell me more about your friends," he said.

"I haven't been seeing much of them lately," she said. "We had a falling out a few weeks ago. You know about that. We still haven't sorted it out. But Sarah's great. She seems strait-laced, but she knows the filthiest jokes. Helen's more ethereal and you think she's a little spacey, but then you get her in an argument and she suddenly becomes alert and incredibly stubborn."

"Pit bull with fairy wings. Got it."

She laughed. "They're complicated," she said. "I guess most friendships that are worthwhile are a little bit complicated."

She turned a little in the seat. "How about you?"

"I've got Gerry."

"Insult Chef."

"Yes, that's a good name for him."

"Why aren't there more people in your life?" she asked. "You seem like a social person. Plus, you're in a profession that requires a lot of cheek-kissing and arm-patting."

He shrugged. "I work too much."

"Yet, here you are, tooling around the countryside with me on a Saturday evening. You aren't answering the phone."

"I'm not always like this, as you already know. I'd like to promise you that I'm often like this, but I haven't made time to spend with anyone before."

He spoke slowly, as if confused and surprised. She was, too, but he looked so bewildered by his admission that she quirked him a smile. "Maybe we should pull over," she said, after a short silence.

They ended up spending the entire night at the Twin Motor Inn. There was no mirror on the ceiling, and the American flag quilt on the bed seemed to be composed of cotton, not man-made materials. Ian seemed cheerfully unconcerned.

"You're a pretty cheap date," he said much later, opening a tiny bag of chips.

"I wouldn't speak so soon. I'm still hungry," Petra said, stretching out.

It was near midnight and they had eaten the bananas and apples that Petra had brought, and that was nowhere near enough. He got up to get some water. His torso was lean and long, and she felt the urge to reach out to brush the sparse, crackly hair on his stomach.

It wasn't just lust, she thought. They *were* good together, despite the fact that he'd been a patient, despite Sarah's naysaying and the disaster that lay ahead with Jim Morrison and Lisa, despite the fact that he was taking up too much of the time and energy she should be using to get out of the red.

She swigged her water and held out the bottle to Ian. "I'll admit that I will have very good memories of this room," she said. "But I'll still want a better breakfast than chips and stale nuts and fruit."

"Anything you want," he said sleepily. "I think you're amazing."

He pulled her close and tucked his head into her neck. She could feel a smile on his lips. She had put that there.

And then he was out, his breaths coming steady and warm against her neck. She lay wide-awake beside him.

–

"So, Ian, what do you do?" Jim Morrison asked in what passed as a gruff parental manner.

Jim Morrison made shirred eggs. Jim Morrison had a gorgeous, sun-filled house with a wraparound porch, high in the hills. Jim Morrison had a signed original concert poster of The Doors in his study because he knew how to chuckle at himself – or that's what he wanted the world to think.

Petra's mother presided over this all in a mint-green dress topped with a little white jacket. It was a far cry from the oversized sweaters and baggy pants that she usually favored.

They ended up having brunch, even though Ian and Petra had eaten eggs and toast at a greasy spoon earlier that morning. Jim Morrison's eggs and toast put the other eggs and toast to shame. There was also apple-smoked turkey bacon and homemade blueberry muffins, and a fruit salad.

Lisa's life was looking kind of ideal right now.

Petra, on the other hand, felt grubby from waking up in a motel with hard water, no shampoo, and a sliver of medicinal soap. Curse Ian for having convinced her to stop over last night. Petra had scrubbed as much as she could in an attempt to get the smell of sex off of her before she met her mother. Ian, on the other hand, had suffered few ill effects. He flashed his teeth and pushed his hands through his hair so that it looked even wilder, and it was such a three-way love fest between Jim Morrison and Lisa and Ian, that Petra thought she would have to dump the water from one of Jim Morrison's Lalique vases on them.

Instead, she glowered and ate a lot of muffins.

She watched her mother, not as a daughter, but as a clinician assessing a patient. There was nothing physically wrong with Lisa. Her eyes were clear, her hair shone, no bruising, no flushing, no strange weight gain or loss. She seemed to be full of energy, although some of it was of the nervous variety. But her mother wasn't cowed or intimidated by Jim Morrison. She met his gaze straight on and even laughed over the fussy way he rearranged the table.

"I'm so glad you decided to come and that you brought Ian," her mother said, waving her arm with one of her fabulous new gestures.

Come to think of it, maybe the green was a better look for Lisa's complexion. Plus, it made the yellow diamond look almost blue. Maybe Lisa had achieved the happiness that she long deserved and she would sit on the porch on the hill and eat shirred eggs for the rest of her life. And maybe Petra just needed to shut the fuck up and let her mother live her life.

Lisa leaned forward to take some bacon and her jacket slipped down for a moment, and Petra saw a bright hickey on her mother's collarbone.

Oh my God, Petra thought. *They had sex, probably this very morning.*

Petra set down her fork and closed her eyes. She was not thinking about this. She could not think about this.

Ian's hand slid across her thigh. Her eyes popped open.

"We were thinking of having a simple ceremony here," Jim Morrison was saying.

It was so pretty, even in winter. She could almost picture it. *Imagine the wedding instead of your mother and Jim Morrison.*

Jim Morrison turned to ask Ian if he knew of any good caterers in the area and Ian promised to look into it.

"When were you thinking?" Petra asked, taking a big gulp of coffee.

Lisa and Jim Morrison exchanged glances. "If it were up to us," said Jim Morrison, massaging Lisa's shoulders, "it would be right away. But there have been some complications."

Lisa looked at her daughter, then plowed on. "We have to wait for Jim's divorce to be final, first of all."

Ian leaned into Petra and tried to touch her shoulders, but she shrugged him away.

"Mom, you're living here and he's not divorced?"

"Well, Petra, I wanted to be with Jim and—" She hesitated. "I sold the house. That was the other thing I was planning to tell you. It'll probably be another couple of weeks before they take possession. There's plenty of room here. It just seemed sensible, given that Jim's place is big enough for us, and for all of the children if you want to come back during holidays. And in this market, a larger property might be harder to sell. It's not as if it was your childhood home," Lisa added.

"Does Ellie know about this?"

A pause.

"We feel, Petra, that maybe the support isn't always there," Jim said evenly.

"Now, let's not—" Ian began.

But Petra was already far ahead. "*You* mean that *you* don't think that *I* am very nice to *you*," Petra said. "Just come out and accuse me, Jim. Just come out and blame me with some pronouns and action verbs. Even though you're the one who's shacking up with my mother even though *you* aren't even divorced yet."

"Petra!"

"I was quiet. I was nice. I gave you a chance. It seemed like you were happy. Now I don't know what I can tell you, Mom. I'm disappointed in you. You told me you had your head screwed on straight, that you weren't being impulsive and taking any chances. I trusted you to be practical. But now, this."

She gestured at Jim Morrison. He looked mildly offended. But only mildly.

"Petra, I'm sorry I didn't tell you about the house. But I hated it. I hated the empty rooms and the ugly carpets, and the bathroom floor always looked dirty because the previous owners had white tile. And I'm happy here, in this place, with Jim."

"Because you've got a view, and he makes you a few fancy eggs? Mom, he's not going to take care of you. Your own house would at least be something."

"He doesn't need to take care of me, Petra. I kept the money. I'm my own woman. Sometimes he makes me muffins, sometimes I make him meatloaf."

"Well la-dee-dah. Maybe you can cater your own wedding, then."

She strode out. Ian followed and said thank yous and goodbyes while Petra started the car. She watched while Lisa tearfully gave Ian a hug. Her mother whispered something in his ear and he shook his head. Jim said something, too, then Ian got into the car with a Tupperware container full of Jim Morrison's blueberry muffins.

—

He almost handed them to Petra, then thought twice about it, and placed them in the back seat.

She waited until they got to the outskirts of town before starting.

"You didn't have to be nice to them," Petra said. "Why the hell were you nice to them? Did you think I was so wrong to say any of those things? You thought I was too hard on her, didn't you?"

"I understood where you were coming from."

"You understood. God, you were all cooing at each other the whole time. She hugged you. She's never hugged any of my boyfriends before—"

He would have liked more details on this – which boyfriends? How many? Had they been serious? – but she didn't seem in the proper mood to divulge.

"You know what your problem is, Ian? You're like some sort of diplomat who only offers half-statements and equivocations. You avoid committing yourself emotionally. If I'm a person who naturally takes care of people, then you're one of those people who tries to smooth over other people's feelings. I've seen you work a room. You avoid conflict, but you also avoid depth and taking sides with people you should take sides with—"

He watched her switch lanes almost angrily.

"Petra," he said.

"What?"

He asked her to pull into a parking lot. She did and she turned off the car. He took her hands in his.

"I made you cry," he said quietly.

"No," she said through tears. "Yes, a little. But mostly, I think my mom made me cry. And I did it to myself, too. And Jim Morrison. That fucker." She swiped at her face. "I don't usually clutch my pearls like that over divorces and houses and money. But it's my mother, and I can't deal with it."

She took a deep breath.

"I am a smoother-over," Ian said. "I try to make jokes and unruffle feathers, and then I get the hell out. There's got to be another word for that. Something in Merriam-Webster. If you can find it, or popularize it, then I promise you, you can have all my underpants."

It wasn't that funny, but Petra gave him a gulping laugh sob. He took one hand off of hers and rummaged in the glove compartment for tissues. Of course, he didn't keep tissues. There were obviously much more important things to store in there, like gas station receipts from 2002 and a used coffee cup. He wiped her face gently with his thumbs instead.

"I'm on your side, Petra. I was nice to them in the end because, well, I'm hoping that I get to see them again. With you. And that it won't be awkward."

"You like them."

"I like *you*. I want to be with you. Maybe I didn't handle that well and I know that you're worried about your mom, but let's not turn this into doubts about us."

Petra took a few breaths. "I'm trying not to," she said, "but it's hard to separate everything when…"

He wasn't sure what she was trying to tell him when she trailed off. All he knew was that it hurt to see her like this and he felt responsible. He tried to keep talking. "You're right," he said, "I don't commit even when I say I have. I avoid things and I disappear. Growing up in my family, it was tough not to do that."

She was staring out the window, trying to wipe her nose. In the reflection, her eyes caught his. He wished she would turn around. He wanted to hold her, not because she was crying, but because he felt alone. But she was still buckled in her seat belt, and he in his.

"My dad worked a lot around the world," he said. "He brought us with him. Insisted on it. My mother, though, she had trouble adjusting. She didn't go out, ever. Even when we lived in English-speaking countries, and eventually, even when we lived in other parts of the United States, she just stopped being able to interact with people. My dad didn't acknowledge all of her problems. He just worked all the time. A lot of it was on me."

He saw her eyes close.

"I was the one who found her. It was probably an accident. She'd gotten on a ladder to clean something. She was always tidying, always cleaning until her hands got blisters. She must have slipped and fallen. Maybe if someone had been there, but my dad hadn't been home for days. I was away with friends, doing God knows what. Leg fracture, the coroner said, which caused a pulmonary embolism."

He rubbed his forehead and took off his glasses. "And, of course, I blame myself. Because what kind of screwed-up, complicated adult would I be if I didn't?"

He attempted a smile. She looked at him through her tears, wiped her nose on her sleeve, then took his hand and kissed it.

Then she hit him on the shoulder. "What the hell?" she said.

He couldn't believe it. "You hit me?" he said.

She nodded and then she took her hand out of his and thwacked him again.

"I am never going for a long car ride ever, ever again," she said, very clearly, looking into his eyes, "because every time I do, it ends up in tears."

Her face fractured momentarily, but she pulled herself up again and looked him in the eye. He popped her seat belt and his and took her in his arms. He rubbed her back and let her snuffle messily into his shirt.

"I know," he said, kissing her hair. "I know."

"I'm supposed to be consoling you," she said.

"I think we're consoling each other." After a while, they switched seats and pulled out onto the road again.

Petra glanced sideways at Ian and waited.

"Well, at least you don't pity me," he said, after a while. "My mother's relatives, my aunts and uncles and cousins, they used to just look at me and shake their heads. I lived with a few of them for a while. My aunt Patty, in particular, would take my elbow every time she saw me and say, *And how* are *you?* as if we were always in the middle of the same conversation, and the conversation was always about my neglectful foreign dad and my weird, depressed mom. Is it any wonder that I hardly visit?

"And then there was the fact that I blamed my mother, for a long time, for her own death. Partly because I thought she was the one who was determined to be unhappy. And my dad, who wasn't even there, he seems to get off scot-free in my mind and in my feelings. That makes me feel pretty guilty, the fact that that happens."

Was he ever going to stop talking, he wondered? Petra looked almost blank from all of his blather and the things she'd had to feel today. She never seemed drained. She could be up all night, or grumpy in the morning, but there was always a restlessness to her mouth and hands, a spark in her eye. Hers was the most animated face that he'd ever encountered in his life. But her visage stayed still now when he told her these things about his family, and himself. And he still couldn't stop talking.

Maybe he was trying to get her to hate him. He had started hating himself.

Finally, they managed to get back to the city. Miraculously, he found a parking space near her building. He pulled her bag out of the back seat and held on to the strap as she climbed out of the car.

He bowed his head.

"The other reason I don't want to be in a car again is I couldn't do this when I really wanted to," she said, pulling him down to her.

He let her weave her fingers into his hair and pull his forehead to hers. Her eyelashes brushed his cheeks once, twice, as she blinked. She kissed him hard and pressed his cheek into hers.

I love you, he thought, embracing her with relief, stunned at the feeling. *I love you.*

Chapter Eighteen

It was entirely too soon to be thinking this way.

She was in love with him. She was in love with his resilience and his kindness and she wanted to soothe his heart.

He had been so young when it happened. He had been left alone, making his way in a strange country. Daily, he was forced to speak a language that reminded him of his dead parent. She could see it in his face. And his face, as he looked past her and told her his story, was so resigned and broken. She wanted to cradle his limbs and smooth his brow. She wanted to kiss his lips and take off his shirt and warm him with her body. She wanted to touch every bump on his skull. She wanted to heal every hurt that he had encountered, because that was the kind of sucker she was for him. After all these years, it was clearly too fresh on his face and from his throat, and she wanted to heal him.

He's my boyfriend, not my patient.

Petra was alone at home, wandering around the mess and eating a bowl of peas. She wore a pair of pajama pants with black and white cow spots on them and a tank top that was stained with, she suspected, Tabasco. The spatter pattern matched the cowhide look. Or not.

She felt unsettled and messy and unsexy. Ian had gone reluctantly back to the restaurant after dropping her off

Sunday night and the last time he'd texted, he'd been embroiled in some kind of refrigeration emergency.

Maybe it was good that he wasn't there. She was feeling irrationally in love. She loved the resilient hairs on his chest and arms and thighs which sprang back into place when she pressed them. She loved the odd scars over his body that suggested a childhood climbing trees or crawling through underbrush. He was happy with her fascination except when, in the motel room, she told him that a mole on his chest was a third nipple. He'd looked down at his chest, so adorably disconcerted that she rolled around on the bed giggling until he seized her and she stopped being able to laugh. They said people who had long been together memorized their lovers' bodies. Despite her curiosity, she would never know enough about his.

She'd known things would be complicated with him. She knew from the start.

She couldn't brood now. She decided that this lonely night was the time to throw out all her medical journals. She read everything online, anyway. If she was going to be conflicted about her feelings for Ian, then she could at least organize and control the rest of her life. She was staring at the pile on her table when the buzzer sounded and her first thought was that she hoped to God it was Ian, coming to rescue her from her reckless ambition. And her second thought was that he absolutely could not see her bowl of mushy peas or her stained clothing. She resembled a giant baby.

Luckily, it was Helen.

"We need to talk," Helen hollered into the intercom. "Let me up."

Petra let her shoulders down in relief. Or disappointment.

After a minute, Helen stepped in and surveyed the wreckage of the room. She grabbed the bowl of peas from Petra's hands and set it in the sink. "I brought chocolate chip cookies," she said. "And a gallon container of whole milk."

She got wineglasses from out of the cupboards and poured them each a generous amount. She motioned to Petra to sit on the couch, and she opened the bag between them.

They ate and drank in silence.

"So yes, I cheated on Mike," Helen said, in a flat voice, as if they'd already been discussing it to death. "And it wasn't the result of reciprocal infidelity, where I catch him with a brunette on our couch and decide to take revenge with the mailman. I just went out one day, saw someone who turned my crank for whatever reason, and I took him home with me to my apartment, and even gave him coffee in the morning. I have no defense for what I did. I wasn't drinking. No one slipped me a roofie or told me to do something I didn't want to do. Basically, the only thing that I can figure is that I'm a horrible, untrustworthy person who can't be in a relationship and maybe doesn't deserve one."

If she believed in magic, Petra would have begun to think that someone had cast a lurid truth-telling spell over everyone she knew: Ian, Helen, Sarah, her mother, Ellie.

"Mike was starting to talk about getting married," Helen added. "Clearly, he had a picture in his mind: Physicians in love, building a future of good health and excruciating smugness. My life felt like such a mess at the time that I couldn't stand myself. The timing was so

193

wrong for me. I could have just broken up with him, like a normal person, but instead, I chose to inflict maximum damage, on him, on us."

Petra looked over at Helen, poor, self-flagellating Helen. "You couldn't have known that I'd get you involved in some debate about dating a patient and that Sarah would choose that moment to go on a rampage and take us all down. Also, if it makes any difference, Dr. Mikey is an asshole."

"He is kind of pompous, isn't he? Why didn't you tell me?"

"I figured you already knew but didn't mind because he was smart. Or, at least, good at what he did. Did you like this guy, this man you slept with?" Petra asked.

"Maybe," said Helen. She paused for a moment and looked down at the cookie in her hand. "This is such a cliché. Do you have any carrots and hummus or anything? What I'd give for Sarah to come over with kale juice. We could purge ourselves of all this crap."

In her roundabout way, Helen was asking after Sarah.

Petra sipped her milk. "Just call her," she said.

"Maybe I'll do that," Helen said.

They both drank and stared ahead.

"So," said Helen, "how's the guy?"

"Ian," Petra said. "We went to see my mother yesterday. My mom wants to get married to a not-yet-divorced guy and she sold her house. Shit hit the fan. We drove away. Then he really opened up to me, and then my heart really broke."

"You love him," Helen stated baldly.

"I think I do."

Helen nodded, then she shook her head. "So, why are you so sad about this? You're making this too complicated

194

and I've got to wonder why," she said. "Look, I get it. You feel guilty about how this relationship started, that he was your patient. But don't you think maybe that's an excuse to not just jump into this relationship? Things change between people all the time. Too much second-guessing and trying to explain things that you can't explain unless you're in his head. Why not just go with it, see how it pans out?"

"Because if I go with it, I'll have to admit that I care for him." Petra paused. "It's too soon," she added. "It's not the right time in my life. I'm just starting out as a doctor. I need to establish myself and not pour my energies into some guy. I don't want to be that kind of fool. I've already made so many mistakes, Helen. I've been practicing for less than a year and I've already screwed up my career so much. Starting up a solo practice right away was one of my mistakes but I love it. He's one of my mistakes and I love him. I don't know how much more I can take."

And for the millionth time in two days, Petra found herself crying. Helen immediately grabbed her and hugged her fiercely, and Petra hugged back. The crumbs from her sleeve stuck to Helen's sweater, but Petra figured Helen wouldn't mind. Or at least, she wouldn't see them.

"If you can cut me some slack about the Mike thing, why can't you do the same for yourself?" Helen asked, her voice muffled.

"I don't know what you mean."

"I mean, stop thinking about your career track and worrying about money and getting ahead. Let yourself be a fool for once and see what happens," Helen said. She looked up at Petra with a tiny smile. "What's the worst that can happen? So you close up shop and find work in a hospital or a clinic. So you break your heart. You're

195

already acting like your heart's broken. How much worse can it get?"

–

The buzzer rang too early in the morning. Petra barely managed to register it, but soon she heard a thumping and then voices came from the living room. Great, she thought, Helen had let someone in. With a groan, she got up and slumped down the hallway.

It was Ian.

Ian and Helen had already introduced themselves, and she shot Petra a glance that indicated that either Helen found him delightful or that she was going to have some sort of seizure. Petra supposed that either were possible. Ian looked delicious and he held a white paper bag that smelled like almonds and butter. Helen was highly susceptible to both stimuli.

Helen, of course, looked graceful and delicate, as usual, with her soulful brown eyes, arched brows, and a swan-like neck. She would have made a lovely victim for the guillotine. A surprising number of men liked that sort of thing.

And Petra, she looked like shit, or like she'd rolled around in it. There were crumbs and bits of chocolate chip smeared on her tank top. She didn't want to think of her sheets.

"I thought I'd stop by before you went to work," Ian said. "I brought almond croissants."

Helen sighed and fanned herself. Perhaps she was laying it on a little thick, but she could hardly say anything to Petra in front of him. Ian shot Helen a charming smile. For a moment, Petra felt jealous, but he turned his bright beams to her, and she forgot all about Helen.

"It looks like you two had a girls' night," he said.

"We laughed, we cried," Helen said. "I'll go make coffee."

She practically winked at Petra before disappearing with the bag. Ian stepped up close to Petra. "I'm sorry I wasn't around last night but by the time I got out, it was way too late. It looks like you had good company anyway," he said, putting his hands on her hips. He gazed down at her mouth.

She supposed she could have told him the truth, that she had been miserable when Helen showed up unexpectedly. And that she'd continued to feel miserable afterward.

She put her hand in front of his lips. "My breath is terrible," she said.

He lapped at her middle finger delicately. "I don't care," he said.

Hell.

"Do you have chocolate on your top?" he asked, stepping even closer.

"It's cheap chocolate from very bad cookies," Petra whispered.

She was supposed to be staying away from him. Her friend was in the kitchen. So much about this was so wrong. But while he was not ideal for her in theory, in person he seemed so perfect.

"How bad were the cookies?" he asked in her ear, his voice velvet.

"So bad," she sighed.

They were joking and yet her body still thrummed. "They were hard," she said, "and I ate ever so many of them."

Ian snickered.

"I was worried for a minute," he said. "There were some things I wanted to talk to you about and I didn't know how to say them."

He touched her cheek, but her eyes shuttered and she drew back.

"I should go brush my teeth," she said.

-

He got an uneasy feeling in the pit of his stomach. What was wrong? He wondered, staring after her like a lost fawn. Did she not feel some of what he felt? He told himself that he'd be satisfied if she had even a fraction of the love he had – it was, after all, very soon – but he knew he wouldn't be content for long.

She seemed so happy to see him. He told himself that it couldn't be faked. Inevitably, she seemed to catch herself, and then, it was like viewing her light through a scrim.

He shook his head. Something was off. He had felt so close to her over the weekend. Even when she told him off and accused him of trying to smooth things over, she was immediate and honest and full of sparks. It was an extension of the sex, he thought, or maybe the sex was an extension of them.

It was bullshit that men could separate love and the sex easily, he thought, his mind flashing over memories of the weekend, of the motel bed. It would be like sifting through her hair, trying to decide which strands were black, which were brown, and which were red.

It did sound like a nice way to pass the time.

With Petra, it was all over her face and limbs: intensity, playfulness, sorrow, joy, happiness, fear, abandon. There were planes and shadings to how he felt when he was inside her, to how he felt when she settled down against him with her eyelids still fluttering and made the world seem softer. He sat down on the couch and pulled a throw pillow over his middle in case Helen walked in.

He sighed gustily and his arm tightened around the cushion.

He shouldn't have left her right away on Sunday. He should have just told her right then and there that he loved her. But Gerry had called and Ian was the only one could deal with it and before he knew it, Sunday night and most of Monday had disappeared.

He found Helen watching him with avid interest. He was still staring at the corridor where Petra had disappeared, like a dog whose owner had gone inside the grocery store. Helen set two mugs on the coffee table and a plate of pastries.

"I couldn't find a tray, so I'm going back for milk and sugar," she said. "I was going to ask how you take your coffee."

"Just milk, thank you."

She remained standing looking at him.

"Are you going to offer me any insight?" he asked.

"I have no idea what you're talking about."

"I need to get a grip. We've been together for, like, a month," he said.

"News flash, she cares about you. She agonized over her feelings for you. She still does."

"Agonized." Ian turned that word over.

"Yes, agonized," Helen said firmly. "For Petra, getting involved with anyone is a big deal because of her mom and dad and other things. And with you, her former patient, it came with putting her in a slightly ethically ambivalent position. It didn't help that she lost you as a patient while her practice struggles – all of which makes her feel even more insecure about her competence as a doctor. On top of that, her friends have been warring—"

"Because of me."

"Men aren't the be-all end-all of everything, Ian. Yes, talking about you triggered a fight but it really wasn't about you. I'm just trying to tell you that even though you clearly make her happy, it's also been a hard time for her. And I don't know how much you know about that. And maybe I'm projecting, but don't try to be one of those jerks who tries to solve her problems by offering her a life with you and smoothing over her issues."

Helen quirked a glittering warning smile and slipped out as Petra came in. She was dressed in her sensible doctor uniform of low heels, button down shirt, and black pants. She also seemed to wear some sort of invisible veil that whispered, "Touch me not." Of course, it provoked him. He felt like putting his hands up her shirt.

Luckily, or perhaps unluckily, Helen slipped in and gave another glare. Ian still wasn't sure if he disliked her, or if he should thank her for the insight. Maybe both. "I have to get going," she said, filching a pastry. She waggled her fingers and a moment later, the door shut.

Petra opened her mouth as if she was about to say something, but Ian didn't let her speak. He half-rose up from the sofa, grabbed her, and kissed her. Hard.

She didn't even try to resist. She tilted her head. Her arms and stomach and lips softened for him almost immediately. He pulled her onto his lap.

"That's good toothpaste," he said.

Petra murmured something incoherent.

"I have to get back to Stream soon, but can I walk you to work?" he asked.

The man wanted to walk her to work after that kiss? He was going to have to carry her liquid remains in a bucket. Luckily, there was a throw pillow jammed uncomfortably between them, or she would have melted into his lap. She managed to nod – or maybe her neck gave out and her head just flopped – and she let him push her up, put a coat on her, and wind her lumpy orange scarf around her neck.

"Where are your gloves?" he asked, frowning as they got outside.

"Bag," she said.

With her tacit permission, he began to rummage. He examined her lip balm and smoothed out some wadded-up tissues. He eyed the large first-aid kit she kept handy. He took out the gloves, and then he reached for another small pouch.

"You've got a bra and underpants in your purse," he said.

He raised a brow.

"You should always have clean underwear in case you have to go to the hospital," she said.

Or in case your boy shorts get soaked because a man who has been kissing you dangles your intimates from his index finger.

This was ridiculous. She'd been having generous amounts of sex with the man for a month. They weren't strangers anymore. She loved him.

But he was eying her carefully now, and Petra remembered that Helen had been alone with him. Had Helen said anything? And if so, what?

"How are you going to put it on if you're in an accident?" he asked, grasping her arm firmly as they walked.

He had her and it should have been the best feeling in the world but she mistrusted it.

"It's for when you've recovered, then," she said, sounding just like her mother.

"Prepared for everything, aren't you?" he murmured.

She made a strangled sound. "No, I'm really not. I'm really, really not."

He considered that. He straightened. "You know that you're amazing, right? You have all this energy – that's the first thing I noticed about you. It was like you were incandescent. And, it's not just that. It's about how much of that light in you is goodness, how much you care about people, how good you are at taking care of people. I really, really respect you."

He looked deep into her eyes.

Petra cleared her throat. "Uh, you're still holding my underwear."

"Oh, right."

He stuffed it in her purse and kissed her quickly as they arrived at her office door. "I'll see you tonight. Now get inside that door, it's cold."

With that, he walked rapidly away, and Petra gazed after him, even more confused. *What the hell had Helen said to him?*

When she got upstairs, she saw that she'd received a text message.

That man is losing his shit over you, Helen had written.

Well, he wasn't the only one losing it.

Chapter Nineteen

Field was lucky enough to book a private party at the end of the February doldrums. Ian stood at the bar, polishing glasses and staring straight ahead. The corporate crowd liked their drinks. Fake laughter clanked like chains around the room.

Ian hated everyone.

For the first time in his life, Ian resented work. Now his staff just expected him to be around to solve all their problems.

He had planned to woo her with picnics and silky underwear. He planned to have sex with her until their hipbones gave out. But after Helen had torn him a new one, he was through with assumptions. He was annoyed that he hadn't seen it before. Clearly, Petra still felt wary about some things. If what Helen said was true, then just dumping all of his feelings on her wouldn't be enough.

Although maybe he could still take her away some-where. He hadn't had a vacation in – well, ever. He was ready.

He stacked the polished glasses and began to cut up some limes while the bartenders continued to serve drinks to the rowdy crowd.

The truth was that Ian also shied away from talking too much about Petra's work because he noticed that she was a little sensitive about her work. With him.

He didn't want her to be secretly worried and unhappy. He couldn't be the kind of man who ignored it – not after what his father had put his mother through. Ian liked to be in some semblance of control of his feelings, and he preferred things to be easier and more harmonious. It was part of the reason he worked so hard and depended on so few: when the only variable was him, things ran more smoothly. But not everything about this relationship depended on him and he was going to have to get used to it.

He had gone for a run in the middle of this afternoon and returned to his apartment to do pushups until his arms felt like they would fall off. He still felt like punching something. Preferably the bartender who'd left them high and dry tonight.

"That glare isn't going to scare these Silicon Valley types from the open bar," Gerry half-shouted above the din. He wiped his hands on his chef's jacket, leaned against the counter, and ordered a club soda.

"Don't you have tiny, tiny bites of food to send out of the kitchen?" Ian growled.

"That's the glory of tonight, my friend. It's all advance work. If any lovely ladies want a show, I can sear a couple of lamb lollipops and help the gals lick 'em clean, but otherwise, it's all mostly done. What's the matter with you, you big lunk, do you miss Dr. Tinkerbell already?"

"Yes," Ian growled.

It was hard to carry on a conversation over all of this noise. And about this particular subject.

He started stacking clinking glasses angrily.

Gerry took them away.

"So it's serious with the little pixie doc."

"You're dating a doctor?" asked a voice behind them both.

Danielle.

"Ugh," said Gerry, summing it up nicely.

"Is that any way to thank the woman who got you this gig?" Danielle asked, gesturing to the room. She looked well. She'd let her hair down this night, so that it flowed in silky waves down her back, and she was smoothly encased in a V-necked dress.

"He's in love," said Gerry. "He's even taken time off from work to be with her. Not enough time, clearly."

"I always thought it was kind of small-time of him to always try to fix problems by himself. Subbing for the wait staff, tending bar, playing handyman."

"He's a bit of a control freak," Gerry agreed.

"Why are you here, Danielle?" Ian asked.

"I'm the one who told our clients about this fabulous place. Insisted we do this here. They're not very adventurous, so I thought this might do. I've got a rep for knowing all about the great places to eat, you know."

"You mean Ian was your ticket to launching yourself as a food groupie," Gerry said, ignoring Danielle's barb to attack on another front. Classic Gerry.

"I appreciate men who can cook," Danielle said, batting her eyelashes. Classic Danielle.

Gerry smiled cynically. "I hear you've appreciated a lot of men in the biz lately. After Ian, there was Ron from Bel Canto, then Juan from Carioca—"

"I introduced you to him," Ian said.

"And he's lovely, thank you. But I want to hear all about the woman who can make the unflappable Ian Zamora completely miserable – so miserable that he doesn't even want to spend time at his precious restaurant. She must be so very special."

He didn't like the way she breathed, "so very special," and he certainly didn't want to give her any ammunition against Petra. Not that Danielle was the kind of person to use it. Or was she? He had certainly misjudged her more than once before. He tensed at the glint in Danielle's eye.

Gerry, however, felt no such compunction. "She was his allergist," he said.

This raised Danielle's eyebrows. "You mean, she was the one who gave you the cat shots? You began seeing her while you were seeing me? And she was your doctor?"

"No," said Ian. He made an effort to be calm and precise. "That's definitely out of order. She was my allergist for, like, a tiny moment. But then, when you and I broke up, I quit going to her. And then a few months later, we met up again. Simple."

It was the truth and he *hadn't* done anything wrong, but stated that way – well, it didn't sound great. Maybe this kind of ambiguity was what bothered Petra about their relationship.

Danielle kept her eyes on him. He wanted to squirm, but he let himself go very still before he quirked his lips up in an attempt to look benign and happy.

She gave a quick smile of her own. "But you liked her from the start," she said, again, very sweetly. "She must be gorgeous."

"She's a fierce little wood sprite," Gerry said cheerily.

"Stop calling her tiny. She hates that."

Ian darted his friend an angry glance. Why was Gerry fanning the flames? There was definitely fire in Danielle's eyes. She certainly still seemed a little too interested, a little too malicious. How could he have ever thought she was a lovely person?

"Doesn't sound like your usual type, Ian. I thought you liked women who were mild and serene, the kind who would smooth your brow and say yes all the time."

She had pointy incisors, he noticed, perfect for tearing apart flesh. He should have shown her more respect. She was a smart woman and he had treated her like a show pony. And now he got the feeling he was going to regret it.

"Is that how you think of yourself?"

"I think you underestimated me," Danielle trilled. "That, and you spent so little actual time with me that you had no idea what I was really like."

Well, that was true enough.

"It's such a lovely story, really," Danielle continued. "Attraction over the examining table."

"Hold on a minute," Ian said. "First of all, as I said earlier, she did nothing wrong. We started this well after I broke up with you and stopped being her patient."

"Did you try anything on her while you were still her patient?"

"No. Jesus, Danielle."

"I'm just saying, I always found you a little distant, as you'll recall. Just trying to determine if there was a reason for your aloofness. I guess it wasn't because there was another woman. It's just how you are."

The problem with having his ex confirm his assessment of himself was that there was really nothing that he could say to counter it. And it was always infinitely horrifying to have one's worst fears underlined by someone he assumed had not known him well enough.

"It sounds like you have nothing to add to that, Ian." She raised her glass. There was a small glint in her eye that indicated she knew that she had wrested a victory from him.

–

"Don't hang up," Lisa said.

The phone number was unfamiliar. Petra was good and trapped. Lisa had left a few messages since Sunday, but Petra hadn't wanted to listen to them.

"Listen, I'm sorry that I didn't tell you about how serious it was with Jim. I'm sorry that I sold the house without telling you. But you have to understand, it has been very difficult for me."

"Everything is difficult for you, Mom."

Petra held her phone to her ear and put on her coat. She'd stayed late at the office, investigating the possibility of adding cosmetic Botox to her list of services. It was a moneymaker, that was true. But she was pretty sure that she was probably not the best person to be doing it.

This morning seemed so far away, she thought as she went through her purse. She tucked away the underwear that Ian had stuffed carelessly back in, found her gloves and her scarf, and walked down into the cold night, her phone still pressed to her ear.

"I suppose it's fair for you to criticize me for not telling you about the house," her mother was saying. "I suppose I deserve that."

"Is this Jim Morrison's phone that you're calling from?" Petra asked.

"Yes. It's his landline."

"Is he there?"

"No. He didn't think I should call. He thinks I lend your opinions too much credence and that you take advantage of it in order to act out. I've stopped being the parent, but you are still acting the child."

"Wow, that's a direct quote, isn't it?"

"He doesn't dislike you, Petra."

"No, I don't imagine that he dislikes anyone."

Petra paused to look in the window of one of the galleries that dotted the street. She'd learn to administer Botox and then she could buy art. She could invest in a few pieces, then they would accrue value and she would not have to worry about paying back her medical school debt, or paying the rent on her office, or supporting her mother when Lisa's latest fiancé deserted her and left her with nowhere to live. She could smooth the wrinkles of worry from her mother's forehead. She could buy that antelope head over there, or maybe that painting of a woman who appeared to be giving birth to a rabbit.

Probably not the sort of thing she should hang in her office. Maybe Sarah would like it.

"Jim felt that I should leave you alone for a few more days, let you get used to the idea. But I just wanted— I wanted…"

Petra waited.

"It has been difficult for me to admit that I've fallen in love. Again. After all this time, and after some disastrous relationships. I didn't want to go to my daughter and have to explain to her that this time it was different. I felt… ashamed of myself for not having better judgment in the past. And to go to you and have you pick it apart this time, as an adult. It was almost too much to think of. So I put it off and I put it off. Jim's the one who convinced me that I had to do this, that I had to tell you the truth."

"At least there seems to be one grown-up in this relationship."

"I wasn't trying to hurt you, Petra. I wanted – selfishly maybe – to protect myself."

Petra started walking again. She could understand the urge to try and shelter herself. After all, wasn't that what she was doing with Ian? She was scared about what dating him meant about her personal and professional judgment. She was afraid of the future. She was terrified of being in love with him.

"The money from the sale of the house is going to a separate account, Petra. Jim won't be able to touch it."

"It's not about the cash, Mom."

"But I just want to show you that I've put thought into this. This isn't some spur-of-the-moment thing. We knew, almost right away, that there was something there, even though I questioned it and even though I worried that my instincts were terrible. Jim tried to make me comfortable. He made me see that we could be practical about the whole thing. It may seem hasty to you—"

"Because you only told me a few weeks ago this was serious, and Ellie has known for months."

"Again, I'm sorry."

Petra walked into the grocery store and took a basket.

"But what I'm saying is that I took steps. I am trying to protect myself. I know I don't have a great track record, and I hate it, but I am trying and I need you to just…"

Petra put broccoli in her basket. She snagged a box of lettuce and some lemons. She'd had enough of frozen vegetables. She needed something new. She needed to feel springtime coming.

"You want me to just what? Tell me what it is now, instead of waiting six months."

"I want you to just accept that I'm getting married, to just accept me," her mother said.

Petra stood looking blankly at the vegetables she had put in her basket. What had she been about to do?

"I need some time," she said. "That's the best I can do, Mom. I need some time."

She hung up.

In reality, she had probably forgiven her mother. But talking with her was like running on a well-worn track. Her feet just fit right into the grooves. They went along without thought. So much had been said already, so many arguments well established and continuing. So difficult not to keep old battles going. She supposed it was this way with parents. Ian's mother and father were dead, but she doubted he felt much relief.

Ian hadn't phoned or messaged her all day. Her fingers itched to call him or text him.

The way his face had looked today, the awkward speech he'd given her about how much he respected her – it was the least romantic thing he could have said, but for some reason it made her blush from deep inside until her whole body felt red and warm.

He was dopamine. He was a surge of norepinephrine. Then there was the fact that clearly, she made him as crazy as he did her.

When they were in bed, it was easy to believe that there was no one else for her. She had never experienced that with anyone and when she looked into Ian's eyes, she was sure that it felt that way for him, too. The feeling left its honeyed residue. Even when they simply talked on the telephone, it was like he was there, stroking her like a cat. But she was a woman of science. She knew about the deceptiveness of endorphins.

She walked home with her bag of groceries. The sky had darkened and it felt several degrees colder than before. And she found Kevin shivering outside her building.

Chapter Twenty

"I wanted to talk to you, but your office was closed," Kevin said.

He looked small and skinny and his face seemed very white. "You said I could talk to you any time," he added.

He couldn't come up to her apartment, inner Hippocrates told her sternly. But clearly, she couldn't stand out here with him in this wind. She glanced down longingly at her grocery bag and wondered if she could just stash her soon-to-be wilting lettuces upstairs. The best place to go would probably be back to her office, but the idea of returning depressed her. Inner Hippocrates be damned, she thought.

"C'mon, you're freezing to death," she said. She put her hand on his shoulder. "Have you eaten dinner? Does your dad know where you are? Why is he letting you wander around?"

"He's working late," Kevin said. "He's got a big case coming up. He gave me some money. I can take you out. I told him I'd hang out with Penny Poole, but I don't want to go there right now."

"I'm surprised that you even know where I live," Petra mused. Then she thought about it more and wasn't surprised at all.

They went to the vegetarian diner around the corner and settled into a warm booth. Kevin kept his jacket on.

"I'll have the fries," Kevin said, without checking the menu.

Petra raised her eyebrows.

"Okay, the sweet potato fries," he said.

"What kind of oil are they cooked in?" Petra asked.

The waiter snorted, but went in back to check.

"You remember everything I'm allergic to, don't you?" Kevin asked. "Even though you have more patients now, you still know."

Still not enough, Petra thought.

"My father doesn't," he says. "He comes home with strawberries and wonders why they go moldy. He buys granola bars with peanuts in them. I'm thinking of asking for my own mini fridge for my birthday. I can hide in my room and I won't have to talk to anyone ever again."

The waiter came back and they ordered their food.

"Your dad has got a lot on his mind. And, well, I've devoted my life to this stuff. You'll understand when you're older," she said.

"You haven't really devoted your entire life to this, have you? I mean, it's okay to be a doctor and all, but don't you do other stuff? What about other dreams? Don't you want to have kids? Or get a car? You don't even have a car, do you? I can't wait to drive."

Petra winced. A busboy brought them tepid water, and she tried not to compare the service to Field. Ian had spoiled her.

"So, what did you want to talk about?" she asked, trying to seem businesslike while sipping water from a Felix the Cat drinking glass.

Kevin fiddled with the salt and pepper shakers. They had pictures of Tweety Bird and Sylvester on them. What kind of crowd was this place aiming for, anyway?

"I think I like Penny," Kevin burst out. "I think I *like* like her."

"So, what's the problem? I thought she enjoyed being with you. She came out to Stream and she seemed impressed."

"Yeah. But I thought we were just friends, right? Then I started texting with Brie Eng. She's really cool, and I thought I liked her, but I think she just thought I was weird enough to become one of those teenage tech billionaires, and she wanted to tell people she knew me back when. So Penny got upset, and she told me that she wanted more, and I didn't because I thought I could hang out with Brie's friends. And then when Penny stopped talking to me, I missed her. She likes the same things I like, she doesn't roll her eyes when I say I can't do something or eat something, and she's really good at things. If anyone becomes a tech billionaire, it's definitely going to be Penny."

Great, thought Petra, eying her water. Confirmed by Kevin: life was not better as one grew older, it was exactly like junior high school and maybe a little bit worse.

"Penny's a lot like you," Kevin added.

The food arrived. Kevin asked for vinegar for his sweet potato fries. He concentrated on salting his plate and licking his fingers. Petra picked at a black-bean burger.

"So, anyway, I was thinking that maybe you could give me some tips on how to convince Penny to like me again. I was going to ask Ian, but he wasn't at the bar and Field was closed for a private party." Kevin wrinkled his nose. "Ian's a good-looking guy," he added, "and he's smart about some things, but he can be a bit clueless, too. I mean, look at the way he was with his ex-girlfriend."

"What do you mean by that exactly?" Petra asked.

God, was she actually asking Kevin (Kevin!) for gossip on Ian?

"She used to make him take care of her cat," Kevin said. "Even though he's allergic. That's why he was seeing you. She was always too busy to go out with Ian. But he would go over and play with the cat and feed it. I heard him talking to her on the phone a lot."

"Do you think he was in love with her?" Petra asked.

Inappropriate, screamed inner Hippocrates, or maybe it was her pride yelling at her. Hard to tell everyone apart at this point.

"I don't know about that," Kevin said. "I think half the time, he didn't mind that he wasn't seeing her, and half the time he just wanted to calm her down."

He snagged a string bean from Petra's plate.

"Do you think I should get Penny roses and stuffed animals?" he asked, brightening.

"Does she like those things?"

"Doesn't every girl?"

"First of all, you probably shouldn't go near roses because of your allergies," Petra said. "And second, what does she like? Do you think she wants a stuffed animal? Do you have any way of showing her that you listened to her?"

"I don't know," Kevin groaned.

Ian had brought her an almond croissant. He took her to trivia night. He helped her find beauty in an ugly motel room. He was nice to her mother despite Petra's displeasure, because he wanted her mother to get along with him in the future. He looked beyond every weird rough surface, every objection, and he still saw her.

It wasn't just charm. He made an effort with her. He probably loved her, too. God, it was frightening.

Joni Mitchell sang "A Case of You" in the background. Petra took a huge bite of her burger and tried not to close her eyes. She should call Ian. She wanted to hear his voice, scratchy from late nights of working too much and maybe from his dust allergy.

Kevin slumped in his seat, a picture of adolescent misery. She probably looked much the same.

"Okay," Petra said, "tell me about Penny."

−

Roses and stuffed animals were not going to cut it for this girl.

Two hours later, Petra was slumped over her water but they had figured out some sort of gift for Penny. Petra wasn't sure what it was, but it involved a game that Penny and Kevin played, a sword, and some sort of power over dusk or dawn. Kevin was explaining it to Petra while texting Penny when Kevin's dad entered the diner. "Uh, doctor?" Mr. Lee said. "What are you doing here?"

Petra sat up straight under Kevin's dad's scrutiny. "Hi, Dad," Kevin said. "Dr. Lale was giving me some advice."

Funny how Kevin managed to string together perfect sentences while still typing madly. Although he had apparently neglected to mention one important thing when informing his father of where he was. "You didn't tell him you were with me?" Petra asked Kevin.

He was a nice-looking man in his early forties. He had some gray at the temples. He wore a rumpled suit. Petra caught a flicker of interest in his eyes that she was not prepared to deal with.

He slid in beside Kevin.

"If I'd known," Kevin's dad said, "I'd have joined you earlier."

Petra shifted in her seat. How was she going to get out of this? *This is what you get for fraternizing with a patient,* inner Hippocrates chided her.

She decided it was time to leave. She opened her wallet. "That's okay," Kevin and his dad said at the same time.

"It's on me," Kevin said grandly. "I would never let a date pay for herself."

"It's not a date," Petra said hastily.

"She was giving me romantic advice," Kevin said.

Kevin's father raised his eyebrows. Petra was getting a very bad feeling about this. And maybe Kevin was sensing it, too. "It's my fault," he hastened to add. "I was waiting for her outside her building. I railroaded her into it."

"You know where she lives?"

"We're all in the neighborhood," Kevin said, squirming.

She hadn't done anything technically wrong, but it looked bad.

Mr. Lee put money on the table, and he and Kevin got up, still arguing. Petra sat for a moment and tried to gather her thoughts together. She still wasn't sure what had happened. The waitress cleared away the cups and dishes and wiped down the table before Petra got up again.

When she got back home, she changed into her pajamas, took a deep breath, and gave Ian a call. No answer. She frowned. He always took her calls. It wasn't so late. They had talked or been together every night since they started seeing each other. Well, except for last night. And the night before. Maybe she'd been spoiled, she thought, although spoiled was not quite the word she had in her brain. She snuggled down in the bed, her iPhone still in hand.

She must have fallen asleep. But when it rang, she had the phone at her ear before she could really even talk.

"I woke you," he said.

"You usually open with underwear," she croaked.

He laughed, a sandpapery whicker, and she was awake and maybe, maybe that meant everything was okay again.

How to talk to the man who had so many faces? The sad man she'd left this morning, the wicked one who made her blood thrum, the calm placater. She opted to do the thing she always did whenever she didn't know what to say: she worried about other people.

"I hung out with Kevin tonight. He showed up at my building looking cold and skinny and, well, even more Kevin-like than usual. He needed romantic advice."

—

Ian lay on his couch. So many questions. Why was it so easy for her to talk about other people's love lives instead of her own? How come Kevin got to spend time with her when he couldn't? Had she been excited? Had she laughed? Had she been scared? Kevin scared him. Mostly, at the moment he was just jealous of the kid. "Did he have a good time?"

"He did," she said hesitantly. "I did, too, surprisingly. But I shouldn't have done that. I should have kept more distance between us. His father showed up and wasn't too happy about it."

"He's a kid. It's hard not to get attached to a kid, even one like Kevin. Cut yourself some slack."

He said that last bit a little too sharply.

"It's not just that. I keep slipping up. First with you—"

"That wasn't—"

"And now this."

She fell silent. "I'm being foolish, right? Too sensitive? Maybe sometime I'll get over my first-year jitters. I'll start prescribing Valium to everyone I meet and have Botox parties in the office. I'll go hang-gliding with all my patients." She sighed. "But right now, especially because of what happened with you and with Kevin just now, I feel like I have to adhere to the rules."

Because of what happened with you.

She sounded like she regretted it. Helen was right.

"Do you think maybe Kevin has a crush on you, too?"

To his relief, she laughed. "He has a funny way of showing it," she said. She added, "My mom called earlier. She wanted to see how I was. She wanted me to give the whole thing with her and Jim Morrison a chance."

"Did you say you would?"

"I told her I needed to think."

"Yes, that seems to be the theme of the day." Then he said, "I should go."

"You don't have to."

"I'm pretty tired," he said. "Long day."

Ian hung up.

Danielle had accused him of being cold and distant. Which he had been with her, he supposed. Of course, she had stayed with him despite all of that. Danielle had also been a little drunk tonight, which explained her burst of vinegar. Still, after his conversation with Petra, he thought increasingly that Danielle was right. First, he'd smoldered silently when she told him about Kevin. Then he cut her off shortly after she began telling him about her mother.

Petra had wanted to keep talking to him and he had hung up like a sulky teenager.

Grow up, he told himself.

He could call her back. He really should. But it was late and he imagined her little face on a pillow, tired but wanting to stay up with him, insisting on one more flick, one more kiss. At least there was passion between them. A wry smile touched his lips; he had been keeping her up late for the last few weeks. Maybe it was best that he let her sleep. He rubbed his head and sat up. He would have to work harder to win her over. She was worth it.

He shut off his phone and skidded it across the coffee table.

Tomorrow he would start anew.

–

Of course, Petra couldn't sleep. Too much had happened, and now the final straw, Ian's phone call left her unsettled. She got up, threw on a robe, and made a cup of tea. Standing over the sink in her frigid kitchen, under a single cold light, she cupped her hands over the mug.

She had other things to consider. She couldn't keep mooning over this. She had applied for privileges at the two nearest hospitals, and she finally seemed to be getting referrals from them. She would make an appointment across town to talk to her old attending to see if it was worth applying there, even though it was hard to get to. Especially – she winced – without a car. Maybe she could do this without adding cosmetic services, without compromising herself even more. And of course, there was still her mother to think about.

In a way, she envied Ian. She hated admitting it to herself, but he was golden and she was still stuck. His businesses were lively. He didn't worry about money. He didn't have to fret about whether he was good at his job because clearly he was. And although it was clear that the memory of them still haunted him, he had no parents to argue with and cry over. He was ready to settle down and she was struggling to stay in the same place. He and Petra were at different places in life. How would this even work?

She drained her cup. She had to get some sleep.

Her phone trilled. She was glad no one was there to witness how quickly she leapt for it. "Hello!" she said breathlessly.

"Petey," Sarah said in an uncharacteristically small voice. "It's me."

"What is it?"

"I'm at the—"

"Sarah, I can't hear you."

"This police officer says he's going to arrest me," she said. "I'm all right. I just... Can you come get me?"

Chapter Twenty-One

"Don't say anything," Sarah warned.

Petra shook her head. She continued to look out the cab window.

"At least I won't be charged," Sarah muttered.

The car stopped and Petra got out. "You're paying me back for the ride," she said. "Here's another twenty to take you home."

Sarah scrambled out. "What has gotten into you?"

"You'd better catch the cab before he rolls away, because you are not invited over."

"Pete."

"You have no idea what the last four days have been like for me – the last month or two, even. But I came down to pick you up at a karaoke bar across town. I brought your spare keys, like you ordered me to, and all I got was a terse, *Don't ask me! I don't want to talk about it!* Not even a hello, not even a fucking thank you."

"Hello. Thank you."

Petra threw up her hands and began to walk to her door.

"Look, I'm sorry, Petra. I'm not used to asking people for help. Neither of us are."

Suddenly, all the fury and all the annoyance and all the responsibility of being who she was crashed down around Petra.

"I am nothing like you, Sarah," she said, jabbing her friend in the shoulder. "I am not the smartest person in the room. I am not perfectly organized and sure of everything about myself and everybody else in every situation. I am barely getting by most of the time. I used to think that I wanted to be more like you, but I'm starting to think that maybe it's best that I'm not."

"A bouncer threatened to send me to jail. I'm hardly perfect," Sarah muttered.

"Yeah, I know, but you've got a good act going, don't you? I was there. I saw how you made that off-duty officer think it was somehow his fault that you were drunk and crazy. Seven feet tall with a giant gun, and a mouthy Asian woman almost has him crying like a baby. I don't know how you did that. I never know how you do that. And let me tell you, I am not about to crumble like the Portland PD under you, all right? I've known you too long and I've taken too much of your shit to let you make me feel terrible. I'm tired of being the one in our friendship who always apologizes and is always wrong, okay?"

"Okay."

"And don't give me any bullshit about asking for help. You are constantly asking me for help, even though you won't fucking admit it, and I am tired of being kicked down for doing it. I am tired of being the fixer. You and Helen have a problem with each other? Who do you both yell at? Me. Who do you both call instead of each other? Me! Who do you tender your regrets and half-assed apologies to? Guess who, fucker. Do you have any idea how fucked up that is?"

Sarah opened her mouth. Then closed it again. "You're a physician. You love other people's problems," she finally said.

"You're a physician, too, and so is Helen. Heal thy own damn self." Petra resumed digging for her key. "I hate other people's problems," she muttered. "It's sick, that's what it is, this stupid thing with you and Helen."

She turned to yell at Sarah again.

"My mother is getting married again, Sarah. For the third time. Do you know what she wants from me? She wants me to simply sit back, trust her decisions, and support and love her. Well, why couldn't she fucking do that for me for, what, her entire life? Couldn't she have stopped worrying, stopped second-guessing me for one minute? She's always asking, *How's business? Are you sure you're doing the right thing?* And what if I wasn't? Couldn't she just accept me? Isn't that what she was supposed to do, because she was my mother and that's what parents do?"

She felt breathless, as if she had been sobbing, but her eyes and cheeks were dry. "Maybe I am tired of shouldering everybody's problems and making people all better. Maybe I just want to be me, faults and all. Maybe I just want somebody to love *me*."

Of course, somebody did love her and she couldn't understand why.

"Petra, it's late. Maybe we should get you inside."

"You're not invited up, asshole."

"Petey, if I create another public disturbance tonight, I probably won't be able to stay out of jail. When they find out you've been doing the majority of the yelling, I doubt that the police will look upon you kindly, either."

Petra stood in the cold.

"I am a total asshole, all right?" Sarah said. "I admit it. Let's go upstairs and I'll make you hot chocolate and we can talk about exactly how terrible a friend I am." She

225

touched Petra's arm. "I'm sorry about tonight. I'm sorry about me and Helen. I'm sorry about your mom."

She took the keys from Petra's hand and opened the door. Petra let Sarah lead her upstairs, then plunked down on the sofa with her coat still on. She still felt chilled and the lack of sleep was starting to catch up with her. Sarah busied herself with finding a box of Swiss Miss in the cupboard and putting the kettle on.

Where had all that anger come from, Petra wondered, as Sarah set a mug in front of her. "All I could find were these gross chocolate chip cookies," Sarah said.

"Helen came over last night for her own meltdown and she left these. I know kale chips and rooibos tea are usually more your style," Petra said.

"Yeah, well, sometimes I need a vacation from myself," Sarah said, taking a cookie.

They clinked mugs.

"What happened tonight?" Petra asked.

"I went to karaoke and I wouldn't relinquish the mike. They were about to call security, so I left. Well actually, I was about to vandalize the door of the club with lipstick and the bouncer stopped me, so I kicked him. He happened to be an off-duty cop. Plus, I did it in front of another cop. I lost my purse in the scuffle. Someone stole my stuff in front of two cops. I'm going to have to cancel all my cards and I don't want to think about my phone. Anyway, they held me there and debated whether to haul me to the station or just put me in a cab – like I wasn't there. I talked the bouncer into lending me his phone and, luckily, remembered your number."

Petra stared at her friend. She was torn between telling Sarah that it was kind of awesome and wondering what the hell was wrong with her.

"Look," said Sarah. "I realize that my behavior tonight was really immature, which is why I kind of don't want to talk about it. But I also realize that you deserve an opportunity to gloat, given what a hard time I've given you. That cop had more important people to attempt to arrest tonight. I wasted people's time and hurt them because I was tipsy and petty. I should hold myself to a higher standard than this. I'm thirty-two and I'm a physician, for god's sake."

Petra was quiet for a moment. Then she started laughing. "God, you're a self-important little prick sometimes."

"Um, yeah, don't hold back, Petey."

"*I should hold myself to a higher standard than this.* Why? Because you're better than everyone? Because you're a physician? You prescribe pills and I stick needles in people. What the hell makes us think that we're such holy healers that we can't be a little human, or a little imperfect sometimes?"

"You saved a woman's life last month."

"All I did was stick a needle in someone. The kind of needle that she could easily stick in herself, I might add. The only thing I really, really did was show her the importance of just doing it on the spot without embarrassment, before something terrible happened to her."

They brooded, lost in their own thoughts.

Sarah drank more hot chocolate. "I love this stuff," she said reverently. "Last weekend, I went to San Francisco and Bryant – he's the new boyfriend, the new ex-boyfriend, actually – bought me some of that Ghirardelli hot cocoa. And it was delicious, of course, but I took three sips and couldn't finish the rest of it. I love this cheap-o Swiss Miss. It tastes like chemicals and drugs."

"The new ex-boyfriend was the cause of this tantrum."

"Well, yes. And no. I accept trade-offs. I know that. I won't be with anyone long-term, so I pick men who are imperfect. Take-away lesson: people always disappoint you. Don't get overly involved."

Petra was quiet. At some point, maybe she had agreed with Sarah. But now, there seemed to be a lot wrong with those feelings. "I don't think it works that way," she said. "In fact, I disagree with almost everything. But I've never really been able to change your mind, and in the condition I'm in, I doubt that'll happen. You're used to these late nights what with birthin' the babies and whatnot. I'm not. I'm going to sleep."

For the second time that week, she left a friend on the couch.

–

The next evening, Petra leaned in the doorway of Ian's office at Field. She had never seen it before. She had never seen him at work before. She pursed her lips as he glared sexily at a laptop screen.

The office was crammed with the kind of touches that his apartment lacked. There was a corkboard covered with pictures of Stream at various stages of construction. A hard hat stood atop the file cabinet, and two shirts in their dry-cleaning plastic hung on hooks on the walls. His long desk held stacks of paper and a lamp, and he sat in one of those fancy ergonomic task chairs that reminded Petra of a bewinged Amazon insect.

"Cuppers," she said quietly.

He looked up. His smile was instant and glorious.

She pushed out of the doorway and took a step toward him. "It was the best I could come up with on short notice," she said. "All in all, I'd say you're much better at coming up with alternate underwear words than I am."

She took off her coat and draped it on a chair. He looked at her, in her tall chocolate boots and short skirt.

"Cuppers," he said, turning the word over slowly on his tongue.

He rose slowly. There was a hint of a smile on his lips.

Petra's heart began to beat very fast.

She almost felt the release of adrenaline into her bloodstream as he started to prowl toward her. But she was frozen, her lips slightly parted. She was in grave danger, half exhilarated, half terrified. Her mouth curved up into a crazy smile.

"Interesting choice," he purred. "I never would have thought to go that way, to go with something that holds your pussy and ass in place, maybe even warms them."

She nodded.

"Which, I suppose," he added conversationally, taking another step toward her, "would make me jealous of the underpants."

He came just far enough that he wasn't touching her, just close enough that he could reach around her to slide one finger down her skirt-clad rear. "'Course, cuppers don't exactly describe thongs, do they?"

"I hate the word thong," she said, her voice coming out as a whisper.

He slid his hand to the hem of her skirt.

"I wanted to talk to you about something," she said quickly.

His hand stilled. Her breath, his breath, rasped.

"I miss you. I want to be around you. But I lose my head around you, and that scares me."

He dropped his hand. "I love you," he said.

Her heart fell into her boots and swooped up again until she felt dizzy.

She closed her eyes to still herself, to stifle the ecstatic smile that threatened to crack her face and overwhelm her whole body. She stamped her foot, hard. "Dammit, this kind of thing is exactly what I'm talking about," she half shouted, half whispered.

Her fingers had curled into fists, but Ian grabbed them and laughed softly. When she opened her eyes again, he was still laughing, and relieved, and dazed, and backing her into the doorway. Without turning from her, he shut the door and locked it. "I love you," he repeated wonderingly, putting his arms around her waist and pressing himself against her.

"I love you, too, but—"

In a moment he had unzipped her skirt. "You aren't wearing any—"

"Don't say it."

"—thing. You walked out into the winter without a single cupper to keep you warm."

"I was feeling optimistic," she said, kissing his neck. "It's a new thing I'm trying."

She gave a wide lick to his throat and started to undo his shirt buttons. "Although I don't think we should settle on cuppers," she added.

He took his hands from her momentarily to remove his pants and shoes. *Naked*, she thought with a shiver. He pulled her into his warm body again. "I was trying it out in a sentence," he whispered in her ear. "As one should."

They worked their way to his dark wood desk. He smoothed his hands across her shoulder blades and down her spine as he kissed her neck. She wedged her arm between their bodies to grasp his erection, but he was holding her too close. She settled for maneuvering her fingers around the head and moving her thumb back and forth, but that was hardly satisfying. She wriggled back and parted her legs. It was difficult to sit on the surface, especially with the laptop computer just inches behind her, so she held on to the edge and arched her back to rub herself against him. Ian complied with her demand. He dropped his mouth to her chest, opening his mouth wide over one breast, while his tongue flicked over her nipple.

She gasped with the pleasure of it and pressed herself forward. She wanted more: more pressure, more lips, more stubble, more teeth, more cock, but he was holding back. She hooked a leg around his waist to pull him closer. She was still wearing her boots, she noticed. That excited her even more, and she rolled her hips, sliding her greedy pelvis against his prick.

He pulled his head up, teeth gritted. "I don't have a condom," he whispered, his eyes flashing almost angrily behind his glasses.

"I'm not on the pill."

"I know." A pause. "I don't see why you haven't written yourself a prescription."

She got off his lap. "That's not really right," she said. "I should really go in for a checkup."

But Sarah was her ob/gyn. Both of them had conveniently forgotten that fact. Petra was going to have to point that ethical lapse out to her... later.

Despite the large outpourings of emotion, the mood had been somewhat dampened. Petra grasped the edge of the desk so that she wouldn't wring her hands. But Ian pried them off. He brought her to the chair and set her gently on the waffled seat. She was going to have red hashes on her bottom, she thought, as he pushed her legs apart and looked at her. He blinked gently. "Scoot a little forward," he said.

"Ian, you don't have to—"

He fiddled with something just out of her sight and the chair rose with a *psshhh* of air. Her knees were now level with his face. His breath skittered over her skin and she squirmed in excitement and embarrassment. He smoothed his fingers up her thighs. "Let me do this," he crooned, turning the chair gently.

He followed the line of her inner thigh muscle with his thumb. She could feel his breath warming her knees.

Why was she protesting? It wasn't as if they hadn't done this before. Why was she afraid of letting him give her this at this moment?

With his other hand, he rounded his palm gently under her and brought her forward. The chair hissed again and tilted toward him and he began to touch her. He ghosted his fingers over the line of her folds, up and down lightly until she felt herself become liquid. She sighed and settled back. Her bunched skirt hid him from view except the top of his head. Sometimes his brows appeared, sometimes the inscrutable shine of his glasses. She saw, briefly, one eye flicked upward.

She felt him open her inner lips slowly, circling, circling until she wasn't sure if she was moving or if he was. A finger teased her entrance and she shifted toward it. She wanted to wrap her legs around his head and pull him in. She wanted so much, so much of everything, but even as she longed for it, it seemed he was moving away. A sob of frustration choked in her throat and she wanted to cry out at him. She almost felt angry. "Please," she said, shifting restlessly. "Please come back."

As if he knew what she'd been thinking, he glided the chair closer and moved her legs, still heavy and encased in her boots, over his shoulders. She dug her thick heels into his back and whimpered. He moved his head closer and licked her and she jolted. She could hear the wet lap of his tongue, drinking her up, sucking her in. She moaned again. Her hips lifted and his stubble-covered cheeks pulled at the skin of her thighs. He delved deeper now, his thirsty sounds driving her wild, until he reached her clit. She could feel the tip of a digit tracing her delicately and she cried out. She was close. He pulled her wider, drawing her apart. His fingers dug heavily into her and his mouth continued to move, licking ever so gently. She wanted him forever, she thought, shivering. Her hands were at her nipples now. She was all open, and every touch from every part of his body made her surge up and up. She couldn't hold together. She was going to fall into pieces under his hands. His lips gave another tug on her and she came with a cry, her body jerking. The chair bumped with her, swinging gently left and right. He had pulled away, although his hands still worked her. His face, appearing above her skirt, was pleased and wondrous.

She was sweating when she fell back into the seat. Ian fiddled with the chair again and it moved down with another puff of air. She couldn't wait for its slow mechanics, so she pulled him into her and kissed him, kissed his lips wet with her. His glasses were smudged and completely askew. He got up and picked her up and sat down himself, arranging her in his lap. They pressed their foreheads together and Petra found her heart slowing and slowing until her body was calm again.

–

Later, Ian had some food packed up in the kitchen. He snagged a bottle of champagne. He wanted to take her home and celebrate properly. They had condoms there. They could have more sex there.

He was happy.

Walking back to his apartment in the winter air, his arm wrapped around her, his body pressed as close as it could be to hers, he fretted over how cold she must be and grinned like an idiot at everyone they passed.

She loved him. He loved her. How simple and wonderful it was. They kissed in the elevator and in the hallway. When they got in the door, they dropped their bag with a clunk and shed their clothes on the way to the bedroom. Afterward, he wrapped her up snugly in blankets and spread the food out on the bed. He opened the warm champagne and they drank it out of mugs. They ate too much and she fell asleep. He watched her and in the morning, they woke up together, fuzzy-mouthed but happy. He insisted on driving her back to her apartment so that she could get warm clothes. He set out for Field for an early start. She went to her office.

And that's when it all started to go off the rails.

Chapter Twenty-Two

The first phone call came from Ellie. "Petra, where the hell are you? I've been trying to reach you for hours."

Petra contained her urge to squeal, *I was with my boooyyyfriend*, and simply said, "I was out."

Nonetheless, a tiny hiccup of delight managed to escape her. Ellie ignored it.

"Well, the divorce came through and Mom and Jim decided not to wait. They're getting married the weekend after next," Ellie said. "You didn't pick up your phone so Mom, in her usual Lisa Lale fashion, assumed you didn't want to talk to her."

A few days ago, Petra would have been dismayed by the news of Lisa's rapidly impending nuptials. Today, it barely managed to squelch her. "I will call her, I promise."

"Pete," Ellie said, "what are we going to do?"

"What do you mean?" Petra asked.

She had a patient arriving in five minutes. She started to go through her notes.

"I mean, it's too soon!" Ellie wailed.

"Seriously? You're getting upset about this now, after screaming at me to be more supportive and stop being negative?"

"It's just so soon. I wanted a little more time to prepare."

"Well, you've had six more months than me. Suck it up."

Petra hung up.

She took a deep breath. Ellie had been preternaturally calm for most of her life. She was entitled to a flip out occasionally. After a cooling-off period, Petra would call again and try to smooth it out. But Ellie was not going to spoil her mood.

She stuck her chin out and gave a determined smile.

Her patients today were the usual mix of the itching and the cursing. She dropped a few shots and rubbed cream on arms. She administered spirometry to a coughing fifty-year-old bank manager and jumped up and down shouting encouragement to blow. It was times like these that Petra wished that her office walls were a little thicker. Three times, they performed the test; the bank manager's forced expiratory volume sucked. Petra told Joanie to arrange for a follow-up appointment.

Before she knew it, it was lunchtime. Joanie was out so Petra took a call from her landlord, Mr. Willand. He told her that the downstairs tenants were moving out and asked if she would she be interested in taking over the space. Petra put down her yogurt and tried not to laugh too hard.

She did not tell him that she was barely getting by, but she did let him know that there would be little chance that she'd need the extra room.

"The downstairs is not that big or expensive. I'd rather have someone take both spaces at once," he started to say.

They had decided on a short-term lease, which although it was unusual for a business, Petra thought prudent at the time. The landlord argued that they could renew at the end of the year. He seemed, at the time, to like the idea of a doctor taking the upstairs office. Now Petra realized that she might have hamstrung herself with her cautious move. It was as if she had expected herself to fail, that she had expected to give up the business, and tried to cut her losses ahead of time.

Willand said something about how much trouble it was to have two separate tenants, how the quilters on the first floor had been pretty much perfect except for the fact that quilting was probably not the most profitable enterprise, and he speculated about how much he could get for the spaces combined, as if she weren't there.

"But you'll renew me for next year if I want to?" she asked, her anxiety kicking to a higher pitch.

She couldn't relocate her practice. She loved this place and it had been hard enough getting people in the door to begin with. How would she do it if she had to change addresses, move delicate allergen bottles, and print new business cards? What if she had to leave the neighborhood? She'd have to get a car. She could definitely not afford a car.

Mr. Willand sighed gustily and gave a wobbly, "Well, we'll see, Doc," which didn't bode well at all.

The third phone call came from Kevin's father's administrative assistant.

She informed Petra that all of Kevin's future appointments were canceled.

–

"Heard that you and the doctor crept out of here late last night," Gerry said, standing in the doorway.

Ian looked up from his computer. In truth, he hadn't been getting much work done, especially because Petra had been sitting naked on his lap on this very chair just last night, and she had told him that she loved him.

He was never getting rid of this chair.

"It's very, very serious," Ian tried to say seriously. He was hampered by the shit-eating grin on his face.

"Oh, I'll say," said Gerry. "You've got it bad." He dropped into a chair. "Am I going to have to go ring shopping with you?"

"It's too early to tell," said Ian. In truth, he had already been thinking about what would look good on her small, cool fingers.

There was his mother's silver ring. He thought about giving it to Petra, later. It was beautiful, and the kind of thing she might like. But he thought about his parents' marriage, the false starts and imperfections, the loneliness. It was definitely far too soon, he told himself.

"I've decided to hire an assistant manager for Field. I need to loosen my grip on a few things," Ian said.

Gerry pretended to choke. Ian ignored him.

"It's hardly a fledgling business anymore," he continued. "Lilah is doing well with Stream. Yet I'm still out there, working repairs and dealing with taxes and permits, bussing tables, and generally just doing anything that needs doing. I realize that I should have just hired people for this a long time ago. It makes no sense for me to be in this place all the time. I thought I'd start to retreat from the business more formally. Maybe take a vacation or go traveling."

Take Petra to Bora Bora and make love to her until neither of them could walk straight.

"Finally, finally, the day has come when Ian Zamora, the seemingly lazy and charming playboy admits that his steely control freak side exists. Whatever will the world do? Will the walls cave in? Will the sun start revolving around the moon?"

"The steely control freak is not amused by your sarcasm."

"Who knew that it would take bringing a woman down here to make you give it up? Maybe the doctor is good for what ails you."

There was a knock at the door.

"We're one short on the floor," called one of the servers. "Jenny's nowhere to be found."

Ian sighed. "I guess I won't be stepping back tonight."

Gerry and Ian went upstairs. The dining room was pleasantly full. Ian moved around and greeted a few regulars. But the servers were definitely a little stressed. Ian sidled up to Winn.

"Any idea where she might be?"

"We've been run off our feet and girl chooses now to disappear. Last time I checked, she was headed to the bathrooms. I think with a customer. A male customer."

Winn rolled his eyes.

Really? Ian thought, heading toward the bathroom. *Really, Jenny?*

Ian rattled the door and called.

No moans, no giggling, no thumping. Despite what Winn assumed, Jenny wasn't having sex in the bathroom. He flushed slightly, wondering what he and Petra had sounded like last night, and wondered if any of his staff had heard them.

But the silence was worrisome. Even if someone had a legitimate reason to be inside, he would have said something. Was someone dead in there? Had something happened?

Ian took out his Swiss Army knife and stuck a long prong in the doorknob. It opened easily.

Jenny was sitting on the floor holding her hands over her chest. The customer, a young businessy-type in a rumpled suit, was leaning over the counter holding a baggie with white powder.

Ian didn't want to know. He didn't want to involve police or ambulances. He just wanted it gone. He made sure Jenny was reasonably well, called her roommate, and sent all of them away in cabs. He was smoothing it over. The thought was fleeting. He put his head down and worked, waiting tables that night for the first time in — well, it hadn't been that long. It might be a good idea to create a list of substitute wait staff, he thought, instead of always trying to do it himself. He would track down some Field alum and see if they wanted to earn extra money on occasion.

Petra was making him more efficient, he decided after the restaurant closed. This was all stuff that he had put off and thought they couldn't afford. It was what he used to do because he could just go and be alone and fix the damn refrigerator for an hour and no one would bother him. He thought of his mother and her incessant cleaning. He thought of his father and how often the man simply disappeared.

But tonight, he was tired of all that. He wanted to take a shower and sink into his couch, or rather, sink into the couch with Petra dozing against him. He wished she were there. He added giving her a set of keys to his to-do list.

The phone call came as he was about to turn down his block.

"Are you busy?" she whispered.

"No. I was just thinking about you. Are you all right?"

Her voice sounded shivery and frail. His heart clenched as he waited for her answer.

"I lost Kevin," Petra said. "I mean, he's fine," she added quickly. "He's gone as a patient. His father's secretary called and told me that they're switching to a different allergist. They didn't explain, but I'm guessing the dad was disturbed because I was out with him.

"The worst thing is," she continued, "I know I crossed the line. I did the wrong thing last night – I made several bad choices. I adore Kevin. I know I'm not supposed to get involved, but how can I help but get involved in his life?"

"You did nothing wrong. Kevin followed you. The man is being a jerk." He switched the phone to his other ear and picked up speed. "I'm coming over."

"You don't have to," she said dully.

"Hey, I know Kevin, I know how the little bugger can get under your skin. I'll just pick up some clothes from my place and be over there in fifteen minutes, all right?"

Maybe he could have a quick shower at her place. Maybe he could convince her to join him. He had never been in her shower before, he realized.

Was he a jerk for thinking about sex when his girlfriend was obviously distraught?

He felt reasonably confident that Kevin would be able to talk his father out of this. This was *Kevin*, after all. The kid was persistent. Ian would give Kevin some pointers tomorrow, he decided, maybe discuss strategy with him.

He had no doubt he could smooth this over, too.

–

Petra looked calm when she opened the door to him. Her face was scrubbed clean for bed, and he loved how bare and soft it looked. He touched her nose.

She sighed and put her cheek in his palm.

"I think I may not be cut out to be a physician," Petra said.

"That's not true."

"I can give people the right medicine and keep up with the research, and all the clinical stuff. But it's more than that. Obviously, I care about my patients, but I just don't know how to strike the right balance. I messed up with Kevin. Sometimes, I still wonder if I messed up with you."

Ian felt an initial shiver. "Let's not go down that road right now, okay?" He guided her to the couch.

"I've lost two patients that I couldn't afford to lose," Petra said. "I might lose more before the year is out."

She told him about her landlord's phone call. Ian shook his head. "You can find another location. I'll help you. I know a good commercial broker and she'll be able to give you better advice about selecting a space and negotiating a lease than your last one did. Patients will follow if you give them enough notice. This has nothing to do with your abilities as a doctor," Ian said. "It's just business."

"Being a physician is also about being a businessperson," she said. "Not that they teach you any of that in medical school. But I can't help anyone if my practice fails. I have a responsibility to my patients in that way, too. It's not something I can compartmentalize. I'm just too much of a mess all over.

"I envy you, in a way," she said, her voice a little muffled. "Things seem to come easy to you."

He pushed up his glasses and rubbed his face. "Petra, if you think things come easy to me, then you don't know me well enough yet," he said. He let a little of his frustration show. "I've had a hell of a day, too, as a matter of fact."

Petra was silent. Then she shook her head. "That was unfair of me. I'm sorry. What happened?"

"Had to fire a server. She was doing drugs in the bathroom with a customer. It was a mess."

"God, I'm sorry, that sounds awful. Is she okay?"

"It's all right. It's done. Look, we can talk to Kevin tomorrow, see if he can persuade his dad to let you be his doctor again."

"I can't do that. It wouldn't be right for me to use my influence on Kevin to undermine his dad's authority."

"Do you always have to be scrupulous about this? Isn't there any wiggle room in these rules for doctors now and then? Aren't you allowed to be human?"

Her face set and she was about to say something again. He held up his hand. "It's okay, you don't have to talk to Kevin."

But he would, he told himself. There was nothing that said he couldn't say anything.

Petra sighed. "Another thing. My mom is getting married on the Saturday after next. I managed to get a hold of her today. It'll be small. If you come, you can meet my sister."

"Of course I'll be there."

He felt tense. He had thought that he would be the one consoling her and that later, he could make her feel better. Instead, he was pushing against her. Their peace seemed to be a delicate line. The only thing that kept them from screaming was his wish that they not fight. He asked if he could use her shower and she nodded. "You know," he couldn't help saying before he disappeared into the bathroom, "you can't use this stuff as an excuse to say everything in your life is shot to hell. Just because one thing is not perfect doesn't mean everything else will be terrible. It's an overreaction. You just need time to let things settle down. It will all be fine."

Ian didn't allow himself to see her face before he went in. He was afraid of how she might look.

When he came back out, she was already in bed. She lay on her back staring glassily at the ceiling. She wore a raggedy Ramones T-shirt. He kissed her and wrapped his body around hers. She stroked his hair. He could tell how tired she was, but he was content to be holding her.

"Yesterday, I was so happy," she said, before she fell asleep.

He lay frozen, with her form heavy in his arms. His mother had said something like that before, on the plane, when they were taking off from PDX after leaving her town again. They were going back to South America that last time. She had mumbled it over and over again. Not long afterward, she was dead.

He turned over and looked at Petra's face.

He wasn't enough to make her happy, he thought. He wasn't enough.

Chapter Twenty-Three

At least she had managed to get enough sleep, Petra thought as she woke the next morning. Ian clutched her particularly possessively. His arm anchored around her waist, his body molded to hers as if to prevent her – or himself – from drowning. She worked herself free and sat up on the side of the bed, pausing for a moment to stare at his still sleeping torso. He really was perfectly formed, she thought, tracing his lats and deltoids with her eyes. Even at rest, his muscles formed crisp lines in his shoulders and arms, interrupted only by the burr of wiry hair on his chest.

Perfect.

Unease wormed itself into her.

She had been goading him last night, and she didn't know why. It was as if she wanted him to admit to some unspecified wrongdoing. Maybe she wanted him to agree with her, that she was at fault about Kevin, that she was a terrible doctor and businesswoman. And she was, of course. Then again, she also didn't want him to agree. She just wanted to see how far she could push him before he got frustrated. He had gotten angry, but not over her, not over what she deemed her incompetence as a physician. He had been unhappy with her unhappiness.

Frowning and dissatisfied, she headed for the shower.

Petra was gone before Ian woke. He had slept badly, tossing and turning through the night.

The first thing he did was pop off a text message to Kevin. The kid didn't reply, but that was okay. Teens went to school, didn't they? Maybe later, Ian could arrange to meet Kevin at Field. He didn't think it would be hard to get Kevin to convince his father.

The easiest of his tasks completed, Ian worked his way through a to-do list that included composing an ad to find a manager for Field, finding a new linen supplier, calling a dishwasher repairman, checking Lilah's tweets for Stream, and, of course, putting together Jenny's dismissal letter and calculating her final paycheck.

Frowning, he added a personal note, asking her to let him know if she was okay.

Ordinarily, he worked through administrative stuff dispassionately, but today, he found it hard not to be angry at the old linen supplier for failing to get the tablecloths white, and at the repairman for ducking Ian's calls, at Lilah for the constant chatter, and at Jenny for jeopardizing herself and her job. He was definitely not pissed off at Petra.

He took a deep breath. He was definitely not pissed.

If anything, he was angry at himself. That was not a new feeling.

His phone rang and he checked the screen. It was Danielle. With trepidation he picked up.

"Ian, I had no one else to ask, and I was wondering if you'd do me a favor. Would you mind taking Snuffy for me?"

"I can't. I'm allergic and Petra is, too."

He realized belatedly that he shouldn't have let Petra's name slip.

"Tsk, tsk. An allergic allergist. It's like the cobbler's children who have no shoes. But I don't really have a lot of options. No one else knows him the way you do."

"Can't you board him?"

Danielle paused. "I was hoping you could take him, you know, for the long term."

"First of all, no. And second, were you thinking that you could sneak the longer term by me? How long are we talking?"

"Well, for a good long time, actually. You see, I've met someone. You know him, actually. Juan, from Carioca. And," she hesitated, "we've decided to move in together."

"How nice for you two," Ian said drily.

"You could be happier for me. After all, you found yourself another girlfriend quickly enough."

Ian tapped on his laptop.

After a short silence, Danielle continued, "Juan is allergic to cats."

Ian groaned.

Danielle continued, "And since Snuffy is used to you, I thought—"

"No, absolutely not."

"Listen, Ian, you know I'm not one of those people who likes to play hardball. I try to negotiate with every side in mind. But I need to do what's best for Snuffy. In this case, I think it's leaving Snuffy with a person who has shown him attention and knows his quirks. Plus, you're such a straight arrow, you'll make sure he's taken care of well."

"But I told you, Danielle, I don't actually want him. If you love him and want to protect him, why don't you keep him yourself instead of throwing him over for your boyfriend? He's a nice enough cat, but I'm allergic and the woman I love is allergic to him."

There was another silence.

"About this woman you love…" Danielle bit off the word and Ian had a moment of regret for announcing it so blatantly. "I wonder what a medical board might say about a doctor who is dating a former patient."

"Jesus, Danielle. We didn't start dating until after I'd left her practice."

"I'm not sure if those are the facts."

Danielle was going to lie. She would actually lie to the medical board. "Why would you do that? Why on earth would you be so malicious toward someone you don't even know?"

"This is about love, Ian, something that you seem to suddenly know so much about now. You know, you never once told me you loved me, Ian. Not once while we were together. Do you know how awful it is to be the 'good enough' woman? Do you have any idea what it's like to be neglected and taken for granted? Now, you're with…" She paused. "…Petra, a slightly unusual name, and you were seeing her before you even dumped me—"

"That's not true!"

"So you allege. And you expect me to feel sorry for her? You're the one begrudging me my love for Juan, when I clearly deserve something after what you put me through. So yeah, love. I'm in love, and I love Snuffy, Ian. I just want to protect him, like any mama would. I know that you will take care of him. You always did. I'll stop by your apartment tonight with the carrier and some food and his toys."

She hung up.

248

He pushed up his glasses and rubbed his face.

She sounded sweet and heartbroken and outraged while she stomped all over his relationship. She made him think that maybe he had been a bit of an asshole. Perhaps it was true, and he owed her an apology for that.

But he couldn't care for her cat.

He thought of Petra and he thought of how she'd taken it when Kevin's father had canceled the appointment. She had almost come close, so close, to saying that she regretted getting involved with him. He had seen it in her face. Danielle's threat would devastate Petra and it had the potential to really hurt her practice. Although Petra had done nothing wrong, maybe her license would get suspended. He could not reopen that wound. He had to protect her. But what was he going to tell Petra about this cat?

Maybe he could keep Snuffy for a little while and bundle the big guy off to someone else. Or maybe this thing with Juan wouldn't last and Danielle would want Snuffy back, eventually. But Ian couldn't count on that.

This wasn't something that could be smoothed over. Not by a long shot.

–

After all the confusion and heartache of the day, Petra wanted to go to Ian and sit in his lap. She arrived at Field, hoping Ian was in, and was surprised to be told that he was working from home. She dialed his number and started out for his apartment.

Strange, no answer.

She started down the street to her apartment, thinking that she would call him again after she'd grabbed a few things. Maybe she could pick up dinner.

She could make him food, she thought suddenly. She wasn't the best, but Lisa had made sure that her girls had survival skills. Petra could boil pasta, or sear a steak. She had even made lasagna once or twice in her life. She wondered about his kitchen equipment. A steak would only require a pan, or something like that.

It was all so domestic, she thought to herself as she put together an overnight bag and contemplated her under-wear. It scared her, negotiating these little details. She wanted things to be better between them. The first night – she considered it their first real night – had been great, the second, wobbly. Third time was the charm, she decided. She had told herself that she would let go a little bit; she could become a more optimistic person. True, she had not been happier today, but she shouldn't fall apart after one or two or possibly three setbacks, depending on how she looked at it. Ian had soothed her. He had wanted to help her. The least she could do was be grateful. She picked up a sleek blue bra she hadn't worn much before. It was a little uncomfortable but it wouldn't be on for long.

Plus, it looked pretty good. A little shiver of anticip-ation rolled through her. It gave her more bounce per ounce. She pulled on a fuzzy sweater and her skirt, the lucky boots and coat, and gave Ian another call.

Still no answer.

It didn't matter, she told herself. It really didn't.

She picked up wine and groceries. She bought tea for the next morning. She picked up a bouquet of gerbera daisies and then put them down again. She picked up a small cactus.

Armed her with bags and wine, she started to feel better. There were things to look forward to in life. She could make a decent dinner – or maybe Ian would take over and cook it for them. She looked cute in her little sweater and skirt, and he would be gorgeous and maybe a little grumpy and rumpled. Even if he had work, she was sure that she would be able to lure him to bed. Luckily, someone was coming out of the building as she came in and held the door open for her.

She was halfway down the hall when a woman strode toward her, a tall, polished woman with sleek hair. Petra watched as she dug in the buttery leather bag she was holding and found a pair of soft gloves. She pulled them on, and the whole while, Petra was conscious of the woman's curvaceous figure, her long legs encased in expensive trousers.

She was the woman that Petra had always wished she could be. She was quite possibly perfect.

Petra had slowed her walk down to a stop, but the woman passed by Petra without giving her a glance. The woman was lost in her own thoughts.

It was hard to feel admiration for her, though. It was hard to feel anything but a cold numbness in the perfect woman's presence.

The elevator doors opened and the woman stepped in.

It might have been fine if she'd been just beautiful, or smug, or well dressed, or if she had a great figure, or all of those elements in greater or lesser quantities. It would not have mattered. But the thing that made Petra want to grab the woman and stop her – the thing that had made Petra take a second hard look at her at all – was the fact that the very perfect woman had come out from Ian's door.

Chapter Twenty-Four

Ian wasn't cheating on her. The woman's vibe had not been post-coital. It had been brittle and determined, as if she had finished a difficult section of a triathlon and had one more event to go. Not that Petra would know anything about that.

She knew Ian. Mostly. It had been about a month, but of course their acquaintance extended longer than that. She trusted him. But it was just...

Petra put the bags down in the middle of the hallway and wiped her face with the back of her hand. She was sweaty from standing in the overheated hallway in her coat, carrying her bags, and her skirt was twisted around her ass. Her hair was probably frizzing. She was a mess. She was a fucking wet, drippy mess in the middle of the tastefully neutral hallway of a fancy glass and chrome building, in a neighborhood that she would never have been able to afford, about to cook dinner for a man whom she should never have fallen for, a man who belonged with the perfect woman who had just left his apartment, rather than with plain, flawed Petra Lale. There was probably a perfectly reasonable explanation for everything, she thought, slowly unbuttoning her coat. All of her insecurities threatened to overwhelm her.

Why hadn't he answered his phone, dammit?

She didn't know how long she stood there, trying to decide whether to walk the rest of the way to his door or not. She flapped at herself, willing the perspiration away. Finally, after one of Ian's neighbors emerged from his apartment and frowned at her, she closed her eyes and made a decision.

At the far end of the hallway, she called him.

This time, he answered right away. "Petra," he said, "I'm sorry I didn't pick up before. I was occupied with something."

Did he sound relieved? Scared? Guilty? Normal? She huddled over her phone although she knew he wouldn't be able to hear how near she stood. "So, what were you doing that kept you so occupied?" she whispered.

A pause.

"It's complicated," he said. "I'll explain it all to you in person."

Was he planning on breaking up with her?

God, where had that come from?

"I was thinking of making dinner," she said. "I picked up some wine and stuff. I'm not the best cook—"

"You're going to cook for me? That's so nice. I don't remember the last time anyone's done that. People are usually intimidated because—"

She was standing in the hallway of the apartment of her boyfriend, the only man she could remember saying *I love you* to, and having an awkward second- or third-date conversation.

"Well, don't expect much. I'm not, like, great or anything."

Another pause. There was the sound of a bump in the background and a hiss.

He said, "Yeah, well, why don't I come over in, say, an hour. I have something to take care of here." Another thump. "And I should clean up a little."

What did he have to take care of? What on earth would he have to clean up? Suddenly Petra's throat closed up and she couldn't speak.

"Petra," he asked, when she didn't say anything. "Are you there?"

"Closer than you think," she said quietly.

"Petra, I'm sorry. I can't hear you."

She had to do this. She cleared her throat and picked up the bags, dragging everything awkwardly down the hallway. "Actually, I'm here," she said.

"I'm sorry, what?"

"I'm right here. Outside your door."

There was a long pause and Petra's heart started thumping.

Bad things were about to happen.

Ian's door opened and he poked his head out. He looked terrible. His eyes were red-rimmed behind his glasses and when he came out into the hallway to help her with the groceries, he sneezed.

"You can't go in there," he said.

She had been about to use her doctor voice on him, but now she didn't care. She didn't care who heard her. She was not going to take this shit anymore. "Why the hell not?"

He sneezed again and gave a snort worthy of Kevin.

"Why the hell not?" she repeated, her voice getting louder.

"It's not safe," he said, finally.

"Ian," she said quietly, "what do you not want me to see?"

He froze and said nothing. She grabbed the key from his pocket.

"Hey," he said, but he couldn't stop her with his arms full of bags.

She threw the door wide, and before he could say anything more, a cat streaked out.

—

For an elderly, fat fluffball, Snuffy was pretty damn fast. Ian shoved the groceries into Petra's arms and told her, "Stow these and I'll go after him," then he took off.

Snuffy had already disappeared around the corner. With a groan, Ian realized that someone had left the fire exit propped open. He clattered into the stairwell and started calling. In a few minutes, Petra joined him.

"I'm sorry," she said. "I had no idea."

"Yeah," was all he could say. He had a headache.

"We could split up," she said, biting her lip. "I'll head upstairs, you head down."

He nodded. That sounded sensible. In a few moments, he heard Petra clucking softly from above him, and he started to do the same.

The stairwell smelled like cigarette smoke. He was glad he wasn't allergic to that.

He considered how upset Petra had looked when she grabbed his keys. She knew he was hiding something, but he'd hardly put on a good show of it on the phone. He was going to have to tell her at least part of the truth, although he supposed he could still conceal the bit about Danielle threatening to go to the medical board. Perhaps it wasn't wise to keep it from her, but Petra was sensitive to this — hell, he was sensitive to this, especially now that she'd lost Kevin. He needed to deal with this on his own. He noticed that another door was propped open, and he swore softly. What the hell kind of building was he living in, anyway? Not that he'd be able to stay in his apartment with Snuffmaster Six there. His throat was threatening to close up, or was that fear? Or maybe he was having a bodily reaction to Danielle, who'd walked through his apartment so smugly after setting down the cat carrier.

He wondered how he had managed to go out with the woman.

He slipped through the door and scouted the hallway. It looked disorientingly like his own, which made sense. He sneezed again and went back out.

At least he could rule that floor out.

He could still hear the echo of Petra calling faintly. Her voice was the voice of longing. He wished he could abandon the damned cat and go up to her and grab her and take her back to his apartment and to his bed and just pretend nothing had happened. They could spend all their days and the rest of their lives there. But he had to protect her from Danielle's malice. He had to keep Petra from being hurt by his stupidity and carelessness.

He found two more open doors and scouted two more sets of surreal hallways. For the first time, he realized that the odd numbered floors had light blue carpets and the even numbered floors, like his, were a faint green.

He reached the exit to the rear of the building and the locked basement door. Either Snuffy was really lost, or maybe Petra had found him.

He didn't know which possibility he hated more.

Ian started to bound up the stairs. If Petra had managed to corner him, the least he could do was keep her from the beast. Not that Snuffy was a bad cat, but he hated to think of Petra sniffling and coughing because he had been an idiot.

He didn't even know how bad Petra's reactions were. Would she be flattened by them? Would her throat close up? He hoped that she'd brought her purse with her into the stairwell. He knew how prepared she was for emergencies. He gave a small smile, thinking of how he'd unearthed a pair of panties from that huge bag she carried.

Bloomers, he corrected himself. *Asslettes, rearlies, good girls.*

Damn, he wished she were here with him.

He went past his own floor, paused for a breath, and continued up, panting now and sweaty. He could hear nothing except the sound of his (admittedly loud) breathing. At a door propped open by a fire hose, he heard it.

Petra was crouched, half singing, half whispering an old Dolly Parton song. Snuffy was a few feet away, tail twitching. He was listening, his delicately translucent ears swiveling at every high note.

Ian had never heard her sing before. She had claimed that she couldn't. But her voice was sweet and soft and the notes swooped around them like liquid. It was a revelation.

He loved her. His heart cracked and overflowed. He loved her so much.

Snuffy apparently agreed. He inched forward and as the last notes died, he allowed Petra to gather him up. She put her nose into his fur.

Then she sneezed.

By the time they got back to Ian's floor, they were watery-eyed messes. By silent agreement, they stowed Snuffy back at Ian's apartment and headed to Petra's.

She was going to dose them both with diphenhydramine, wash her face, and burn her clothes. That seemed like the only sensible solution.

She left the groceries at Ian's. She was in no mood to cook now.

They did not talk, although there were things to say. The woman leaving Ian's apartment was the ex-girlfriend, the woman for whom Ian had decided to brave immunotherapy. Now Ian had her cat.

Petra tried to wrap her mind around it. She tried to imagine the steps that had led to this, but her brain simply stuttered on Danielle's beauty and expensive glamor, then shut down entirely. She sniffled and felt in her pockets for a tissue. Ian handed her a travel packet and she accepted. He took out another for himself. He'd had time to prepare, she thought dully.

At least the cold rain felt good against her itchy face.

Ian was trying to shelter her from the water. She could feel him moving in closer to cradle her under his arm, but she moved away and stared at the buildings.

They entered her apartment and she left him to go to her room to take off her clothing. The fuzz of her sweater had undoubtedly mated with Snuffy's fur and was now producing dander babies. She ripped the offending garment from her and stuffed it deep into her laundry bag. It probably had to be dry-cleaned. She didn't care.

Ian came into her room. She was still in her skirt and boots, and on top she still wore the blue bra she'd been so happy with only a few hours before.

Ian came up behind her and put his hands on her hips. He smoothed his hands up her waist, up to her breasts.

"Don't," she whispered.

He dropped his hands.

She pulled on a sweatshirt.

"I saw her leave your apartment," she said.

She didn't look at him.

"Did she say something to you?"

"No, why would she even know what I look like? What would she have to say to me?"

Ian was silent.

"Ian, why do you have her cat? I didn't think that you agreed to be friends. Why are you even seeing her?"

Ian rubbed his itchy eyes and face.

"She sort of coerced me into taking the cat."

Petra whirled around.

"How? And how long are you going to have him? You can't stay in your apartment as long as he's there."

Ian stifled a sigh.

"She's angry with me over how things ended. I was careless of her feelings and making me keep Snuffy is sort of her revenge."

"You mean you have to keep the cat forever?"

"I'm figuring it out."

It was true. He had been thinking frantically about how he was going to take care of this, but none of his solutions looked very good.

"I'm allergic to cats! Hell, you're allergic to cats! What does this mean for us?"

He was only answering ten percent of the questions she was asking, and still there were more and more and more. She shucked off her boots and skirt now and this time, Ian didn't bother to hide his groan.

"What does she have on you? You didn't do anything dishonest, did you?"

"I didn't do anything dishonest."

"Tell me."

"I can't."

Another pause. Petra said, "One of us has to give something here. And it's not going to be me."

Ian said nothing.

"Does she want you back?" Petra asked.

"No."

"Are you still in love with her?" she asked, averting her face, almost as if she expected to be hit with something awful.

His heart almost broke. He reached out for her slowly and ran his fingertip along her jaw. She allowed that much.

"No, definitely not. I love you."

She pulled away again. She rummaged in her overstuffed closet and pulled out a pair of sweatpants. He noticed that she did not say *I love you* back.

She was waiting.

"Danielle was in the restaurant the other night," he said.

"You saw her before tonight, and you didn't think to tell me?"

"It didn't matter. I didn't ask her there. Gerry let slip something that I wanted to keep private, and she... she used it as leverage for me to take the cat. She's moving in with a guy who's allergic."

"You should have told me. It's kind of a big deal."

"But I didn't think she'd do anything about it. She was angry with me for being happy and in love with you. I never was there for her and we both knew it."

"What is it that she knows about you?"

Ian paused. "I don't want to tell you. I just need you to trust me that I'm trying not to hurt anyone."

Petra shook her head. "I don't know if I can accept that. You need to tell me more. I don't know that you're giving me enough."

Ian tried another tactic. "Look, he's not a bad cat," he said.

"He's sweet, but..."

"We could get shots."

It was the wrong thing to say.

She was shaking her head again and backing away. Ian found himself unable to stop his own mouth. "I can't believe you're an allergist who doesn't want to get immun-otherapy shots."

"It's not that simple. You're asking a lot, Ian."

"Why is it so much? Just tell me why. I'm willing to go back to Dr. Singh and grovel for Nasonex and a resumption of our visits. Just tell me why you won't invest in this. You could do this for us."

"No, I would not be doing this for us. I will not be railroaded into this by you and your ex for mysterious reasons."

"This would solve the problem."

"No, it would be temporarily smoothing over the problem. At this point, there are so many cracks in this story that I don't even know where the problem begins. This takes care of one symptom, not the underlying disease. Classic Ian Zamora."

"Just trust me."

"The point is that I don't," Petra said, the words cracking out like a gunshot.

She did not meet his eyes.

"I don't know if this is working out," she whispered.

"Petra, don't say that. You're under a lot of pressure now."

"That's the point. This whole relationship is too complicated. There was too much wrong with it to begin with. There's too much wrong with it now."

He balled up his fists. "Don't," he said. "Don't you think this is worth it? Petra, look at me. Please tell me you think this is worth it."

She did not look at him. "I can't talk to you right now."

"Petra."

She pushed him to the door. "Oh, and take this," she said, handing him a pill without looking at him. Her fingers barely skimmed his. "It's a Benadryl."

She shut the door.

Chapter Twenty-Five

She didn't know what was worse, the idea that he hated her, or the fact that she still loved him even while she was incredibly angry.

And she was angry.

What was this all about, anyway?

At work, she plowed through a pile of paperwork and harangued an insurance carrier over the phone. The billing codes were just fine, she argued. She used the same codes all the time. They appeased her like she was a madwoman. They gave her victory. Not that she was wrong. She was right, of course.

Joanie seemed wary of Petra's new forcefulness. Perhaps she was somewhat more aggressive than usual. Joanie did not get any reading done during work hours. The drug rep was similarly terrified and gave Petra extra samples.

Maybe this is what people had when they said they needed a spark to be successful. But her lonely triumphs didn't make Petra feel better.

Ian called several times but she ignored him. Or rather, she slammed her smartphone facedown on her desk. (On top of piles of paper. She wasn't far gone enough to damage her precious toy.) By Thursday, he seemed to have understood that she was not going to pick up and he left her alone for most of the day. She was not afraid that he would show up downstairs at her office or outside her building. She left at the time she always left. She took long runs along the water and did everything that she usually did, except talk to people.

He didn't try to see her.

She couldn't say if she was disappointed.

Of course she didn't want to see him. She didn't want to see his face, the hurt in his deep brown eyes.

At night, she tossed and turned, consumed with fury and sadness and lust and – was guilt in there, too? Her feelings made no sense. Most of the time, she reminded herself to be livid, incandescent with rage. She tried to hold on to the feeling for as long as she could, afraid that she would forget she was angry. If she didn't, she might leap right at him and tug his face down to hers.

It was never going to work out. It had been wrong from the beginning. She had started off stabbing him with needles and they had ended impaling each other's hearts. And popping allergy pills.

She wondered if he was sleeping at the office. She supposed he had no choice.

It was never going to work out.

Even though he protested that he wanted to stick around and work through this problem, this was Ian. The self-confessed smoother-over. If it caused too much trouble, if it went too deep, then he removed himself. Or was it herself she was describing?

Eyes burning, she stared at the dark ceiling.

–

She must have fallen asleep. She picked up the phone, barely awake, and when it turned out to be Sarah, she felt the disappointment that is wasn't Ian, then relief.

Not Ian. Sarah.

Luckily, her friend read nothing into Petra's silence. "I'm not on call tonight," she was shouting.

Evidently, Sarah had been up all night, delivering babies. She was always exuberant after a birth, as if she'd stolen the new mother's hormones. "I wanted to thank you, really thank you, in case you took all my grumbling and yelling for ungratefulness," she said. "Can I take you out?"

Petra closed her eyes. *Now*, after being up almost through the night, she felt like she could sleep. "I'm not really up to going out tonight," she muttered.

"Why? What's wrong?"

"Sarah, no offense, and really, this isn't about you at all. I think I just need to be alone this evening. Also, you're shouting."

"Sorry," Sarah bellowed cheerily. "I just pulled a little girl out. I *never* get to deliver babies with my Pronto patients. I love this! The parents named her Tara, which rhymes with Sarah. So far no one's named a kid after me, but I'm giving myself half a point for this one."

"I'm going back to sleep, Sarah."

"You do that, you pussy."

The morning and afternoon wore on. She stuck more people with needles and yelled at Jane Wu for overusing her bronchodilator. The girl cried and Jane Wu's mother yelled at Jane, too.

At the end of the day, Petra went home and went to bed.

Her apartment doorbell rang. She had not buzzed anyone up. Terrified and half hopeful that it was Ian, Petra checked out the peephole and Helen peered back at her. Behind her was Sarah.

Petra pulled open the door.

"If you're going to turn this into an arena fight, don't bother," Petra said, holding up her hands.

"You have got the ugliest sleepwear I've ever seen in my life," Sarah said, shouldering past her. She was carrying a pillow.

"We're having a pity party," Helen said, "and we're using your place."

Petra looked from Helen to Sarah and back again. They were acting suspiciously normal around each other, as if the last month had been erased.

"Don't the girlfriends usually come bearing affirmations and snacks?" she asked.

"Blah. You don't like my food. Plus, we knew you'd already be loaded up," Sarah said. "We didn't think we'd need more."

"Actually, I brought something," Helen said.

She pulled out a tray of the terrible generic cookies. Petra nodded a couple of times. She considered bursting into tears, but whether it was over the fact that her friends had come together even though things were still tense, or because she cried a lot nowadays, or because the cookies were just that bad, she wasn't sure. It was probably a combination of the three.

"I'll make some cocoa," she said.

"No, I'll make it. You sit down and wallow," Sarah said.

Helen had already put on her flannel long underwear. She patted the seat next to her.

"So, Sarah called you."

"Yes. I'm really glad she did. We tried to fill in some blanks together, but I'd rather hear it from you."

Petra shook her head. "I feel really stupid," she said.

"Why?"

Petra shied away. "I should have known better. I should know what this is like."

"What?" Helen asked.

"You know, all this love stuff. I should have understood that it wasn't going to work out. Not with a former patient, not now, not ever."

"Why?"

"I swear, if you ask me another one-syllable question, I'm going to beat you with one of these incredibly hard cookies."

Helen sighed. "Never say that you don't believe in love."

"I believe in it just fine. Funny, isn't it? My dad walked out, my mom's about to be married for the third time, and I've had my heart crushed, but I believe in the emotion. I just don't know what to do with this thing with—"

She couldn't say his name.

Luckily, Helen didn't expect her to say it. "Well, what do you want from it, then?" she asked.

Petra thought for a moment. "I want…" she stuttered. "Well, things to be different from how they are right now. I want love to make me happy."

She knew she sounded young and immature. Maybe she was. Helen looked at her, but if she thought Petra was being stupid, she didn't say anything. "It can if you let it. It probably did at some point."

Petra lay down. She could not lie and say that Ian had never made her happy. Transcendently, exquisitely, *obscenely* happy. But life had a way of intruding on it.

"Are we talking about boys, yet?" Sarah asked, carrying in three mugs.

"You know, for someone who fucks and leaves, you attach more importance to men than you should," Helen said.

"At least I—"

Sarah sucked a deep breath in through her nose and let it out again.

"Maybe you should just tell us what happened," Sarah said in a perfectly normal voice to Petra.

She picked up a cookie, sniffed it, then put it down again.

Defiantly, Helen stuffed an entire one in her mouth and couldn't say anything for a while.

"He told me he was in love with me," Petra said. "Then, he kind of showed me that he couldn't be in a relationship with me. I chose him over my ethics and professionalism. He chose a cat."

Except that wasn't the whole truth, was it? It was that he refused to tell her why he had taken the cat. It was that his ex had been gorgeous and sophisticated and expensive, and Petra's own life had been circling a cosmic drain. It was that she was scared and angry that she was going to do too much to be with him – get shots, forget transgressions, forget who she was. It was that it was easier to blame her professional troubles on him – on his brown eyes and velvet voice – than it was to blame it on the fact that she hadn't thought long and hard enough when she'd decided to open a solo practice. Even now, she felt willing to try to be with him, willing to just abandon everything else.

She tried to explain more, minus the desperation and abandon.

"So why did Ian accept the cat anyway?"

"He said Danielle had something on him, but he wouldn't tell me what it was. He told me to trust him. But by that time, I was so jerked around and angry, I just wanted—"

She stopped. She didn't even know what she wanted. She wanted to be back together with him, but in the time before the cat had arrived and her landlord had called and Kevin had canceled, and after Ian had said he loved her. She wanted to be back in those brief hours before life had intruded. Or no, she wanted to meet him before she had become his doctor. She wanted to go back to the moment she'd gotten her dad's money, stuff it in a retirement account, and go to work for Pronto!Docs. She wanted to burn it all down and start the whole thing anew. But that could never happen.

"I wonder what it was he was protecting. His business, most likely," Sarah mused. "It's probably really the only thing that guy really cares about. Maybe there's something fishy going on there."

Petra felt a flare of indignation. "He's clean. He works hard and he tries to be fair. I've seen him in action. Besides, it's hardly the only thing he cares about. I've seen him be wonderful with Kevin. And he's affectionate with the cat even though he's allergic to it."

And he's good to me, she thought.

"That's true, he does care deeply about things. Maybe too much," Helen said. "Not to mention, he's crazy about you."

Petra put her hand over her eyes. "Well, he's got a funny way of showing it."

They were quiet.

"I don't want to talk about this," she said. "Let's talk about something else. My mom is getting married next weekend and I just don't know what a girl should wear to her mom's third wedding."

She appreciated the effort Sarah and Helen made. It was a strain for them, Petra could see. But she just couldn't really be honest with them about Ian – or herself. She could barely stand the voice in her own head.

"So you love him and he loves you," Helen said, when Sarah went to take a phone call in Petra's bedroom.

"That's your takeaway from all this? Because mine was: next time don't sleep with your patients, current or ex."

"I think that's Sarah's takeaway. I think that you're being overly scrupulous and blaming yourself for things that aren't necessarily wrong or your fault – which is so like a physician. You're a good doctor, Pete, and you try hard and I think you're fine, ethically. Maybe I'm biased because of my parents. But Sarah is biased because of her issues, too."

"Right. How's it going between you guys?"

"How does it seem, Dr. Changes-the-Subject-Unsubtly?" Helen sighed. "Look, I'm not going to pretend that things are perfect, but we know each other and understand each other, and there's something to be said for that. And I know that part of her is sad that she hurt me, even though the only part she lets me see is her shit-ass judgmental attitude. And part of me – a lot of me – is really sorry that hit one of her hot buttons and disappointed her… and me."

"Yeah, fuck you," Sarah said, coming back in.

Helen gave her the finger and ate another cookie. "These are terrible," she said, her mouth full.

–

Petra escaped to the bathroom. She pretended that she wanted to shower. They were talking about her, she knew it. After she excused herself, she heard Sarah's voice go low. She peered at them through the crack in the door. Their heads were close together and she heard Sarah hiss the words *bastard* and *balls.*

That was Sarah, always leaving the guesswork out.

Petra shut the door again and took out her toothbrush. Sarah was probably of the opinion that Ian had cheated with Danielle. Helen was probably convinced of Ian's love for Petra, but maybe not so much of Petra's for him.

She sat on the none-too-clean floor of her bathroom and wished that they all could stop having this conversation. They understood her well, that was the problem and it was the wonderful thing about her friends. She *knew* them.

She knew Ian, too.

She knew, for instance, that he didn't know anything about American football, even though he pretended to follow the conversations at Stream. She knew he was handy, despite affecting an air of ease and nonchalance, and that he had constructed the bars at Field and Stream himself. He had built a tree house years ago, too, he said, that was almost like a real house. She knew he had not seen his Oregon relatives in nearly ten years, although he still called his aunt every now and then. She was elderly. She liked to play online poker.

Petra knew the feeling of his arms and his hands. She knew his corded muscles, the scar between his thumb and index finger. He nuzzled her shoulder blades and kissed her neck when he thought she was asleep.

She knew about his mother. She knew that he had been the one to call the police, to arrange the funeral. His father had left it all to him, even though he was still a boy. He had done the hard things that people had to do in life. He had not simply abandoned anyone, even though he thought he had. He had followed through on everything.

When she had said that she didn't trust him, she'd lied, and that was the worst knowledge of all. She didn't trust herself.

Chapter Twenty-Six

Petra went into the office on Saturday morning and sat in her chair, chewing over the numbers. She could move her office. She had many months to prepare. Ian's real-estate broker had called to introduce herself, and Petra wondered if Ian had made the call before or after their breakup. She was inclined to think after. He was that kind of person.

Of course, she could figure out easily how much she'd have to spend on the move, how much new prescription pads and appointment cards would cost. But whether she'd lose business by shifting locations, that was hard to tell. There was the fact, too, that if she stayed in the neighborhood, she could end up right next door to Stream or Field. And she did not think she could do that. It was bad enough that she was tensed to run into him at every moment. The thought of him so close by would break her.

Maybe she should close up shop.

She glanced at her phone. Past noon. She needed to eat something.

She treated herself to an expensive sandwich from the hipster coffee shop across the street. She'd been spending lots of money lately: on a dress for the wedding, new shoes. She felt reckless. A sandwich wouldn't break her. The shop was full of lazy weekend coffee drinkers, so she wandered outside holding her recycled paper bag. She wasn't going to return to her office.

It was dry but brisk this morning. The wind hurried her along to a little park. She sat on an empty bench and looked around. Well, it wasn't as if people were clamoring to sit outside in this weather, she thought, as the wind blew her hair around. At least she wouldn't seem sad out here. She would look almost brave.

Idly, she watched some men and women playing soccer in the park. It looked like a pickup game. Backpacks were being used as goal posts. Bodies scrambled across the turf in grubby mismatched sweats and muddy sneakers. The field was a mess of mud and most of the players sported dark streaks across their torsos. It looked like a detergent commercial. She watched the players without following, almost sightlessly taking in their movement, glad for the break they gave her overworked brain. She wondered how the players managed to keep track of which team they were on. They were indistinguishable, their shouts barely heard above the stiff wind. Then, she saw him. He had broken from the scrum to maneuver the ball toward the goal and she recognized his run, the elastic motion of his limbs, the calm purpose of his head.

Ian launched himself forward. She clutched her sandwich messily and her heart started pounding. She stared harder to make sure, and then he slipped and fell and her heart leaped into her throat.

There was an awful pause.

She was standing. She was ready to run to him.

He sat up.

He was shaking his head as a couple of guys stopped by him. He refused their hands, and he got up easily and started walking up the field, right toward her. Had he seen her? She didn't think he had.

He was fine, he was fine. More than fine. Apparently, he wasn't lying on the floor of his apartment, wheezing to death as Snuffy's dander flew up in a maelstrom around him, nor was he buried in spreadsheets or abusing a belt sander. Or spying on her as she played soccer.

She got up hastily and threw the rest of her sandwich in the trash.

She was not running away. She was beating a strategic retreat. She pounded the sidewalk, almost breaking into a run for several minutes. Her breath came short. Finally, when she got around the corner, she slowed. She had stolen to safety, she thought, when rapid footsteps came up. Someone grabbed her arm.

–

He ached. There was no other word for the hollow feeling in his stomach and breastbone. His ankle felt a little tender, but nothing compared to the dull pain he felt without Petra. He sat on a bench in the park and watched the rest of the game, not that he could tell what was happening. His glasses were in his backpack and he didn't care enough to retrieve them. He'd hardly been able to concentrate while he was playing. But the mud and the air had done him good. At least for a few minutes he hadn't been thinking about her, or trying to call her, or hoping he'd run into her.

She would probably call the cops on him if he waited outside her door again. He couldn't blame her.

He wondered what would have happened if he'd told her the truth, that he had taken the cat to protect her. She still would have broken up with him anyway for telling Danielle about how their relationship started. Petra had scruples. She always had reservations, and Danielle's threat would probably confirm her feeling that something was fundamentally fucked up about their relationship.

There probably was, and he didn't care, he just didn't. He still wanted her.

He rubbed his face. It hurt that she didn't trust him. It hurt that he wanted her back. The other day, he had thought of another good word for underwear and he had been about to pick up his phone, when he realized that she would never answer.

It had been a damn good word.

He bought a new punching bag. He bought a better air mattress for his office. He made appointments with Jatinder Singh again, in hopes of being able to once again live in his apartment, although he didn't want to return to that empty, lonely place. Before, it had been bare and the bareness reminded him of how solitary he was. Now, it was filled with memories of her. And cat dander.

Fuck it.

The last thing she'd given him was a pink capsule. Like she still thought of him as a patient.

He hadn't swallowed it. He wasn't carrying it in a vial around his neck like a douchebag. But neither was he happy with being dismissed so easily.

He couldn't continue with his life the way it was. For one thing, he was paying rent on an apartment occupied by a cat and the ghost of a living woman. His life was ridiculous. He needed to connect with someone. For the first time, he wanted to talk.

He got up and pulled out his phone. "Gerry," he said, wiping mud from his forehead. "You and Lilah will need to help train the assistant manager. I'm going out of town."

–

It wasn't Ian, Petra knew that much. But for a split second, she wondered. She turned around.

Her throat closed again.

"Kev," she said.

He looked small and sad and worried.

"Kevin," she repeated. "I'm so glad to see you. How are you?"

"I'm sorry," he said. "I'm sorry. I wanted to keep you as my doctor, but my dad… It's my fault. He thought it was weird you were with me and talking like a friend. And then he found out I'd been at Stream with you—"

"You didn't ask him if you could go?"

"You tried to warn me, but I wanted to hang out with you so badly. The whole thing was my idea. I fought with him, really hard, but he shut it down."

Petra took a deep breath. It was almost too much. She was furious that she was in this position, but she couldn't blame Kevin and she was tired of blaming herself. Still, she had to be a professional.

"It's okay, Kevin. It's definitely not your fault. I was the grown-up and I should have known better – I did know better. I should have found a better way of helping you that day. How is Penny, by the way? Did she like your gift?"

For the first time, Kevin's face split with a big grin. "She loved it. It was so cool."

"So everything's okay with you guys."

"We're working on it," Kevin said. "Rome wasn't built in a day."

Petra had no idea what to say to him. They continued walking.

"Do you like your new doctor?" she asked.

"Dr. Ham is fine," he said. "His practice is a little farther away, and they banned talking on the phone in his office. I'm a little bored, so I read and text. They have a TV, but it's on mute with the subtitles on. Usually a news channel. That's annoying. You were right that it would be stupid. They should show comedy."

"It's hard to find things that everyone will like."

"But nobody likes the news."

"Are there a lot of people in the waiting room?"

"Yeah. Once I couldn't even find a seat."

Petra stifled a sigh.

"Ian said I should hand out your business card next time that happens," Kevin said. "He said it sounds like Dr. Ham has more patients than he needs."

Petra stilled. "You talked to Ian?"

"Yeah. We hang out. He seemed like he needed some cheering up."

Petra clamped her mouth shut.

"Maybe he needs a new girlfriend," Kevin added. "I should hook him up."

"Oh, dear God."

Kevin eyed her. "I do know people other than junior high girls," he said. "I know you, for instance. If you're wondering why I've never tried to introduce you to the gentlemen, it's because you're a very elegant lady. I can't pick just anyone for you."

"It's inappropriate for you to introduce me to people," she mumbled. She was *not* going to cry. Crying in front of patients was probably a no-no, too.

Kevin paused. "You know, I know you two like each other, you and Ian," he said. "You can tell me these things. I am very intuitive anyway."

"Not—"

"—appropriate. I'm not your patient anymore. We can be friends now," Kevin persisted.

"You could always become my patient in the future, Kevin," she said. "And you're still a minor. The boundaries stay up, for your own good. This is what your dad was concerned about."

Kevin set his chin. He looked a little red. Petra eyed his scarf. She hoped there wasn't any wool in it.

"Well, that's stupid," he said. "What if when I turn twenty-one I want to go to Stream and have a drink with you guys? What if I want to be in a band with you? What if you find me handsome in the future and want to go out with me?"

"I can't end up abusing your trust, exploiting you."

Ian had always suspected that Kevin had a crush on her. Maybe he was right. Inner Hippocrates tried to say something, and she gave him a swift kick.

"The point is," Kevin said, "you're one of the only people who cares for me just the way I am. I *am* your friend, even though I'm younger than you and you have a medical degree. You've fed me and bandaged me up and told me the truth about almost everything. You know more about me than almost anyone. My father has no idea who I am. He can't even remember what I'm allergic to and I'm not sure he cares. I'm alone, Dr. Lale. You're one of the few people who just let me hang out and who listened. You just let me be me."

"I know people who need an allergist," Kevin added. "All the kids in my school have allergies. Medication is, like, the thing that unites our generation."

"You must be a real overachiever, Kevin," she managed to say.

"I am," he said, seriously. "I'm going to make this up to you, Dr. Lale. You'll see. This isn't the end."

It seemed she *was* going to cry – was crying – but she had finally realized one sad fact: Kevin was never going to be her patient again. She was going to have to cut them both free. "Kev, I'll always be concerned for you…"

"Don't," he said desperately.

"And you have to believe that I am looking out for you…"

"Don't. Don't say it." He screwed up his face and looked like the child he still was.

"But your dad cares about you, too, more than you know. And Penny, and Penny's mom, Mrs. Poole, and even Ian. You aren't alone at all, Kevin, even if it feels that way."

Kevin's face dissolved. "I'm not going to let you say we can't be friends." He turned and tore away. She worried that his asthma would be exacerbated by running in the cold air. She worried that he'd be blinded by tears and stumble and fall. But he was already near his building. She had to let him go.

Her heart was shredded. There was nothing left. She had done the right thing. Why did it feel so terrible?

Chapter Twenty-Seven

Petra drove up to Astoria by herself on Friday night, singing loudly to all the boy-band, teen pop-sensation music that she was ashamed to admit she owned. But nothing else would do right now. She couldn't risk crying to Patsy Cline and running her rental off the highway.

The car smelled new and she was glad to be away from the city. But in the static silences between songs, she felt herself gripped with an overwhelming sadness that even the brassiest synthesizers and sunniest choruses couldn't dispel.

It was normal to feel a little off before your mom's wedding, right?

She pulled into the parking lot of the bargain bed and breakfast she had booked for two nights. No one knew that she had left town already. Her sister and the girlfriend were set to arrive tomorrow morning. They would all meet Jim Morrison's kids and have lunch together on the porch. Not a lot of people had been invited to the wedding, which suited Petra just fine.

Her mother had said Petra could wear anything she wanted. Lisa had also said something about Ian, and Petra told her in a choked voice that he wasn't coming. Then her mother had said something else, which Petra didn't catch, but sounded suspiciously like an oath, and she hung up the phone. Lisa Lale never swore or hung up on people.

It was kind of great that she'd started and Petra hoped it would happen many times again when she was more in the mood to appreciate it. Petra supposed she had Jim Morrison to thank for that one, too. That, or bridal nerves.

The chatty innkeeper led her up the stairs to a room with a huge canopy bed and large walnut wardrobe. The bathroom had a claw-footed bathtub, the kind of thick, fluffy white robe that was always way too long, and, best of all, towel warmers.

It was low season, so it hadn't been horribly expensive. She didn't care about money anymore. What was the point when she didn't have any?

Petra had the night planned. She would soak in the tub and paint her fingernails. Then she would read a book until she was sleepy, and her evening would be perfect and uninterrupted. She just wanted to go missing for one segment of time. In a clean room with linen that smelled like lavender and brand new soaps, she could pretend she was someone with a whole heart.

The problem was that this room looked perfect for sex. Too bad she wouldn't be getting any of that again for a while.

–

The day sparkled like a diamond (although not like the diamond in her mother's ring, Petra noted, because that one forever had a disturbingly jaundiced cast) and threatened to become one of those unseasonably warm days that had people shucking off their clothes indecently, believing that spring had arrived, perhaps even summer.

Jim Morrison and Lisa had decorated the porch with tulips, pots and pots of them, until the place looked like a Dutch postcard. There was a white tent off to the side and chairs already set out. Jim Morrison greeted her at the door with a kiss on the cheek, a blueberry muffin, and a mimosa, and told her to go up to her mother. Ellie and her girlfriend had not yet arrived.

Everything was perfect.

Jim Morrison was possibly perfect.

Petra had to admit, she was warming to him. After all, he made Lisa happy, he had bought up her favorite flowers, and Petra suspected that the orange juice in her drink was fresh-squeezed and the champagne was real champagne. (Not that she was able to tell this sort of thing. Ian would probably have known.) And if Jim Morrison were indeed Dr. Evil, then the weather machine that he had invented was working splendidly. She raised her flute in a toast and downed the entire glass.

Lisa scrunched her eyebrows and cleared her throat a little nervously.

"Relax, Mom, I won't suck down too much alcohol. But you have to admit, it's really delicious."

"I'm not having any," her mother said.

"Oh dear God, you're not pregnant at your wedding, are you, young lady?" Petra trilled laughter. Hmmm, maybe she had already had too much to drink. Petra set the flute down on the nightstand and took a big bite of blueberry muffin.

Her mother had laid out three suits on the bed and she was walking around, picking them up and holding them to herself and putting them down. She peered at herself in the full-length mirror and wrinkled her brow.

"You look great, Mom. Any one of those colors will be nice on you."

"I had the hairdresser come yesterday, and I slept with a scarf tied around my head. It was very uncomfortable. I have dark circles under my eyes."

"Do you have a makeup person, too?"

"No. Should I?"

She looked so chagrined that Petra moved to soothe her. "Don't worry. I was kidding. Again. Ellie will know what to do. I hardly see the circles. If you hadn't said something, I'd never have noticed."

Her mother began to pace and Petra wished for an entire pitcher of mimosas.

At least the room was gorgeous. Jim Morrison had installed his bride-to-be in a huge room at the back of the house. Sunlight poured into two gabled windows and a set of French doors opened out to what her mother said was a rug-shaking porch. Petra liked that. In summertime, there were probably wonderful views of trees and green lawns and hills. Maybe if she played her cards right, she could house-sit one weekend. It was beautiful but comfortable, and it spoke of the kind of old money that she'd never had. In a place like this, she would never contemplate sadly the fact she'd never have sex again; it was just not something she'd care to do while she was in Jim Morrison and Lisa's house, anyway.

"I just can't decide," Lisa was saying helplessly. "Which one makes me look nonthreatening and yet respectable?"

"I didn't think that was the statement that brides generally wanted to make."

"His children at lunch," Lisa moaned. "I just want them to like me."

Petra almost told her that the suit would be the least of Lisa's worries. Luckily, Ellie slammed through the door and burst into her mother's arms.

"You look beautiful," Ellie wailed.

"No, I don't," Lisa bleated back.

They erupted into noisy sobs. Petra sat on the bed, careful to avoid the suits. After a moment, Ellie disentangled herself from her mother and slid next to Petra. "Oh, Petey," she said, snuggling into her, "I missed you so much."

Petra laughed and kissed Ellie on the cheek.

"Missed you, too. Where's Jenna?"

"She's eating muffins, drinking mimosas, and salivating over Jim Morrison's Jim Morrison poster. I think it's like heaven on earth for her right now."

"Where are you staying tonight?"

"Oh, I think we're all bunking here, right?"

Ellie looked at her mother for confirmation.

"I'm not," Petra said.

"You could stay here."

"Aren't Jim Morrison's kids also staying? That would be like a weird slumber party. I've got a great room at the bed and breakfast in town. Or, I mean, I hear it's a very nice place."

"C'mon, it'll be cozy," Ellie said.

The mention of Jim Morrison's kids had sent their mother pacing again. She was wringing her hands and scrutinizing her outfit choices again. She muttered under her breath.

"What did you say to her?" Ellie asked in a low voice.

"What? I've been perfectly nice. Okay, I made one crack about her being pregnant at the wedding, but it was more of a lame joke than a bitchy zinger. Besides, you're the one who was more recently freaked out about Mom getting married." Petra rose from the bed and said loudly, "I think we need some dance music to put us in the mood.

Plus coffee. I'm going to go downstairs and see what I can find."

She shut the door behind them and closed her eyes.

She was… okay. Considering her mother was getting married, her sister was blaming her for imagined ills, and her own heart felt shredded. They still had to get through lunch with Jim Morrison's kids – her new stepbrother and stepsister, she reminded herself. They were both in college. She glanced at her jeans and boots. They'd do. She didn't want to look overly formal but was her outfit too casual?

She cut herself off before she could go any farther down that rabbit hole of self-doubt. She was already older than all of the other kids. Her poise and confidence would have to pull her through – or more mimosas. Plus, it wasn't as if they had to like *her*.

They probably wouldn't.

Low expectations were so refreshing sometimes. So were mimosas. She hurried down the stairs and almost ran smack into Jim Morrison.

He was also wringing his hands. Cute. It looked like he had learned a few tics from Lisa. It must be love. "How is your mother doing?" he asked.

"She's fine. Worried about her outfit. Outfits, I should say. Wedding nerves."

He shot her a sidewise glance. "Did you two manage to talk? I hope that there wasn't too much anxious chatter. This is, after all, a joyful occasion."

Why was she receiving warnings from everyone? She deserved to get drunk at this point, dammit.

"I was a cheerful little earful," she said. "Now why don't you tell me all about my new step-siblings?"

Lacey and Laird Morrison arrived about an hour later. They were arguing when they climbed out of the car. Petra had been having a surprisingly good time with Jim Morrison and Jenna. Jenna wanted to become an orthopedic surgeon and had spent the time grilling Petra and Jim Morrison about medical school, the hours, specialties, money, and patients. Privately, Petra thought Jenna was probably a little too laid-back to be a physician. Kid was definitely smart enough, and she had good grades, but she needed that extra kick of aggression and anxiety. Or maybe she could become a shrink.

Jim Morrison had been in the kitchen with the caterers until his kids arrived. As soon as he heard their car in the drive, he shot out and the lines in his face deepened.

Interesting.

Jim Morrison was hard to ruffle, but his kids clearly knew how to do that. Lacey Morrison was pretty, with soft, light hair and eyes. She had a big bag of laundry. Laird Morrison was golden-haired, golden-eyed, and just plain gorgeous. He seemed to know it. He unloaded a surfboard.

Petra had seen the pictures throughout the house, but most of them had been taken when the kids were young. She was curious to know what their mother looked like.

Laird moved lazily behind his sister and leaned the board against the side of the porch.

"You can't leave that there," Jim Morrison said shrilly.

It was the first time she'd heard him lose his mild, professional tone.

The twins hugged their father perfunctorily.

"I was going to bring it to the shed," Laird said. "It'll be fine out here for a while. Guests aren't due till six, right?"

"Five," Jim Morrison snapped. "Five o'clock."

He seemed to remember himself, and introduced Jenna and Petra to his children.

Laird eyed Jenna's Sailor Moon T-shirt then transferred his gaze to Petra's modest chest. She resisted the urge to kick him and asked the twins about their ride up. Jim Morrison pushed them indoors.

"I thought we'd eat in the dining room. That way we won't disturb anything for the ceremony. Just a simple sandwich buffet."

"Where's your beautiful bride-to-be?" Laird asked.

"And your sister?" Lacey said to Petra. She displayed a set of even white teeth.

"I'll go get them," Jenna said, springing up.

Great.

"Maybe you guys would like to go get settled. I can help Jim Morrison set out lunch," Petra volunteered.

"Oh no. It's our house, *our* dad," Lacey said. "Our job."

She flashed another tight smile then reached to get her laundry bag. The swinging motion knocked a few tulip pots over. She didn't bother to right them.

Lisa appeared downstairs in the blue suit, which was a pretty color. It should have made her eyes look bright. Instead, her gaze darted tensely between Laird and Lacey and Jim Morrison.

Well, at least it was nice that Petra wasn't considered the troublemaker anymore. If anything, she wondered if Lisa had had the same words with Jim Morrison about his children that he had with Lisa about Petra.

Jim Morrison had managed to regain his normal tone, although his eyes looked strained. He kept one hand on Lisa at all times, probably to steady her, but it almost looked like he was keeping her from flying off into a nearby bush and hiding. He tried to get her to eat, but she just shook her head. Laird made a none-too-subtle crack about delicate flowers, and Ellie hissed at him like an angry mongoose. Lacey laughed. Jenna held Ellie back, and Petra suddenly wished Ian were there to smooth things over.

Because that's what he did. Beautifully. More than that. Sadness closed around her suddenly, like a clamshell.

It was funny, she thought, sipping a glass of water. Her mother and sister were unhappy right now, but at least they had people to hold their hands. The tulips waved outside on the porch and Laird and Lacey weaved in and out of the conversation like a pair of stinging bees. Here was her mother so brave, trying once again to find love, and her sister being soothed by the gentle hands of her girlfriend. The whole blond group of them already looked like a family. Even though anger and tension and argument swirled all around her, Petra felt very still and very alone.

She looked at them, dry-eyed, and she wished she had done things differently.

—

People were gathering on the lawn. Laird had forgotten to move his surfboard, although it did look rather beautiful leaning there, its red and white stripes blending with the brightness of the tulips. In any case, Jim Morrison was too busy and too worried to notice. As for Laird, he had disappeared somewhere and Petra knew better than to touch someone else's board.

She went to get a bottle of water for Ellie and a sandwich for her mother. It would be bad business if her mother passed out during the ceremony. It didn't matter if she got crumbs on her wedding dress.

The caterers were in the kitchen, pulling pans out of the oven. They had covered the granite countertops with trays in varying stages of being assembled. The dining room beyond had also been co-opted. It was a good thing that lunch had broken up so quickly – Petra was still not sure what had been said – because it seemed like every single space on the cabinets, in the refrigerator, and even on the floor, was occupied and humming and warm with activity.

She took a step back. Probably best to leave them alone.

But as she moved, she saw out of the corner of her eye a tall man in a charcoal suit approaching her. Her heart zoomed up, then went plunging down into her shoes.

Ian.

–

She looked calm and beautiful. He had never seen her in a blue dress before. It brought out the soft duskiness of her skin. It skimmed her shoulders and breasts and draped lovingly around the curve of her bottom. But an embroidery pattern of leaves and branches unfurled around the skirt, making her look like a cool winter scene.

Only her eyes said something different. She looked at him, tired and sad. He wanted to pull her to him and enfold her in his arms, but he didn't want her to run away. Instead, they just looked at each other.

"Jim asked for advice about a last-minute caterer. Then, he and your mother wanted me to come," he said.

"That was nice of you."

"Not particularly. I wanted to see you."

He was going to say more, but she held up her hand. "I need to get something for my mom. She hasn't eaten all day. And maybe some water."

Ian nodded and flagged down the woman in charge. He smiled and said something in her ear and within minutes, she produced a plate with hors d'oeuvres and two squat water bottles. Petra thanked her and Ian, and he nodded. "I'll find Jim, then," he said. "See how he's holding up."

He watched her walk down the hallway and curled his fist. He was stupid. Of course she wouldn't want to talk to him at her mother's wedding. She was probably feeling terrible about the whole thing. She would be busy through the night, chatting with guests, shaking hands, and catching up with old friends. She was exhausted and unlikely to be charitable. She had hardly reacted when she saw him. She hadn't even bothered to say hello, or touch him, or kiss him.

A kiss would have been nice.

He straightened his collar. He had no ammunition to beg for a second chance. Nothing had changed. He still had the cat. She still, obviously, didn't trust him. At least he'd left town for a week and hadn't had to worry about choking on a furball in his sleep. Kevin had arranged for a delighted Penny to sit with Snuffy, although she had strict orders to change her clothing if she went to visit Kevin afterward.

But he had worried about Petra for this day. Even as he sped along the road, he'd thought of Petra. He thought, too, of his father and all the travel and the neglect. He thought of his mother. He considered all the mistakes they had made and how much he hadn't wanted to end up like them. He had gone to see his relatives earlier in the week, and it wasn't terrible. He had expected epiphanies, closure, seraphim and cherubim, earthquakes and floods. *Something.* But all he felt when he cleaned out his aunt's eavestroughs, or helped his uncle change the oil of his Chevy, was the heavy ache of missing Petra. As he drove around the winding highways along the coast, he remembered himself as a teenager, and all the things that he had wanted to do with his life. Despite the mess of his parents' marriage, he had wanted to find a home, and love. Now, it seemed, he had gone in exactly the opposite direction. He had nowhere to live, and the only woman he would ever want didn't want to speak to him. At this moment, he was worse off than his mother and father.

He promised himself that he wouldn't let her go without one last chance to say his piece.

In the meantime, he probably needed a drink.

Chapter Twenty-Eight

"I think she has the dry heaves," Ellie whispered loudly.

Petra knocked on the door. No answer.

She set down the plate of hors d'oeuvres and banged on the door.

"Mom, are you okay?"

A pause.

"Mom, answer me if you're conscious. Just make some sort of sound."

She heard a sob.

Great.

It wasn't fair that her mom got to freak out in the bathroom just when Petra needed to splash cold water on her face.

Petra paced in front of the door and looked at herself in the mirror. Her mouth jerked tremulously. Her hands opened and shut convulsively. Her heart, she was sure, was wrung out, spent, and left in messy knots.

"You could have warned me," she muttered to the door.

But how could she have prepared about how for how the dark suit complemented Ian's hair, made his eyes look darker, his torso look leaner and more dangerous. His shoulders were hugged perfectly by the wool. His mouth was sexier, his face more pleading. After two weeks of not seeing her, he seemed like a better version of himself. While she just looked short.

"His kids hate me. You hate me," Lisa whimpered.

"I don't hate you, Mom. I just wished you'd told me Ian was coming," Petra said. She kicked the door.

"His kids think I'm a gold digger. They were practically putting Post-it notes on everything. They asked him to make sure he'd updated his *will*."

"I mean, I could have worn heels," Petra said to herself. "I thought I'd sink into the lawn during the ceremony but at least for that moment in the kitchen, I would have looked taller."

"All Jim did was stroke my arm and try to get me to eat more."

"What could Ian possibly want to talk to me about?"

"I don't want to be stroked like some pet cat."

"I hate cats."

Ellie was looking at the door and back at Petra. "You don't mean that," Ellie said.

"I don't mean it. They're usually fine. But they like to rub me, and I'm allergic."

"Is that why we couldn't get a cat? Because you hate them?"

Lisa wailed, "What if I end up divorced again? A third time!"

"I don't hate cats, Ellie. I just feel like my life is being ruined by one right now."

"Who is this Ian, anyway?" Ellie asked.

Lisa burst out of the door. "I can't do this. Not yet, not now."

She had her lipstick on, but no eye makeup. She had teased her hair a little higher and changed into another yellow suit, with a scalloped peplum. She looked a little bit like a daffodil. A very upset daffodil.

"We're leaving," Lisa said. She went to the closet and grabbed a suitcase. She stuffed the other suits in it. "Go to the bedroom and get my underwear," she told Ellie. "It's in the dresser, top drawer to the left."

"Uh, Mom. Is this a good idea?" Ellie asked.

"Elizabeth Ann, go get my damn underwear," Lisa almost shrieked.

"I'll go," Petra said. She whispered to Ellie, "I'm alerting Jim. Try to get her to eat something. Don't let her go anywhere."

Petra went down the stairs and out onto the porch. Laird was right there, his arm around his surfboard as if it were his girlfriend. "Looks nice, don't you think?" he said, gesturing at the yard.

"Where's your dad?"

He smirked. "Problems? Need Dad to prescribe the bride some medications?"

"She's got me for that. Where's Jim?"

She scanned the small gathering anxiously and took a deep breath when she saw Ian coming her way.

He looked from Petra to Laird and back. Deliberately, Ian put a hand on her arm. She let out a shaky breath. Her nerves felt calmer even as her skin prickled over. She stepped away but cold air rose like a column between them. She had forgotten to put on a jacket and the heat lamps that surrounded the tent didn't reach this far. "Hey," he said, "what's wrong?"

"I need Jim. My mom is—" She didn't want to say anything more in front of Laird.

Ian understood. "I'll get him. You go into the house and get warm."

He shot a glare at Laird and strode sure-footed toward the back.

"Get that surfboard in the shed," she snapped at Laird.

She stepped back in. Safely inside the front door, she closed her eyes.

She couldn't hear anything from upstairs. She could only assume that Ellie had calmed Lisa down. Or that Ellie had killed Lisa in frustration and was now stowing her mother's body in the suitcase.

She was really glad Ian was here.

And he was here for her because he knew it would be hard. Why had she condemned him for being someone who smoothed things over? She could get used to him easing her way.

Don't be weak, she chided herself. Still, she let herself slip down onto the stairs.

The door opened and Jim Morrison hurried through followed by Ian, Laird, and Jenna.

Jim glared at Petra openly. For the first time, and she was struck by how Laird resembled him. For a moment, it pleased her to know that the cocky kid would lose some hair and his face would get paunchy and wrinkled.

But Jim must have caught the glimmer of her smile, because he said, "What did you say to her?"

He took a step toward Petra, but Ian put himself in front of her, almost casually.

"Hey, Jim," Jenna said at the same time, her voice soothing.

She liked that Jenna. She also had feelings about Ian that she did not care to define at this moment.

Petra wobbled to her feet and peeked around Ian. "Mom's upstairs. She's scared."

"And whose fault is that?" Jim Morrison snarled.

Ian's shoulders tensed. Petra said quickly, "Let's not start on this, okay? I didn't say anything. She gets worried. Just go to her, talk to her."

She stepped around and laid a gentle hand on Ian's arm. Her fingers curled into the chill of his jacket. His gaze dipped to her hand and they remained still. Until Jim Morrison pushed past her to go up the stairs.

Ian looked ready to punch him.

A few minutes later, Lisa and Ellie came barreling down with Jim Morrison in pursuit. "We're leaving!" Lisa said.

Her face was flushed and her eyes were bright, but her voice was surprisingly steady.

"Lisa, let's sit down and be calm," Jim Morrison pleaded.

"Don't talk to me like I'm one of your crazy people," Lisa snapped.

"Was she one of your crazy people?" Ellie asked. She looked around. "I mean, I could imagine Mom in a shrink's chair more easily than Mom on a dating site. I always thought that story was a cover. Don't tell me you didn't think that, too."

Petra certainly had.

"First of all, they aren't crazy. Second, I would never do that with one of my patients. That would be unethical," Jim Morrison declared.

Petra winced. Ian looked stony-faced.

But Lisa whirled around. "Ethics, shmethics," Lisa said. "You *act* like I'm one of your crazies, which is worse. You talk to me in that mild tone of voice like I need to be soothed at all times before you slip me some pills."

"My patients are people with legitimate medical problems, in need of counseling and medication, Lisa. I do not use a voice on them. I admit that sometimes we need to help people see their issues and we need to communicate this in a non-accusatory manner."

"You sounded plenty accusing to me," Petra murmured.

"*You* have no say in this conversation," Jim Morrison said, whipping around.

"*She* may say whatever she wants," Lisa said, stepping between them.

Ian had tensed and inched closer to Petra. Even with all the anger flying around them, Petra found herself imagining she could feel his hipbone against her waist.

She cleared her throat. "Jim's right, Mom. I really have no say. Maybe you should go into the study and talk."

"Oh, how very reasonable," Jim Morrison said.

"She's being serious, Jim. Besides, she hasn't done any more than your own children have," Lisa said, stepping in front of Ian and Petra. "All you've done is defend Laird and Lacey, even though they've been crank-calling the house, and whining to their mother, and threatening to have me investigated, just because I've been married a couple of times before."

"Let's leave them out of this," Jim Morrison said.

"Yes, let's leave them out of everything. Let's have some understanding for the poor dears even though they're painting me to be some sort of man-eating siren."

Petra choked. It was hard to think of Lisa Lale as a man-eater.

"Sarcasm is not becoming, Lisa. And it doesn't aid with clarity of communication."

"Oh, stuff it, Jim. You understand me perfectly well."

She turned on her heel, and before anyone could understand what had happened, she barreled out the door. Only the sound of the car engine and the squeal of tires alerted them to the fact that Lisa Lale had escaped her own wedding.

-

She had stolen Ian's Prius. Tiny, anxious, law-abiding Lisa Lale, wringer of hands and worrier of warts, had stolen a car. Not only that, Lisa was more canny than Petra gave her credit for. Ian's vehicle had been the last one on the driveway and while arguing, Lisa had scouted that out and lifted Ian's keys when she'd slipped by him earlier. Luckily, Ellie and Jenna had their beater and Petra had her rental. She and Ian hastily organized a search party. They told Jim to stay to placate his guests.

Ian pulled out in Petra's car and began gunning in the direction that Lisa had taken. From the way he gripped the wheel, he looked prepared to perform fishtails, cause multi-car pileups, and plow through buildings. Before the pyrotechnics came out, however, Petra's phone rang.

"The wedding is off," Lisa said.

"Mom, where are you? Are you talking and driving?"

"No, I am at the Round-Up Diner on Commercial, waiting for a BLT."

Petra heard her mother thanking someone. Lisa Lale had good manners, even under duress. "Mom, you have to come back. Jim Morrison is waiting. Your guests are—"

"Of all people, I'd think you'd be the one to sympathize, Petra. You hated Jim from the start. You told me to be careful. You told me that I didn't have good judgment—"

"I never said *that*."

"You implied it. And you were right. He puts his kids before me, even though they're overgrown brats. He encouraged me to give up the house—"

"You hated that house."

"I can't believe that you're taking his side! Well, I'm not going back, I'm not getting married, and you can't make me."

Petra sighed. "Eat slowly, Mom," Petra said. She hung up and looked over at Ian. "How much of that did you hear?"

"Let's just say, after hanging out with Kevin, I'm starting to develop his eavesdropping skills."

After conferring with Ellie, they asked her to break the news to Jim Morrison in person. It would also give Ellie and Jenna an opportunity retrieve their luggage from the house. They agreed to rendezvous at the bed and breakfast that Petra confessed she was staying in. Ian and Petra drove to the diner to find Lisa. And because things never went smoothly during a spur-of-the-moment getaway, Ian and Lisa followed Petra to the inn where they met Ellie and Jenna who, judging by Ellie's glazed look, had a difficult time breaking the jilting to Jim Morrison. Jenna was also moping because she realized that she had left a pair of sneakers under the bed at Jim Morrison's house. Ian pushed everyone gently to Petra's room so they could confer, away from the prying eyes of the B&B host.

Petra could sense Ian eying the canopy, the white expanse of the bed, the gorgeous bathroom beyond. His gaze settled on the underwear she'd discarded over a wing-back chair.

He gave her a look that she hadn't seen in a while – a look that she ached for – and she felt herself warming through.

Focus, she thought.

But it was hard. Her mother was starting to realize just how impulsive she had been, and her back was so rigid that it was nearly trembling. Ellie and Jenna hadn't eaten for hours and they seemed exhausted. And Ian, poor Ian, had been dragged into this and yet hadn't uttered one complaint. If anything, he was the only one who seemed to have his wits about him. She took a deep breath.

The main question to deal with was where they'd go. Ellie didn't want to leave her mother, but Lisa couldn't stay in the dorms. They could all fit into Petra's apartment, but it would hardly be comfortable.

Petra met Ian's eyes. He nodded and asked one question. "Lisa, Jenna, Ellie, are you allergic to cats?"

–

Ian took off early to prepare his apartment, and Snuffy, for guests. Jenna drove Ellie and Lisa. Petra was by herself.

She had good, long time to think.

They converged on Ian's apartment. He had been busy. There were blankets on his couch and new towels in his bathroom. Best of all, he'd stopped at Field. When they came in, he had shut Snuffy in the bedroom and unpacked containers of lamb stew with polenta, and beets and frisée with goat cheese, and pork chops and mashed potatoes and spinach, and cheesy pasta with bits of fried sage on top. There were white plates on the table and shiny new silverware, and there was red and white wine.

"I figured we needed some comfort food," he said.

Lisa put her arms around him and burst into tears.

Petra pushed Ellie and Jenna into chairs – they both looked beat – and began filling a plate for her mother. Petra poured out generous glasses of wine, and she mouthed a thank you to Ian. He was patting Lisa on the back and pulling out a chair for her. He held one out for

Petra, too, and sat down beside her. His thigh brushed hers and she closed her eyes as all the feelings she'd been pushing aside all day seemed to rise to her throat.

He took her hand and squeezed it.

_ Lisa began to eat, and eat, and eat. The more she ate, the more she talked, and the more energy she seemed to gain. Jim was so annoying, she said. Jim only drank one cup of coffee in the morning, and then didn't have any for the rest of the day. Jim never wore socks, not even in winter. Jim didn't like music, at all.

Lisa missed him already, Petra realized. Lisa was remembering all his faults because she didn't want to feel like she had made a mistake. But she loved him and missed him.

Ellie drooped like a flower and Jenna, poor Jenna, was made so uncomfortable by Lisa's tirade about Jim's nostril-hair trimmer that she slid her long, gawky body down her seat and hid her entire face in her plate of polenta. At least she was also enjoying the food.

"We should let you get some sleep," Ian said, after Lisa finally paused to take a gulp of wine. "It's been a long day for all of us. And Petra's reacting to the cat."

Petra felt grateful. Grateful wasn't even the word. She wanted to cry about how tired she was and laugh about how ridiculous the day had been. She wanted to pound on his chest and ask him why he had come for her after she dismissed him. She wanted to burrow into him. She also felt an edge of panic. After all, Ian wasn't using his own apartment. He had probably been sleeping in his office again, or staying with Gerry.

Should she ask him over? She felt that twist of pain again and her head dropped.

She kept her mouth shut.

He helped her with her coat and she could see him almost reach up to fix her collar. He pulled his hand back and grabbed her travel bag instead.

She kissed Lisa goodnight and gave Jenna a big hug. Ellie, despite being drained, gave Petra an unsubtle wink toward Ian. At least the whole fiasco had spared her an interrogation, Petra thought. She wondered how long that would last.

They walked out into the light rain and they both breathed a sigh of relief to be out of the cat apartment and in the cool, fresh night.

"My mom's still in love with Jim," Petra said.

"Yeah, I was getting that."

She peered at him. "You don't sound too okay with it."

"I understand that he's frustrated, but I didn't like the way he became so hostile to you," he said.

Petra laughed, hollowly. "Funny how your explanation for why you're worried is my excuse for his behavior. Besides," she added, "he didn't try to pummel me. He just yelled."

"I can't believe you can be so forgiving. You hated him just a few weeks ago."

A few weeks ago, everything had been different. She could not look at him.

"Do you think they'll get back together?" she asked, pushing her hair back. It was shiny and wet from the rain.

"I wouldn't be surprised by anything," he said.

They walked in silence for a little longer.

"You're a lot alike, you and your mother."

"I'm sorry."

"Jim Morrison was nervous that this was going to happen," Ian said. "She was skittish the whole time. I think he thought bringing me in would neutralize any threat you might pose."

"You don't admire Dr. Evil for that move?"

"I can admire him without liking him," Ian said.

Petra breathed in again. "I mostly am okay with the thought of them being together. Even if it's weird and full of false starts. If he can be reasonable, and she can be reasonable, and they just work hard enough, it can be perfectly imperfect."

She looked him in the eye and he met her gaze. He took her hand.

They had reached the door of her building.

Her glove lay in his bare fingers. They felt so warm. She felt warm.

She heard herself saying, "After all you've done today, the least I can do is offer you my couch."

"I don't want you to bring me home because you're grateful or because you feel you need to take care of me."

His eyes were searching her face intently. She could feel his gaze. She almost turned, lifted her brows, her cheeks, her chin to bask in it. But she shook her head. "I don't like to think of you sleeping in your office," she said, hoarsely.

"I bought a new air mattress. It's forest green. Blows up in two minutes."

She groaned and dropped his hand. "Are you sure you're not trying to make me feel sorry for you? Because you've definitely got the pity."

"Actually, I don't know if your couch is any more comfortable. Your bed, on the other hand..."

Damn him. Her hands trembled as she searched for her keys.

"Anyway," he said lightly, "your mom is welcome to stay there as long as she wants. Snuffy could use the company. She would actually be doing me a favor because I still haven't figured out my living arrangements."

Petra avoided the question in his eyes. "I need a little time to figure things out. So much happened today, and yet, so little has changed. You still have a cat. I'm still failing as a doctor."

"I still love you and you still love me."

"Yes," she said, sadly.

"You aren't failing. This is normal when you start something big and important. And for the record, I am Jatinder Singh's current patient, again, which makes it highly unlikely that I'll ever go back to you for my medical needs. I'm not going to let you scare me off from him this time."

He tugged her to him.

"Come upstairs," she said, pulling away. "My couch may not be forest green, but at least we don't need an air pump to make it comfortable."

Chapter Twenty-Nine

On Sunday morning, the phone woke Petra. "Why didn't you ever mention Ian?" Ellie asked.

"Things have been a bit fraught."

"How could they be fraught? He's gorgeous, like, for a dude. He obviously adores you, and he was going to whup Jim Morrison for you. Ian left us pear crumble, Petra. And a bowl of *cream*."

"He has Snuffy. Ian took the cat in despite knowing I was allergic. As a favor to his ex-girlfriend."

But that wasn't the whole truth, either, Petra thought as she lay in bed, listening to Ellie process this information. She was misrepresenting it to Ellie, making it seem like he didn't care for her and the future. He wasn't still hung up on his perfectly perfect ex, Petra knew. Ian was in love with her.

Because more than anything, the way he took care of her family, the way he treated her so tenderly, showed her that he loved her, no matter what she threw at him. She could lean on him, and it felt good to do it. She wasn't surrendering herself if she let herself forget her troubles, if she let him take care of a few things. Worse, if she didn't let go of all of the insecurity and the worry that clouded her, she would lose him again. She would never be happy.

She wanted to be happy. It was tearing her apart, how much she wanted to be happy.

"Mom wants to talk to you," Ellie said abruptly.

She wasn't going to argue with Petra or try to worry her with this argument or that. That was the difference between Petra and her sister. Petra fretted. Ellie just waited. Ellie was pretty smart.

"Ian says you can stay there as long as you want," Petra told Lisa, who had taken the phone. "He won't use the apartment as long as he keeps the cat. So if you feed Snuffy and empty out the litter box, you're doing him a favor."

Lisa sniffled a little. "Snuffy is a sweet little cat. Please tell Ian thank you. He's a good man."

"Yes," Petra said. "I'm seeing that."

She could sense that Lisa was about to launch into a discussion of pros and cons, the deep brown of his eyes versus the length of his nose.

"Do you think he can do anything about his teeth?" Lisa began. "Restaurants are a risky business. How much of his place do you suppose is paid off?"

Petra was not having this conversation anymore *ever*. Her eyes narrowed. "We're not second-guessing Ian," she said, firmly. "Let's talk about Jim Morrison instead." Lisa let out a breath. Before she could speak, Petra said, "You have to tell me what to do in case he shows up at my office."

"Call the police on him," Lisa yelled. She set off on an angry rant about how irrational he'd been at the wedding, when he should have reined in his own kids, and how he belonged in a cold, hard jail cell sharing a bunk with a man named Jude.

Petra waited until she'd finished. But she did not join in.

"So, you still love him?" Petra said.

And Lisa burst into tears.

Petra burrowed farther into her pillows and closed her eyes.

"I don't know what's wrong with me," Lisa wailed.

"There's nothing wrong with you. You can't just turn off your emotions," Petra said.

"I don't want to make another mess. I don't want to disappoint my children, and I don't want to be hurt anymore. What should I do?"

"I don't know, Mom," Petra said slowly. "But Ellie and I are old enough that you should just think about making yourself happy. You don't have to find me a father."

"But your father hurt you so much."

There it was, the irritating nub of pain that they had both polished and rubbed until it gleamed like the most valuable jewel.

"Dad hurt us," Petra said. "But I can't let it influence my decisions and my feelings about people any longer. I can't let it make me believe that people can't be trusted and that I can't trust myself with them."

"What does that mean?" Lisa asked. "What does that mean I should do? You have to help me, Petra."

Petra's heart felt heavy. Her mother sounded terrified and anguished. Ian appeared at her bedroom door and hesitated. Petra sat up. "You'll just have to figure it out for yourself, Mom," she said gently. "Take some time. Maybe you should stay a while in the city. In Ian's apartment. He can live here, with me."

She gazed at him and he looked back at her. His face brightened slowly.

Lisa took a gulping breath and twittered nervously. "It sounds too good to be true. I mean, I would pay him, of course. I got the money from selling the house, but is the rent expensive? I don't know if I could afford it. How do you think he'd feel about that?"

Petra wasn't paying attention. Her body was lightening and she slowly started to feel peace seep in. She kept looking at Ian, and her smile grew.

"I think we can work something out," Petra said. "I'm going now, Mom. I love you."

She hung up.

That's all she had to do – she just had to hang up the phone.

It was a simple solution, but that didn't make it less difficult. She took a deep breath. And just like that, she let it all go.

–

Ian watched her put her phone down slowly.

"How is your mom?" he asked.

Petra was sitting up in the messy bed, wearing a faded blue T-shirt that hugged her small breasts gently. He would never get tired of watching her, he thought, as he eyed her tousled curls and the crease in her cheek from her pillow. They both looked hesitant, although they were both smiling.

She got out of bed, went to him, and kissed him gently on the lips.

"She'll figure it out," she said, holding her arms around him. "Apparently, it's a fine balance, trying to know when to leave a person alone and when to get on their case."

He stroked her back and led her gently to bed. They got under the covers.

They had not talked last night. But they needed clarity, and morning seemed to bring it.

"What does Danielle have on you?" Petra asked, when they were both lying down. "You're just going to have to trust me with it."

"You're not going to like it," he said, his nose in her neck.

"It was a shock seeing your ex-girlfriend," Petra continued. "The reality of her, her face, and the way her hair shone, and her expensive coat and bag and how together her life seemed. She looked polished and *competent*, so much the opposite of how I was at that moment. When I realized that you were keeping her cat, I couldn't help my insecurities. It wasn't even about you, at that point."

"That's changed?"

"Yes, it has. But now I need to know why you agreed to take the cat."

Ian continued to hold her. "I'm afraid to tell you," he said finally. "Because I'm terrified if I do, you'll kick me out of this bed and I'll be alone. I just can't do it ever again."

She held him tighter.

Eventually, he spoke. "Gerry let slip that I used to be your patient. She was attending some event at Field. She blackmailed me by threatening to go to the medical board and stir up trouble if I didn't take Snuffy. I couldn't let that happen."

Petra let a deep breath whoosh out of her lungs. "Wow," she said shakily. "Wow, she really hates you."

"I was kind of a jerk to her," he said.

"Still, that's just… malicious. And it's not even true. She would have lied."

313

Ian felt tense, as if another blow was about to fall. But she looked thoughtful as she kissed him gently on the temple.

After a moment, he managed to speak again. "I didn't know how you'd take it if I told you. I knew you felt like we were on shaky ground because I had been a patient. I really hadn't taken your concerns seriously, though, until Helen said something to me. And then Danielle threatened you. I'm sorry about that."

He shook his head. "Then your landlord happened and your mother was getting married and you lost Kevin and it seemed to bring all that stress and anger to the surface again. So I kept it to myself. I needed to protect you from another blow, but I should know from experience that that never works. Denial didn't protect my mom. I probably should have told you from the start. I should have said more. I'm just not used to confiding or sharing myself or my problems. I'm used to just burying the burdens myself. I'm sorry."

She stroked his hair.

"I can't pretend that I'm not scared," she said. "But it's some kind of a sign that maybe I'm not approaching this the right way. Maybe if I lose my lease and more patients, and the medical board decides to review me, then I should rethink how I do this. I've been thinking of closing the practice."

"No."

"I'm starting to get that because I made one bad business decision doesn't mean I'm not the best businessperson. And that, in turn, doesn't mean I'm a bad doctor. I have to stop beating myself up for every mistake I make. I intend to have a long career and I'll make mistakes the whole way. Besides, now that I can take a

314

step back from the whole situation, I'm sure the board won't rule that I did something wrong. I'd hate for there to even be questions, but if there are questions, I won't crumple."

"I still don't see how you did anything wrong."

"I did screw up a few things and I have to take a good hard look at my boundaries and learn from all that's happened, especially with Kevin. And that makes me sad but I have to move forward."

She was speaking briskly now and Ian found himself getting turned on – more turned on – by her determination. "In the meantime," she continued, "you've put at least a degree of separation between us by going to Jatinder Singh for shots. I wrote that awful dismissal letter. It's got to be worth something, right?"

She pursed her lips. "I've had time to think about why I've reacted the way I have, and all I can say is that I was scared. But I don't want to be that way anymore. And I won't have to, because of you. You've shown me that it's okay to trust myself enough to let go and put myself in someone else's hands every now and then."

He traced a fingernail along her scalp.

"You've been here for me in so many ways this week, even when I was so angry at you," she whispered. "You found someone to help me with a new practice location. You talked to Kevin. You helped my mom and showed up for this stupid wedding. You fed everyone. You even let a cat kick you out of your apartment. And you did this all for me."

"It's the new chivalry," he said, a little sadly. "Ultimately, I didn't solve anything."

"Ian, you're not supposed to shoulder everything, not by yourself. And I'm not supposed to solve everything by myself, either. So let's move on from here. We can both get the immunotherapy shots. Maybe we can eventually become cat parents together. Or maybe we won't."

He took her chin. "I don't know how I'm going to top a romantic speech like that."

Petra shook her head. "Let's see where this takes us. I don't want Danielle to report me, but I'm choosing not to be paralyzed by fear and self-recrimination anymore."

"I would feel terrible and responsible if anything happened to you because of her."

"Now who's the worrier?" Petra said, caressing his cheek. "We don't have perfect solutions, but at least we have some practical answers. My mother can help by offsetting the maintenance you're paying on your apartment and taking good care of Snuffy. Who knows, maybe he will end up being the love of her life."

Ian laughed. He fell back on the bed. "Who are you?" he asked, a little bewildered.

"I'm a woman who's working on letting go of things," Petra said.

She took another deep breath.

"Of course, that doesn't mean that it'll happen overnight. Sometimes I am going to castigate myself and I'll have doubts, but I will get over it. Remind me about this, to help me get over it."

"And sometimes I will shut down and try to do everything alone," Ian said. "I'll need you to pester me into talking."

Petra sat up and stretched her arms slowly up. Ian's eyes zoomed toward her, and she inched her T-shirt up her torso. "I'll help you get over it," she said.

She tossed the shirt aside.

"Yes, I'd say you were doing pretty well," he whispered, licking her ear, her jawbone, her neck.

"I'm a quick study," she agreed, as his hand closed around her breast. She hummed happily.

He peeled off her underwear and laughed at the little air kick she gave to help him. He grasped her ankle and kissed her instep. She laughed again and threw her arms up.

He hadn't seen her this free since, well, perhaps ever. He slid up along her, closing his eyes at the almost vicious way his body remembered hers, and smoothed her hair. "Are you sure this is all right?" he asked. "Are you sure this is what you want?"

"This is what I want," she said, rolling him on his back.

She pinned his arms up, weakly, but he let her, and she bit his neck and dragged her breasts along his chest. She was already wet. It had been too long.

He bucked. His erection rubbed at her entrance and they both exhaled sharply.

He freed his hands and rolled over to grapple for a condom while she rubbed herself against his back. Finally, he turned again, lying on his side, facing her. He pulled one leg over his hip and she guided him, and he pushed inside.

She whimpered.

They bumped gently against each other for a few minutes, in almost careless delight in the slip and slide of their bodies, whispering about how much they'd missed this, kissing, panting. He felt her tighten around him and she opened her mouth, asking for more. He held on to her hips and Petra put her arms around the back of his neck. She rolled herself on top and rode him, slowly at first. He began to take over, pumping harder into her and she drew her head up and moaned. He paused and drew both her legs wider and he seated himself deep inside her. She gasped. "Too much?" he whispered tightly, his teeth gritted.

"A little," she whispered, and he let one of her legs go. "Perfect," she breathed. Her body settled.

He pulled his hips back and began to thrust steadily now, and she curled down to meet him, their breaths rasping with every movement, every meeting. He could see the tension in her neck, in her shoulders, the look in her eyes almost unbearable as she moved towards breaking.

Her back arched suddenly and she cried out and her eyes opened wide in wonder and he felt her haunches move furiously above him, her muscles clenching and loosening, her hands scrabbling for purchase. But he couldn't look away from those eyes, the deep, glittering gray. He felt himself rush deliriously upwards as if the roof had opened up and he had been thrown straight into a big night sky where there was no air and no sound and nothing but starlight.

He was breathing again and Petra's hands in his anchored him to the earth.

His throat felt hoarse, his ears tinny. His glasses were very smudged. Or maybe his vision was permanently affected.

Petra's eyes were glazed and she was still breathing hard, too.

He pulled her to him fiercely. He swallowed a deep lungful of joy and let the smile that had been threatening to erupt spread across his face.

She smacked him softly on the chest. "Stop that," she murmured, bending to cover his body with hers.

He pulled her into his arms. "What?"

He felt her grin against his chest.

"Stop smiling like you just got laid," she said.

He laughed. He couldn't help himself.

Epilogue

Lucky for them, moving day proved warm and sunny. Petra, clad in red shorts and a worn T-shirt, looked around her at the chaos of friends, drop cloths, bags, and crates, and twitched her mouth into a grin.

Moving wasn't so bad, now that she had gotten used to the idea. It was a good thing, too, because her practice would probably be next. Her patient base had grown as the spring months came, and now that Petra had won a part-time position at a hospital across town (made easier by the fact that she had use of Ian's car), she wasn't as afraid of losing people or of being crushed by debt. Her mother had settled surprisingly well into city life. Jim Morrison occasionally drove in to take Lisa to dinner or to squabble with her. The relationship remained tempestuous. Apparently, Jim Morrison had hidden depths. Now, Lisa had decided to move back to Astoria.

Field thrived, and Stream had grown so much that Gerry and Ian considered expanding into the space next door. They also toyed with opening another restaurant. Petra's suggestions for names included Scientific American and The Atlantic Monthly.

In the meantime, she and Ian found a narrow old Victorian house just ten minutes from the restaurants and Petra's office. It needed a little work, like everything in their lives, but Ian was already relishing the idea of using his power tools.

Everyone was at their new place. Helen retied the bandanna around her head, while Gerry watched admiringly. Lisa lounged on the couch. Even Jenna and Ellie had driven down to help. Although the only person currently doing any work was Sarah. Good old Sarah, peering at boxes, moving them around the new house, following the directions on the stickers she'd placed on them. "Blue for the bathroom, green for the kitchen, red for the bedroom, and yellow for delicates," she repeated.

"About that," Petra said, "we may have crammed additional items into boxes which didn't quite follow sticker protocol."

Sarah muttered something under her breath and continued to work.

Petra looked around for Ian.

He had just come back from his office. He looked tousled and dusty, and a streak of dirt ran down his calf. He looked better than anyone had any right to look.

He smiled as he caught sight of Petra. A small box sat on his shoulders. In the other hand, he balanced some pizza boxes.

"I like a man who can carry a big load," she said.

He grinned and put the food down on the dining table, which was conveniently jammed in the middle of the hallway, waiting to be moved. "I think you're just sweet-talking me for the carb injection," he said.

The troops crowded in, ready to eat.

"Sarah," he said, "I managed to find a kale, tomato, and garlic pizza – no cheese – for you."

I love him, Petra thought, as Sarah blew him a kiss.

"Are you going to miss Petra's old place?" Ellie asked, munching on a slice of pepperoni.

"No," Ian and Petra replied, together.

It had been tough at first. The apartment was small for two people, and Petra found herself strangely reluctant to part with her clutter. Suddenly, her World Book encyclopedia set seemed useful, even though she just Googled everything nowadays. The ratty duvet cover that she'd thought to make into curtains still sat in the linen closet. The tennis racket seemed too new to give away, the baseball bat too old.

And Ian kept bringing home rocks.

When Petra asked – nicely – why he was doing this, he said it was because he needed to add to his collection.

When Lisa noised about moving back to Astoria, Ian made a decision to sell. He and Petra were doing well with immunotherapy. They offered to take Snuffy back, but Lisa seemed reluctant to part with him. They considered a cat custody arrangement.

Petra wandered into the kitchen, trailing her fingers on the appliances holding a slice of pizza. Sarah was washing her hands in the scratched farmhouse sink.

"Things seem better between you and Helen," Petra said, settling herself onto the counter.

"Yeah. We aren't avoiding each other anymore. It's easier now."

Sarah dried her hands on her jeans.

"So, why are you in here?" Petra asked.

Sarah laughed. "Because I need to declutter, my friend. Don't get between me and my label gun."

"You know, if this physician thing doesn't work out, you could organize moves for a living. In fact, I'm going to have to ask you to do this again, since I'll probably have to pack up the practice in a few months."

"Does the landlord have a new tenant already?"

"Nope. But I've decided that I'm not going to worry about it. Ian's broker is culling places for me. She thinks she can find something in the area. If not… well, I had an informational interview with a practice across town."

Sarah toyed with her box-cutter. "I've been thinking," she said. "My contract with Pronto!Docs is up next month and I don't want to stay. I have money saved up. I wondered how you'd feel if I became a partner in your practice?"

"An allergist and an OB?"

"Well, it's not like I'm a veterinarian. We still work on the same species. We'd just be a multispecialty place, share the same receptionist, offices, some of our equipment. Plus, I'd be giving you a fresh infusion of capital and sharing the rent. My presence would provide some foot traffic to yours, and vice versa. Although, uh, maybe with just two docs, calling it 'multispecialty' would be pushing it. Plus, with the money that I put in, maybe we'd be able to keep the office in its location. And I'd be a lot happier than I am now."

"It sounds like you've thought this through," Petra said. "I would love to have you. But I speak from experience. It's a big outlay. You'd have to buy your own ultrasound equipment. And having your own practice won't always make you happy, especially because you feel such ownership. Although if you bought in, we could invest in hiring a nurse, which would be so great.

"Listen to me," Petra added, gleefully. "I sound so seasoned. It's like I know what I'm doing now. At some point, I might actually become a decent physician."

"You're getting there," Helen said, sticking her head in the door.

"Sarah was talking about purchasing a share of the practice," Petra said.

"Cool. Hey, maybe I should go in, too."

Sarah snorted. "I've been running numbers, picking up used equipment on the sly, and secretly sounding out my patients for months, and you just march in and are, like, *Hey, cool, I should buy in, too*. God, sometimes I can't stand it."

"Sarah, you mean, *Sometimes, I can't stand you*, Helen. Sometimes, I can't stand *you*," Helen said placidly.

Petra sat on the counter, her slice still uneaten. She stared at her friends.

"Well, say something," Sarah said, turning around.

"This may be awesome, or my very worst nightmare," Petra said.

"Probably a little of both," Helen said, still cheerful. "Send me some numbers. We can talk about it next week."

Sarah muttered again.

Helen said, "I *heard* that," and Petra slid down and left. She was glad that there were many rooms in this house.

Ian was sitting at the table in the hallway, alone. Petra pulled up a box beside him.

"Where is everyone?" Petra asked.

"Gerry decided they should get dessert. He's got his heart set on some sort of Italian ice. Jenna offered to drive and your sister is giving Gerry a much-needed lecture about intersectional feminism. They could be a while.

"Don't you want to know what's in the box I brought from the office?" He pushed it over to Petra.

She peered inside. A photo album of his parents' wedding. Some loose pictures. "This is you when you were a little kid," she said, delighted. "I thought you said you couldn't find these."

"I started looking through everything, finally, and I discovered them."

He pulled out a black and white photograph of a smiling young couple. "They seemed happy there, didn't they? I figured we could put some up, of your family and mine. I also found this."

He took out a beautiful filigreed silver ring. "It was my mother's engagement ring. It wasn't the happiest marriage, but I look at it and I feel like it deserves a second chance. If you don't want this engagement ring, it's okay, I won't be hurt."

She tried it on. It was a little big.

"It would need to be cleaned, and resized, of course," Ian said.

"I love it," Petra said serenely.

They sat eating pizza. Ian eyed her with darkening intent. "Where are Helen and Sarah?" he asked, a little too casually.

She tried to ignore the warmth that flooded her. "They're right in the next room," she said.

He nodded and leaned into her. "How about *happy pants*?" he asked.

"That might be the least clever name, yet," she breathed, darting another glance at the door. "The absolute worst."

"Maybe so," he said, reaching for her, "but happy pants make for happy endings."

Acknowledgments

My eternal gratitude goes to Galois Cohen and Marjorie Schulman for their eagle eyes and thoughtful comments.

I am indebted to Daniel M. Lavery, Nicole Cliffe, and Nick Pavich. Much love goes also to my fellow Toasties, especially members of the writing group, for keeping me on track and sending virtual hugs.

I am grateful for the firm shoves (and Teddy Roosevelt quotations) from Carol Peckham, a great boss and even better role model. And finally, to my husband, thank you for reading, giving me the time to write, and most of all, for believing in me.